MURDER IN
CUCUMBER ALLEY

Murder In Cucumber Alley

A 1920s Mystery

MICHAEL SINCLAIR

By Michael Sinclair in the 1920s historical mystery series:

An Unfortunate Coincidence

The Consequences of Murder

Murder In Cucumber Alley

MURDER IN CUCUMBER ALLEY

© 2022 by Michael Sinclair
All Rights Reserved

ISBN: 978-1-78324-260-3

Published by Wordzworth Publishing

Author's Note

Cucumber Alley is located in the historic stockade district of Schenectady, New York. The stockade contains many homes dating back to the 1600s. Cucumber Alley got its name from cucumbers that were once grown there, and the name remained. Schenectady was fondly referred to as *the Electric City* and *the City that Lights and Hauls the World* due to the prominence of General Electric and the American Locomotive Company. Dr. Ernst Alexanderson was a real person, a pioneer in the development of television. Born in Sweden, he worked at General Electric from 1902 until his retirement in 1948. He died at age 97 in 1975. The kidnapping of his six-year-old son, Verner, actually occurred in 1923. He was found unharmed three days later near Watertown, New York. The lecture and demonstration by Dr. Alexanderson as depicted in this novel as well as the other events and people are fictitious and are simply the imagination of a mystery novelist.

Michael Sinclair

CHAPTER ONE

February 1927

The Hotel Van Curler, Schenectady, New York

Rodney Longworth wondered at the plethora of injustice in the world. Certainly, in his own life, he had experienced more than his fair share.

Sitting at his desk, during a momentary lull at the end of a chaotic workday, he wondered what else could go wrong. He had completed numerous assignments for a manager who was out sick and another who was at a convention in another state. After spending an inordinate amount of time on these endeavors, he then dealt with the whims of several guests, complaining of cold rooms and drafty windows. Furthermore, he was called to the banquet hall, to straighten out the arrangements for a party for that evening, including securing a dance band (as the scheduled band was stranded in Buffalo due to a blizzard) and setting the ballroom in order. Schenectady's popular radio station, WGY, and the *Schenectady Gazette* predicted ten more inches of snow, curtailing his plans to spend the hours with his companion at a local dance hall.

The evening guest clerk, Mrs. Stella Bradshaw, who had been with the hotel since opening day, stayed until eleven last night to help with today's arrangements. Rodney thought of calling to see if she'd come in but decided against it. Poor Mrs. Bradshaw, she needed a day off too! Finally able to catch his breath, he lit a cigarette and leaned back on his chair.

At twenty-seven, Rodney Longworth was sensible and dependable, diligent, and intelligent. Rather tall, with fine slicked-back brown hair, and expressive green eyes, he exuded the movie star images comparable to Conrad Nagel and Charles Farrell. A native of the Electric City and proud of his hometown, he enjoyed the advantages of city life, including partaking of restaurants, theaters, coffee shops and dance halls. His companion Theresa Hayes lived in the village with her mother, so it was ideal to remain with his parents in their home on Washington Avenue, given the proximity to all that was important to him. He graduated summa cum laude, from Union College class of 1921, with a degree in finance and mathematics. While employed as a desk clerk at Schenectady's elegant Vendome Hotel, he saw a better opportunity at the new Hotel Van Curler and upon its grand opening, he applied and was soon hired as an assistant manager. Although he wondered, on tumultuous days like today, why he ever became a hotel manager in the first place.

But then he thought light of it. It was a busy and prosperous place, so what did he expect? Recently Governor Smith, Amelia Earhart, and John Philip Sousa were guests at the hotel, among other dignitaries.

So, it was all in a day's work. Nothing really out of the ordinary. No major catastrophes. It wasn't as though someone from the hotel had been murdered. Turning off the banker's lamp on his desk, he would later regret thinking in that direction.

As he prepared to leave for the day, at almost five o'clock, he was nonplussed when his phone rang. It was Mrs. Wainwright, the secretary of the general manager, with an urgent request to come to his office at once.

Of course, Mr. Lennox knew he'd be leaving at five o'clock. But there must be a good reason for this sudden meeting. He assured Mrs. Wainwright he'd come immediately. From outside his office, he could hear the scraping of shovels on the sidewalk. Would it ever stop snowing, he thought grimly? He butted his cigarette in his desk ashtray, straightened his tie and vest, and then ran his right hand over his slicked-back hair. He then hastily left the office on the ground floor on his way to the seventh. Too impatient to wait for the elevator, he entered the stairway, climbing two steps at a time.

Arriving on the seventh floor, he took a deep breath, opened the stairway door, and proceeded down the hall to the general manager's office, ready for anything. Would he be promoted or given a raise? Certainly, Mr. Lennox knew of his arduous work, his diligence. Would he be dismissed? Was there a complaint he didn't know about? Injustice was cruel, he thought, as he knocked on the general manager's office door.

"Hello, Mr. Longworth," Mrs. Wainwright said looking up from an expense report. She was seated at a desk in the outer office, an efficient, no-nonsense woman of fifty with a flapper-style bobbed haircut and firm if not pleasing looks. "Mr. Lennox is expecting you." She nodded toward his inner office. Grudgingly, Rodney knocked and upon hearing a deep command to enter, turned the door handle and walked in.

"Come in, Rodney," Mr. Lennox grumbled, behind his desk.

As though crossing a foreign land and fearing attack, Rodney entered and sat in the chair in front of his desk. He glanced at the large man in front of him. Mr. Lennox was nearly seventy and had been in the hotel business for over thirty years. He came to the Van Curler from various hotels in Boston and New York City. Although dressed appropriately for a general manager of a luxurious hotel like the Van Curler, Mr. Lennox was more sullen, aloof, and not too social. His bald head, dark, wrinkly face, and even darker eyes were downcast and morose. He smoked a cigar and the room smelled of it. He moved the candlestick phone on his desk to one side as though stalling for time and then cleared his throat and began to speak.

"Rodney, we have an issue," he spoke gravely. "Something serious has happened to an employee." He had the evening edition of the *Schenectady Gazette* on his desk. He picked it up and folded it back to the front page, handing it across the desk to Rodney. "Since you're the only manager on duty now, I wanted you to be informed. When McKee comes on duty shortly, I'll inform him as well."

Rodney took the paper and scanned the area where Mr. Lennox pointed. After reading the article, he looked up in horrified shock. Mr. Lennox held out his hand for the paper, lit a cigar, and leaned forward in his chair. He carefully studied Rodney's startled face.

"Mrs. Bradshaw was murdered last night." He added nothing more, drawing heavily on his cigar, leaving Rodney to fumble for words.

"But I saw her leave when her shift ended! She lives within walking distance."

Mr. Lennox nodded. "As do many of our employees." He paused. "I called a contact at the Schenectady police. He told me she was stabbed in Cucumber Alley, around midnight just as it states in the paper." He paused. "It'll be announced on the radio if it hasn't already."

"Her shift ended at eleven," Rodney added thoughtfully. "I left close to eleven-thirty, so I didn't see her after she left. She always walked the same route."

"Do you know why she'd go to Cucumber Alley?"

Rodney shook his head. "I know she'd pass it on her way home." His mind flew to Mrs. Stella Bradshaw; a diligent, kindly woman in her late sixties, living in the same house as when she married, only to be widowed young, childless and never remarrying. Her countenance and disposition were always pristine as well as her appearance, if a trifle overweight, but Rodney always appreciated her good humor, her sense of decorum, and her work ethic.

"Was it robbery?" Rodney asked, clearly disturbed.

Mr. Lennox shook his head. "No, her purse and wallet were still with her. She wasn't mugged or assaulted." He paused, as though for dramatic effect. "My contact told me her body was discovered by a policeman on patrol. He called for an ambulance, but she was already dead."

Rodney shuddered slightly. "She didn't say anything about going to Cucumber Alley. She mentioned she'd go straight home. There was a radio program she wanted to listen to."

"I haven't told anyone else," Mr. Lennox said. "Mrs. Wainwright and a few of the other managers, of course." He paused. "Do you know anything that can shed light on this?"

Rodney hesitated. "No, Mr. Lennox. I wasn't close to Mrs. Bradshaw. We worked together, but other than that I didn't know too much about her."

Mr. Lennox put his cigar in an ashtray. "Negative publicity doesn't look good for us. Hopefully, guests will not cancel their reservations. We can't afford to lose business, Rodney."

Looking at his contorted face and troubled eyes, Rodney thought he made it seem as though the hotel's reputation was more important than the unexpected fate of Mrs. Bradshaw. He asked Mr. Lennox if there was anything he could do for him now.

Mr. Lennox shook his head. "No, Rodney, that'll be all. I suppose you'll mention this to your parents. It's not a military secret, of course, people are bound to find out." He picked up the newspaper again. "The police will be here on Monday. I imagine they'll wish to speak to you since you were the last employee to see her alive."

Rodney felt his throat go dry. "Of course, Mr. Lennox. I'll be here for my shift Monday at nine." He could tell the meeting was over, and he was glad. He stood and said good night to Mr. Lennox and to Mrs. Wainwright in the outer office.

Bolting down the stairs and arriving back at his office, he saw the evening cleaning crew had already started to vacuum and empty waste-paper baskets and ashtrays. Momentarily he sat at his desk, deeply troubled. Mrs. Bradshaw, murdered in Cucumber Alley? Such a kind, dependable lady. Who'd want to kill her? His parents would read about it in the evening paper. And Theresa and her mother, too. There must be a killer loose in the village. He worried about Theresa, walking home at night by herself. He'd call her at the library when he arrived home.

He put on his coat and his cap firmly on his head. He left the hotel by the main entrance and once outside, lit a cigarette. He saw his breath in the frosty air as he looked around him, taking in the city scene. It was the rush hour in downtown Schenectady. The early evening twilight, the fresh snowfall, and the chilly air invigorated Rodney as he waited on the corner of Washington Avenue and State Street. Trollies were going to and from the General Electric facility, traffic clogged the streets and pedestrians littered the sidewalk. Crossing to reach the other side of Washington Avenue, Rodney pondered the disturbing thoughts swirling through his mind. Dodging a businessman rushing to catch the trolley and a woman with her two small children, he puffed incessantly on his cigarette and repeated the question nagging at his mind.

Who would murder a gentle, unpretentious woman like Mrs. Bradshaw—and why?

As the last of daylight was slowly fading behind thick, ominous clouds, it was a hectic day at the library in the Nott Memorial at Union College. The Nott Memorial, a remarkable sixteen-sided stone-masonry building, as well as the centerpiece of the campus, served as the library and gathering place for students. It was an atrium in style, with the second floor visible from the ground floor. The ideal place to study was often crowded and today was no exception.

Students searched the card catalog, locating books in their scholarly research. Librarians helped with the *Reader's Guide to Periodical Literature* and the *1927 World Almanac*, among other valuable sources.

Theresa Hayes, the assistant circulation supervisor, was literally up to her neck in books. She was in the process of checking out several volumes at the urgent request of a history professor. Always urgent requests, she thought grudgingly, finishing the last of the titles and then stacking them in a pile on a corner of the circulation desk.

Theresa was a pretty twenty-five-year-old, who lived with her mother in the village, close to the home of her boyfriend, Rodney Longworth, and his parents. Her blonde hair, blue eyes, and petite size made more than one male look at her appreciatively. She wore a light blue dress with a new string of pearls, which she fingered absently while reviewing a journal.

She and Rodney had been an item for three years. Unlike Rodney, she was not an alumna of Union College. She was first hired as a library clerk and then secured the position of assistant circulation supervisor. At times exhausting dealing with demanding students and professors, she tolerated her job and smiled, when necessary, but really could have cared less about the whims of spoiled undergraduates and even more spoiled professors.

The best part of her job, she thought with a malicious smile, which she kept hidden from Rodney and even her mother, was her recent unquestioned access to college papers and archives. More than once, she assisted in the administration office of the college president. As part of her duties, she sorted through confidential records, enabling her to learn information about individuals and events that otherwise she would never have known. While charming in person, Theresa was cold and manipulative when she wanted and enjoyed wreaking havoc for others, if it suited her purpose. She admitted to herself that she had made a few enemies in the past, but she simply brushed it off. Her mother's bitter divorce taught her to take care of herself because no one else in this stinking community cared about her. Rodney's parents had plenty of money, so she knew her future was secure, at least financially. A housewife role wouldn't bother her, until she got tired of it. And she'd have dear Rodney wrapped around her finger, too.

She glanced out the window at the falling snow and wished she was anywhere than Schenectady in February. Bleak, bitterly cold, endless rounds of snow, limited sunshine, she thought there must be a better place than this winter wonderland. She looked up and spotted Dr. Simon Longworth, Rodney's father, looking through a reference book. My future father-in-law, Theresa mused. He smiled and walked over to see her.

"Hello, Theresa," Dr. Longworth said pleasantly. "I stopped by to see if you had the latest issue of *Scientific American*."

He waited while Theresa assisted a student with a reserved book. Dr. Simon Longworth was a retired scientist from General Electric, with a natural intelligence that made his career an outstanding success. After completing a doctoral degree in Engineering from Columbia University, he began his career at General Electric in Schenectady. At seventy, he had an outgoing personality. His fair hair was tinged with gray specs, his blue eyes alert and inquisitive and although he stood at medium height, his stature in the scientific community made him a towering figure among his peers by his mere presence. He was a virtuoso researcher and technologist. After his retirement, he lectured frequently at Union College and enjoyed researching in the library, for scholarly articles he wrote for publication.

"Someone's using *Scientific American* at the moment," Theresa told him, checking the journals requiring a time limit. "Did you want to reserve it?"

"No, I'll return tomorrow. Are you and Rodney going out this evening?"

Theresa shrugged. "If the weather continues like it is, I don't think we will."

"Mrs. Longworth and I plan to vacation in South Carolina in the spring."

"How nice," Theresa said with a tinge of envy. "Is Rodney going too?"

"No, Rodney couldn't get the time off from the hotel. Spring is the start of the busy season so he's not sure when he'll take time off."

"Well, hello Dr. Longworth," a crisp female voice said, from behind him, a little too loudly for the library, causing a few heads to turn her way. "What brings you to the library?"

It was Mrs. Edna Grey, a retired nurse and part-time teacher at the college, coming to check on a few reserves. Mrs. Grey was a tall, gaunt woman, with a serious but friendly demeanor, a mop of unruly gray hair, and large, expressive brown eyes, rather hidden behind thick spectacles. After retiring from Ellis Hospital, she was hired as a part-time teacher in the science department.

"Hello, Mrs. Grey," Simon said. "I came here to research as usual." He didn't know why he felt he needed to explain his presence in the library to this nosy woman who knew he also taught part-time at the college. Can't people mind their own business? His glance turned to Theresa, standing patiently behind the circulation desk, with a slight grin, wondering what Mrs. Grey wanted now. Her presence usually meant more reserves or some such nonsense, requiring more work on her part.

"Hello, Theresa dear," she said amicably. "Do you have the nursing journals I reserved? You mentioned they'd be available today."

Theresa nodded and disappeared into the back room, returning shortly with the latest issues of the *Nursing Times*, the *American Journal of Nursing*, and the *American Journal of Public Health*. She handed them to Mrs. Grey and reminded her she could use them while in the library only. Mrs. Grey explained she needed the information for the course she was currently teaching, but Theresa explained the library rules regarding journals and periodicals, which the older woman already knew. Mrs. Grey smiled, rather demurely, as though realizing she could not win the battle. She thanked Theresa for the journals, bid goodbye to Dr. Longworth, and disappeared upstairs to the second floor, where the science and nursing collections were kept. Simon looked after her and then back at Theresa.

"Journals aren't allowed out of the library," Theresa commented. "Just yesterday an English professor wanted six journals to take home." She shrugged. "Sometimes I wonder why I work in academics."

Simon Longworth grinned. "You're a good sport, Theresa. And so is Mrs. Grey."

"Why, Professor Longworth, fancy seeing you here," another female voice said.

Simon turned and saw Agnes Brennan, his sister-in-law.

"We're reading the *Art of Poetry* by Horace," Agnes beamed, coming up to him.

Mrs. Agnes Brennan, an enthusiastic professor of Latin at Union College, was in her thirtieth year and showed no signs of fatigue or an inclination to retire. A young sixty, with well-kept brown hair and vivid blue eyes, she excelled in her craft and had won numerous academic awards. Her persistence in increasing the enrollment for Latin required the college to offer a Latin class on Friday evenings, which was unusual. Soon the Science, Art, English, and History departments offered Friday evening classes, and its popularity increased, to Saturday morning course offerings, thanks primarily, Mrs. Brennan boasted proudly, to her initiative.

She and her husband lived on Union Street, in a pleasant neighborhood called the General Electric Realty Plot, once reserved for executives of General Electric. Her husband, Jerome, still worked at the facility and like his wife had no plans to retire. She beamed at her brother-in-law and Theresa. She had just arrived at the library and her cheeks were flushed from the cold. "The brisk weather does me good! I walked here instead of taking the trolley. Alice should be here shortly. I spoke to her earlier."

And at that moment, another familiar face appeared at the circulation desk. It was Alice Longworth, Agnes's sister, Simon's wife, and Rodney's mother. She shook the snow from her expensive fur coat and smiled pleasantly. As Theresa looked at the Longworths and Mrs. Brennan, she thought all they needed was Rodney and Mr. Brennan to make this family picture complete.

"Hello, dear," Alice greeted her husband, then looked at her sister. "Agnes, you're early. Doesn't your class start at seven?" She looked at Theresa. "I'm not late, am I, Theresa?"

"No, Mrs. Longworth," Theresa said, as though this arrogant woman was ever late.

Alice took off her fur coat, draped it casually over a chair, smoothed down her pretty gray dress, feeling satisfied with her trim figure and looked around the library, as though she had never been there before.

Mrs. Alice Longworth was sixty-five years old, with a comfortable self-possession about her that came from a solid marriage, a successful husband, excellent health, more than enough money in the bank, and a well-furnished house in an affluent neighborhood. A retired English and French teacher from a local, elite private school, she doted on her son and husband, keeping her home pristine as well as her looks. Her gray and brown hair was worn tastefully in a well-kept bob. Rouge, lipstick, a string of pearls and a waft of Chanel No. 5 accentuated her appearance.

A life-long Schenectady resident, she was active in church functions and community events. She considered the library an integral part of her life. It was appropriate that upon her retirement from teaching, she'd volunteer at the college library. That way, she'd keep an eye on her husband and Theresa, the girl her son was foolish enough to get involved with.

Agnes excused herself from her sister, brother-in-law, and Theresa, as she wished to look at the Classics section on the second floor. Alice told her she'd be there shortly as she planned to start shelving. Simon said goodbye to his wife and Theresa, explaining he wanted to get home to have dinner ready for Rodney. Theresa marveled as they seemed to get along so well, at least in public. Although she could tolerate the sisters in the same place for only so long.

"Rodney and I are going to a dance tonight," Theresa said. She watched Alice get a cart of books to shelve. "But because of the weather we may see the new Clara Bow film instead."

Alice looked at Theresa as she wheeled the cart toward the stacks. "Rodney needs to help his father and I this evening," she said curtly. "He won't be available."

She pushed the cart full of books toward the shelves and disappeared into the first-floor stacks. She then glanced up to the upper floor of the Nott Memorial and noticed her younger sister, Agnes, looking down at her, a rather hard, meaningful look on her face.

It was after six o'clock when Rodney arrived home. As he opened the front door, took off his cap and coat, and hung them in the hallway closet, he detected the fresh smell of roast beef wafting from the kitchen. He cleaned his snowy shoes on the doormat and then walked down the hallway to the kitchen, where his father stood at the stove, about to cut into a roast.

The Longworths lived in a handsome brownstone house on Washington Avenue in the village, the historic stockade district of Schenectady. Centrally located, it was on the trolley line and neither Rodney nor his parents owned a car. A needless expense, Rodney concluded. He walked to the Hotel Van Curler, so a car would've been more of a nuisance.

"Hey Dad," he called as he approached him at the stove. "Mother's at the library tonight, isn't she? Bad night to be out, with the snow coming down." He wanted to mention the murder of Mrs. Bradshaw but decided to wait. He didn't want to spoil the delicious meal his father had planned or cause him any worry, at least not before dinner. He may have already seen it in the evening paper or heard it on the radio. He'd wait to see if he'd mention it first.

Simon smiled at his son. "Well, I don't think the weather will bother your mother, Rodney. You know how much she loves the library. I don't think she could live without it."

Rodney looked at the sumptuous roast. "Is that for just us?"

"No, I invited your Uncle Jerome for dinner. Your Aunt Agnes is teaching a class this evening, otherwise, she'd be here, too."

"You sure cook a good pot roast, Dad," Rodney said. He glanced out the kitchen window, which gave out onto a small patio and city garden. "I should call Theresa to see if she wants to go out tonight."

"Maybe WGY will announce any cancellations," his father suggested.

Rodney agreed and entered the living room, turned on the radio console, and turned the dial to WGY. Symphonic music filled the room followed by the news report. As he expected, the announcer mentioned the death of Mrs. Stella Bradshaw, found murdered in Cucumber Alley last night. He lowered the volume as he did not want his father to know about it just yet. Finally, the weather. Ten inches of snow by morning and sleet mixed in before tapering off late in the day tomorrow, just like he heard earlier. Rodney grunted and turned the radio off. He then returned to the kitchen to join his father, where Simon was setting the table.

"Anything new on the weather?" he asked his son.

Rodney sighed and sat down. "I don't think Theresa and I will be going out this evening." He sat, fuming, until he rose and decided to call her at the library, realizing he told himself to do that earlier. At the same time, the doorbell rang. Rodney put the candlestick phone back on the hallway table and opened the front door, welcoming his Uncle Jerome inside.

"Good evening, Rodney," Jerome Brennan said, taking off his Fedora hat and winter coat and handing them to his nephew. "Nasty evening. Have you heard the weather report?"

"Ten inches of snow by morning," Rodney told him.

"Mrs. Brennan called before I left," Mr. Brennan said. "Terrible night to be out."

Rodney agreed. "Doesn't Aunt Agnes teach a class this evening?"

Mr. Brennan nodded, as he followed Rodney down the hallway to the kitchen. "At seven. She loves her Latin class tonight. She told me it's the best group she's had in years."

Simon greeted his brother-in-law amicably and invited him to sit at the table while he and Rodney served the dinner. He asked him about news at General Electric and Jerome began to fill him in on what was happening at the facility.

Jerome Brennan was married to Agnes, Alice's sister, and Simon's sister-in-law. He got along well with both Simon and Alice. He and Agnes often joined them in bridge games and dinners out. He was a tall, conservative gentleman of sixty-two, who, judging from his extremely good looks appeared more fifty. His brown hair was worn tastefully, his green eyes sincere and alert. He and Agnes had no children, so he enjoyed spending time with his nephew, Rodney when his schedule permitted. Like his wife, he had no desire to retire. Jerome and Simon became friends while employed at General Electric, even before Simon married Alice and Jerome married Agnes.

Rodney poured three glasses of ginger ale while Simon serviced the delicious pot roast. Talked ensued; more General Electric news, the sisters working at the college, so late in the evening, something both husbands did not relish.

"Especially when the weather isn't good," Jerome added, sipping the ginger ale.

Simon agreed. "Did you hear anything on the radio about cancellations?" he asked Rodney.

"Nothing," Rodney replied. "I meant to call Theresa at the library. Maybe we'll see the new Clara Bow film."

"You and Clara Bow," his father teased. "I think you're in love with her."

Jerome intervened. "He isn't the only one, Simon. I'm in love with her, too!"

The men laughed, while Rodney excused himself from the table, to go to the hallway to finally call Theresa at the library. He asked the operator to call the library at Union College and in no time was connected to the circulation desk.

"Hello, Rodney," answered Mrs. Fillmore, the evening librarian. She had met Rodney several times before. "What can I do for you?"

Rodney cringed as he was not fond of Mrs. Fillmore. She was forty-odd at a guess, precise, very bookish, and at times brusque in manner, especially with students and young people.

"I'd like to speak to Theresa if she isn't busy."

Mrs. Fillmore looked around before speaking into the phone. "I don't know where she is at the moment. She should be here at the desk." She wondered if Theresa was too long on a break or worse. If she were caught dead to rights at something? "I'll ask her to call you when she comes back. Are you home?"

Rodney told her that yes, he was at home. Did he wish to speak with his mother? Mrs. Longworth was busy on the second floor, shelving books and periodicals, but she'd get her for him if he wished.

"No need, Mrs. Fillmore," Rodney told her. "She gets off duty at eight, so she'll be home soon." He glanced at his watch and saw it was almost seven. "Ask Theresa to call me, okay?"

Mrs. Fillmore assured him she'd have Theresa return his call. Rodney then replaced the handset on the candlestick phone and joined his father and uncle in the kitchen. He had momentarily forgotten about the murder of Mrs. Bradshaw.

It was almost nine-thirty. After finishing dinner and washing up afterward, Rodney, his father, and his uncle were relaxing in the living room, with coffee and cigarettes. Simon had turned on the radio to WGY and the soft sound of symphonic music filled the room. Rodney thought he heard someone at the front door but upon opening it and finding neither his mother nor Theresa, he realized it was just the wind rustling the branches of the trees against the house. He noticed it was snowing heavier creating white-out conditions. He collected the evening paper and joining his father and uncle in the living room, left it on the coffee table, not realizing his father would inevitably see the article about Mrs. Bradshaw's murder. He had been waiting for Theresa's call, but so far had yet to hear from her. Far from being political himself, Rodney listened while his father and uncle carried on a lively discussion about President Coolidge.

"Governor Smith should be our next president," Simon said, a staunch Democrat.

"There's talk Coolidge won't run," Jerome told him, knocking ash from his cigarette into an ashtray on the coffee table. "We need a democrat for sure. Hopefully, Al Smith will get the ticket next year."

Simon puffed on a cigarette, then put his coffee cup to his lips. He listened as the grandfathers' clock in the hallway chimed the half-hour. He looked at his son and brother-in-law and then put his cup on the coffee table.

"Alice isn't back yet from the library," he said, with concern.

"I wouldn't worry, Simon," Jerome said. "Most likely she's waiting for Agnes when her class gets out around ten."

Simon shook his head. "No, she'd call and tell us she'd be later than usual."

Rodney felt a chill run up his spine. Of course, nothing happened to his mother or Theresa. They know their way around town. But then, so did Mrs. Bradshaw. He hadn't told his father what happened to Mrs. Bradshaw and in some respect felt bad that he hadn't mentioned it yet. He still wanted to wait, although, at this point, he wasn't sure why.

At that moment, the phone rang, and Rodney practically jumped up to answer it. Scrambling to the hallway, almost knocking over the small telephone table in his haste to answer it, he expected to hear his mother's voice. Instead, it was Theresa's mother, Mrs. Hayes.

"Rodney, I'm so sorry to be calling rather late, but I haven't heard from Theresa. I called the library and Mrs. Fillmore said she couldn't locate her. I thought she might be with you."

Mrs. Flora Hayes lived with her daughter in the stockade village on Washington Avenue, not far from the Longworth's house and the home of Mrs. Edna Grey. A robust middle-aged woman, with a pleasant disposition, her auburn hair tastefully arranged in the current bob style, her brown eyes were expressive and alert. Always well-dressed in the latest flapper fashion, she was divorced with no inclination to seek out a second husband. She cleared her throat and asked Rodney if he had seen her daughter. Her voice held a mixture of worry and anger, as though Theresa was up to something she didn't know about and that Rodney, as her boyfriend, knew more than he told.

"No, she isn't here," he responded truthfully. "I'm sure she's on her way home." He paused. "We're supposed to go out this evening, but with the storm, I don't think we will."

Mrs. Hayes agreed. "Another reason why I'm concerned. Did you read about the woman from the hotel who was murdered in Cucumber Alley last night? You must know her, Rodney."

"Yes, I knew Mrs. Bradshaw. But I wouldn't worry, Mrs. Hayes. Theresa will be on the trolley, so there'll be plenty of people with her." He tried to convince himself that what he was saying was true. He assured Mrs. Hayes he'd call her right away if he heard from Theresa, then ended the call.

Returning to the living room, his father and uncle appeared speechless and in shock. The radio was still on, and the evening paper was open on the coffee table, so he realized they must have read about the murder or heard it on the radio. There was a moment of comparative silence until Simon cleared his throat and addressed his son.

"Rodney, did you know what happened to Mrs. Stella Bradshaw? She was murdered last night in Cucumber Alley."

Rodney admitted Mr. Lennox told him about the murder before he left the hotel today. He didn't want to alarm his father with the news yet, especially before dinner. He told his father and his uncle that he had no idea what happened to Mrs. Bradshaw. He also told his father and uncle that he had just spoken with Mrs. Hayes, who was worried about Theresa.

Simon nodded. "Thanks, Rodney. You're a good son in waiting to break this terrible news. I would've preferred if you had told me sooner instead of my hearing it on the radio and then reading about it in the evening paper."

"Sorry, Dad," Rodney mumbled, feeling bad.

"Now I'm concerned about your mother. She should've been home by now. Unless the trollies aren't running in this weather."

"Suppose a murderer is lurking about, preying on women?" Rodney asked.

"It doesn't do any good to worry," Jerome pointed out. There was a moment of awkward silence. Jerome then glanced at his watch. "I do need to get going, Simon. Agnes's class gets out at ten and I want to be home when she arrives."

"Do you want me to go with you, Uncle Jerome?" Rodney asked.

Jerome shook his head. "I'll be fine, Rodney. I'll catch the trolley here on Washington that'll bring me to Union Street." He walked to the hallway, returning with his coat and Fedora hat. He bid goodbye to his brother-in-law and nephew as they accompanied him to the door.

"Don't worry, Simon," Jerome assured him. "Alice will be home any minute now."

He waved to them as he walked north on Washington Avenue, to await the trolley, which was arriving as soon as he got there. He boarded and was soon on his way.

Rodney closed the front door and followed his father to the living room, where the fire was heating the room comfortably and the radio continued playing symphonic tunes. Simon started to read the evening paper again, absorbing himself in the political news. As usual for Simon, he occupied himself with reading, rather than let himself fret over his wife's late arrival.

Rodney lit a cigarette and paced back and forth, glancing out the living room windows, too restless to sit. Pulling back the curtains and shaking his head at the steady snow, he wondered what had become of his mother—and Theresa.

In the dining room at the Hotel Van Curler, Russell Banks, his son, Steven, and daughter-in-law, Wilma, had finished eating dinner. Mr.

Banks lit an after-dinner cigarette with satisfaction. Another excellent meal at the hotel. An exquisite dining experience, the restaurant featured gourmet meals and boasted two European chefs, serving the most opulent foods and desserts.

Russell Banks was pleased with his stature in life; his rewarding banking career, his charming brownstone house in the stockade village that he shared with his son and daughter-in-law, his circle of business associates from the numerous civic organizations in which he was a board member. At fifty-five, Mr. Banks was a well-known figure in the city, respected for his business acumen and forthrightness. As a bank manager, he advocated for his clients and ensured they invested wisely. The stock market was growing rapidly. And Russell made the most of it, too. A new 1927 Mercedes-Benz and a vacation to Florida were just a few of the profitable results of his stock market investments. Appealing, handsome, tall and rather heavy-set, debonair, with black hair, brown eyes, and this evening wearing an immaculate brown suit, he was the epitome of the successful businessman. His ex-wife divorced him years ago and remarried, moving to Buffalo. Numerous women in Schenectady regarded him as an eligible 'catch.'

He looked across the table at his son and daughter-in-law. At times he pitied them and other times, wished they'd get their own place. They had struggled when first married but their finances had slowly improved. Russell opened his house to them, an arrangement that worked well.

Steven Banks was thirty and employed at General Electric as an electrical engineer. He had been with the company for just three years and had made excellent progress. Frequently he worked with Jerome Brennan, who not only was a colleague but a friend, despite their age difference.

Russell put down his coffee cup and was about to speak to his daughter-in-law, Wilma. Sometimes he wondered why his son married her. Wilma Banks was twenty-nine and had no pretensions to beauty, she was too smart and clever for that. Currently employed at the United Cigar Store on Jay Street, she completed her undergraduate studies at the State Normal School in Albany with a degree in English and hoped to secure a position at the Nott Memorial library at Union College. She was plain, with little to no make-up and a bob hairstyle, messily arranged. But Russell liked her even from the first time he met her. She was caring, serious and attentive but considered herself a flapper, something Russell didn't quite understand.

"Should we call the waiter over for the check, Dad?" Steven asked his father.

Russell sipped his coffee. "Don't worry, son, I'll take care of the bill."

Steven and Wilma expressed their gratitude. Wilma mentioned she and Steven would reciprocate someday soon, but Russell told her not to worry about it.

"As long as you bake that fabulous chocolate cake of yours," he told her with a smile.

Wilma sipped her coffee while she looked at her father-in-law. "Of course, Russ. Steven and I appreciate living in your house. Although we should look for our own place."

"Nonsense," Russell told her. "You're welcome to remain with me. I enjoy the company. Otherwise, what would I do with that big house? Besides, you have an excellent assortment of cigarettes at the United Cigar Store. Camels are the best."

She agreed, accepting one from his almost empty packet and letting him light it for her. Was there anything better than a cigarette with an after-dinner coffee?

The Banks lived in a brownstone on North Church Street in the stockade village. While not as pretentious or dignified as the brownstones on Washington Avenue, it had character and charm. Three floors, with four bedrooms, and a large living room and kitchen. It was convenient to their employment and restaurants and theaters, and the Banks frequently spent time out, enjoying all the diversions downtown Schenectady offered.

The waiter soon appeared with their check. Steven asked him if by chance he had a copy of the evening paper. He soon returned with the *Schenectady Gazette*. Russell curiously asked his son why he wanted to read the paper at that moment.

"I want to see what's playing at the theater," he told his father. He put his cigarette in the ashtray on the table and folded back the paper. "I see Mary Pickford's new film is playing along with Clara Bow in *Wings*. Want to see it tomorrow night, Wilma?"

"Sure, if this weather improves," Wilma said, putting down her coffee cup. She took the paper from her husband and looked at the movie listings. She turned to the front page and scanned the articles. Then she gave a sharp cry, causing not only her husband and father-in-law to ask what was wrong, but a few other diners turned in her direction. She merely held out the paper to Russell and pointed to an article on the first page.

Russell read about the murder of Mrs. Stella Bradshaw in Cucumber Alley last night. He was stunned, in disbelief. He wasn't acquainted with Mrs. Bradshaw but had seen her in the village several times and when dining here at the hotel. He knew she was a hotel employee.

"Such a nice lady," Steven said, flicking ash from his cigarette into the ashtray. "Who'd want to kill her? And in Cucumber Alley? Didn't she live on Washington Avenue?"

Russell nodded. "It says the police are investigating."

"I'm sure Theresa would know more," Wilma said, sipping her coffee.

Russell and Steven looked at her in surprise.

"She's a busybody," Wilma added. "I don't know what Rodney sees in her."

"Let people make their own mistakes," Russell said, finishing his cigarette. "Besides, Mrs. Hayes and I have enjoyed time together. I'm sure Theresa can take care of herself."

They collected their coats from the cloakroom attendant and after the bill was settled, stepped out in a steady snowfall onto Washington Avenue to catch the trolley. It finally arrived and picked them up, along with a sizeable crowd, heading toward Washington Avenue and the stockade village. Wilma looked out the trolley window and thought she saw Theresa Hayes, walking steadily in the snow on Washington Avenue, furtively, as though on a secret mission. As the trolley passed her, Wilma looked back but lost her from sight.

"She must be up to something," she thought irritably, absently looking at her husband, father-in-law, and the other occupants of the trolley as it crawled up Washington Avenue. "I don't trust Theresa Hayes. I'll put a stop to her wickedness if it's the last thing I do."

Cucumber Alley, so named because of the wild cucumbers that once grew along the banks of the Mohawk River, contained a few brownstones and a small riverfront area. A desolate place with few pedestrians, especially in the evening, appearing sinister in its dim lighting and quietness.

The snow came down like a great white mist as the evening progressed. In the stockade village, theater patrons scurried to catch the trolley or return to their cars, anticipating arriving home, to shelter and warmth. None of this pedestrian traffic was evident in Cucumber Alley until a woman arrived. She looked behind her and up and down Washington Avenue before heading along the alley toward the river.

Clandestine meetings were never appealing to her but when money was involved, she didn't mind. She made her way down Cucumber Alley steadily despite the snow and stood at the foot of the Mohawk River, shivering, glancing at her watch. She then smiled to herself. She was clever and cunning, rather smart, but wise. Extra money never hurt.

She then heard a noise that shattered the stillness. The snow crackled under heavy steps. Right on time, she thought. She'd make it quick as soon as the money was handed over. No need for idle chat. She started to speak, hoarsely, but the words caught in her throat.

Suddenly she saw the glimmer of a knife coming toward her. Her heart leaped with genuine fear. In that brief awful moment, she resisted fiercely. The knife pierced her repeatedly, weakening her futile attempts to defend herself.

She continued to struggle, but the agonized end finally came, slowly, painfully, inexorably. The lifeless body lay on the ground as the snow continued to fall. Heavy footsteps retreated staggeringly. And then all was silent in Cucumber Alley.

CHAPTER TWO

That night, Rodney slept fitfully, tossing and turning. He was too tired to stay up any longer, so he told his father to wake him when his mother arrived or if Mrs. Hayes called about Theresa.

The next day, Saturday the nineteenth, in his bedroom on the second floor, he woke up, stretched, brushed his left hand over his face, and glancing at the alarm clock on the bedside table, saw it was only six-thirty. Still sleepy, he plopped his head back on the pillow. He then smelled the aroma of coffee from downstairs. He also heard a low murmur of voices. Immediately he flung back the covers, jumped out of bed, grabbed his robe, rushed out of the bedroom, along the hallway, and almost tumbled down the stairs in his haste to get to the kitchen. He stood in the kitchen doorway and saw his parents at the table with the morning paper, coffee cups, and cigarettes. Simon nodded upon seeing his son.

"Good morning, Rodney," he said pleasantly. "You're up early on your day off."

Rodney continued standing in the doorway, taking in the scene before him. His parents were casually having breakfast, as though nothing out of the ordinary had recently occurred. He started to speak, but his words were a mere mumble. Alice got up from the table, poured him a cup of coffee, and told him to sit down while she prepared breakfast.

"Mother, what time did you get in last night?' He was finally able to articulate words.

Alice turned from the counter and looked at her son. Rodney thought his mother appeared fresh and alert as always, even at such a Godawful hour as this.

"You must not have had a good night's sleep, dear," she said to Rodney, taking in his tired eyes and tousled hair. "Why did you rush down the stairs so early?"

"Because I smelled coffee and heard voices," Rodney explained, gratefully taking the coffee, and lighting a cigarette. "Mother, will you please tell me about last night?"

Alice began making scrambled eggs at the stove. "Well, after I left the library at nine, I decided to visit Aunt Agnes in her Latin class. I stayed till ten o'clock and then she and I took the trolley home. Not the same trolley, of course. We walked to Union Street, and she took the southbound trolley, and I caught the northbound trolley."

As she placed the plate with the scrambled eggs before him and sat down across from him, she picked up the morning paper that Simon had finished reading and added nothing more. His father looked up at him from the business section of the paper and asked him what was wrong.

"There's plenty wrong," Rodney exclaimed, causing his mother to put down the paper. "Dad, why didn't you wake me up to tell me mother had arrived? I told you to do that, remember?"

Simon told his son that he indeed remembered. "I thought it'd be better if you got a good night's sleep, Rodney. Your mother got home close to eleven and spent an enjoyable evening with your Aunt Agnes and her Latin students."

Alice nodded. "Yes, Agnes and I chatted—in Latin and French—with some of the students after class and before we knew the time, it was almost ten-thirty. That's why I got home later than usual." She continued looking at Rodney's troubled face. "What is it, Rodney?"

"Mother, are you aware that Mrs. Bradshaw was murdered in Cucumber Alley?"

Alice glanced at her husband and then back to her son. She spoke quietly, not wishing to upset herself. "Well, yes, dear, your father told me when I got home last night. Before we went up to bed, we listened to the news and I heard it then, too."

"I was the last hotel employee to see her Thursday night," Rodney said, with a worried expression. "Mr. Lennox told me about it last night before I left for the day."

"It doesn't say in the paper that it was robbery," Simon said. "Her purse and belongings were still with her. I don't know why she'd be in Cucumber Alley so late at night unless she was visiting someone there."

"There are few houses there," Rodney reminded his father.

"Well, whatever the reason, dear, it's best not to speculate," Alice said calmly, sipping her coffee while buttering a muffin. "We don't know what happened."

"Your mother has a point, Rodney," Simon told him, folding the rest of the paper, and placing it back on the table. "The police will investigate and find whoever is responsible."

"Did you see Theresa when you left the library, Mother?" Rodney asked her.

Alice finished the muffin and took her time replying. "No, dear, I didn't see her. I spoke with Mrs. Fillmore, who also hadn't seen her."

"Mrs. Hayes called last night," Rodney told her. "She was so worried about Theresa because she hadn't heard from her, and she hadn't gotten home yet."

"Mrs. Fillmore and I looked for her in the library, but we couldn't find her." Her tone implied it was a lost cause and didn't further interest her.

Rodney sighed, finished his cigarette, and crushed it in the ashtray. He ran his fingers through his brown hair and rubbed his tired eyes. He was about to ask for more coffee when the telephone from in the hallway started to ring, surprising them. Rodney glanced at the wall clock and noticed it was just seven-fifteen. Who in the world would call so early on a Saturday morning? Theresa, of course, to let him know she was fine and to apologize for not calling last night. He pushed back his chair and told his parents he'd answer it.

Entering the hallway, he picked up the handset on the candlestick phone, expecting to hear Theresa. It wasn't Theresa. It was her mother. Rodney tried to allay the disappointment in his voice as he greeted Mrs. Hayes and wondered why she'd call at such an early hour on a Saturday.

"Hello, Rodney dear," she said with a slight quiver. "How are you doing?"

Clutching the handset, Rodney figured she'd get to the point eventually. She certainly didn't call to make small talk. He. He thought he heard her crying softly.

"I'm fine, Mrs. Hayes."

"Have you been listening to the radio?" she asked him.

"No, I had just gotten up and had breakfast with my parents." He paused, rather irritably. "We don't have the radio on." He glanced into the living room where the radio console stood against the wall near the fireplace. "Is something wrong, Mrs. Hayes?"

"Rodney, dear, it's Theresa."

He waited for her to continue. Alice and Simon joined their son in the hallway and by the look on his young face, they could tell something was definitely wrong. Holding onto the hallway table for support, Rodney listened to Mrs. Hayes and thanked her for calling, placed the handset back on the candlestick phone, and then looked up at his parents.

"Rodney, what is it?" Simon asked his son, noticing his stunned expression.

Rodney took his time in replying. "That was Mrs. Hayes."

"Theresa got home?" Alice said, in relief, looking first at her son and then her husband. But after looking at Rodney's horrified face she realized that was far from the truth.

Rodney had gone ashen white and for a moment Simon thought he'd pass out. He looked again at his son and begged him to tell them what was wrong.

"No, she never got home last night," he told them. "Mrs. Hayes said it was on the radio this morning." He glanced again toward the radio console in the living room. "The police have already been to her house and questioned her. We would've heard about it on the news."

"Rodney, what are you talking about?" Simon demanded, clearly agitated, knowing something was indeed wrong.

Rodney fought to hold back tears. "Theresa was murdered last night. Her body was found early this morning in Cucumber Alley."

Mrs. Edna Grey sat at the kitchen table in her comfortable brownstone on Washington Avenue. She had finished breakfast and was expecting her elderly neighbor and friend, Mrs. Norris, to visit any moment. She pushed some gray hair back from her wrinkled forehead. Glancing at the window above the sink, she heard the wind howling. Another cold blustery winter day.

She had already finished preparing her lessons for the science classes she taught part-time at Union College. She admired the Friday evening class as it seemed a different breed of students. She imparted her love of science and nursing and was a popular teacher in the department.

She got up from the table and went to the stove, to make another pot of coffee for when Mrs. Norris arrived. In a brief time, the doorbell rang. Walking heavily to the front door, Mrs. Grey opened it and was glad to see her friend and neighbor, Mrs. Marion Norris.

"Edna, dear," Mrs. Norris said, stepping inside and stomping the snow off her shoes. She took off her coat and cloche hat and left them on a hallway chair. She was a serious but pleasant woman in her seventies, who lived in the village. Like Mrs. Grey, she was retired and kept busy at the local church doing volunteer work. And like Mrs. Grey, she was widowed and childless.

She followed Mrs. Grey down the hall to the kitchen, where the coffee was just starting to boil. Mrs. Norris sat at the kitchen table while Mrs. Grey poured the coffee and brought over two cups, one for her friend and one for herself.

"You look rather flustered today," she said dryly, stirring sugar and cream into her coffee.

"Edna, haven't you heard?"

"Heard what, dear?"

Mrs. Norris stammered. "About the murders? Right here in the village."

Mrs. Grey looked at her friend through thick spectacles and wondered if she had lost her mind. "Murder in the village here? What are you talking about, Marion?"

Mrs. Norris stammered. "Mrs. Bradshaw and Miss Hayes were murdered in Cucumber Alley! It's in the paper and was on the radio. Edna, I'm so afraid. A madman is running loose around here. We've got to be careful."

Even Mrs. Grey showed distress. She exclaimed she didn't know what happened to Mrs. Bradshaw or Miss Hayes, as she hadn't read the paper or listened to the radio. She'd been too busy teaching her night classes, writing her lesson plans, and reading her magazines to do much of anything else. Composing herself, she asked Mrs. Norris to explain in more detail.

"Well, do you have this morning's paper? It's on the front page."

Mrs. Grey reached over for it on the corner of the kitchen table, unfolded it, looked past the political and world headlines, and noticed in the bottom right of the front page, a startling headline.

Schenectady Gazette
February 19, 1927

Second Murder Victim Found in Cucumber Alley

Police discovered the body of a young woman last night in Cucumber Alley. The victim, Miss Theresa Hayes of Washington Avenue in the village, was found lying at the base of the Mohawk River. She had been stabbed. This accounts for the second murder in two days in Cucumber Alley. Thursday evening, Mrs. Stella Bradshaw was also murdered in the same manner. Police are asking anyone with information to please call headquarters.

"Very disturbing, Marion," she managed to say, stoically. "I hadn't seen Mrs. Bradshaw in quite some time. I saw Miss Hayes yesterday at the library before my class started."

"A madman is around here," Mrs. Norris repeated, trying to keep the edge out of her voice.

"There, there, dear," Mrs. Grey placated. "There's no reason to become hysterical. The police in this city are quite good. Wasn't your brother-in-law a policeman in the city? They'll find whoever is responsible, I'm sure."

Mrs. Norris shook her head. "This is different, Edna. Times have changed. All these gangsters and flappers, plus those speakeasies, even here in the village. I've never seen such nonsense. Girls smoking and drinking alcohol, too. Spending time with boys and acting wild. Whatever happened to morals and values?"

Mrs. Grey nodded. "I'm afraid those have gone out the door, dear. The young people of today are uncouth and unreliable. The flappers are most distressing."

"What should we do, Edna?"

Mrs. Grey looked at her friend. "What do you mean, Marion? I'm certainly not staying locked up in my house. I teach in the evenings and plan to continue to do so."

Mrs. Norris smiled wryly. "I admire your nerve, Edna. I'm afraid I'm not as brave."

Changing the subject, to take their minds off the recent murders, they chatted about the rummage sale at the local church, the plays at Proctor's Theater and shopping on State Street. Mrs. Norris mentioned she planned to visit her sister in Albany soon. She then glanced at her watch and noticed the time that had gone by. She wanted to shop at H.S. Barney's, Wallace's, and Carl's Department Store, to look at the spring sales.

Mrs. Grey accompanied her friend to the front door and tried to comfort her as she put on her coat and cloche hat. "Don't worry, dear," she said soothingly. "Just call me if you need me."

The friends hugged, and Mrs. Grey opened the door, waving good-bye to Mrs. Norris as she walked on the snowy sidewalk to catch the trolley to State Street.

Mrs. Grey closed the door and shivering slightly, walked back to the kitchen. She thought of visiting Mrs. Flora Hayes, who lived not far from her, on Washington Avenue, but then decided against it. She'd be in shock still and having a neighbor with whom she was not on particularly close terms stop by to pay condolences would hardly help.

She poured a fresh cup of coffee and settled in her favorite armchair in the living room with the morning paper and the latest issues of *True Story* and *Love Story* magazines. She smiled at her favorite reading material. Perhaps silly to read such sentimentality, but it provided some diversion. She started to read an article but found even that didn't help. It was a peculiar situation, to say the least. The room was warm and made her feel sleepy. She had had a difficult night sleeping and found that despite the morning hour, her eyes were heavy, and she soon dozed, the newspaper falling off her lap, onto the floor. The article on the Cucumber Alley murders on the front-page lay face up prominently at her feet.

The General Electric Realty Plot, one of the finest neighborhoods in Schenectady, was rich in prestige and stature. Obviously, it was only people with good incomes who could afford to live there and enjoy the serenity and prosperity of the magnificent homes, lawns, and gardens. Jerome and Agnes Brennan, along with numerous General Electric executives, as well as politicians, bank managers, and other thriving businessmen felt at home in such an affluent neighborhood.

"There's been another," Jerome Brennan said gravely to his wife.

Mr. and Mrs. Brennan were having breakfast, in their grandiose home on Union Street. A two-story, opulent mansion, it had a wide-swept well-manicured lawn, with a spectacular garden and patio in the back yard. The paperboy delivered on time each morning, as did the milkman, ensuring that the Brennans, along with their neighbors, were always well cared for. These amenities contributed to the comfortable lifestyle the Brennans enjoyed.

Mrs. Brennan, at the kitchen counter, turned and looked at her husband, uncomprehendingly. She wasn't sure she heard him correctly.

"Another what, dear?" Agnes Brennan asked her husband, pouring coffee. She set the cups on the table, along with the cream and sugar.

Mr. Brennan was reading the morning paper and looked up at his wife. He folded back the front page, handed it to her, and pointed to a small article on the bottom. At first, Agnes wasn't sure what she read, then blinked several times and read it repeatedly. Finally, she looked up at her husband in disbelief.

"Didn't you say you saw Theresa yesterday in the library?" Jerome asked his wife.

Agnes nodded. "And Alice and Simon, too. Alice stopped by my class when her library shift was over and stayed until the end when we practiced Latin and French with a few students. We left about ten-thirty." She paused. "I didn't see anything out of the ordinary at the library or with Theresa yesterday."

Jerome took the paper from his wife. "We don't know what happened, Agnes."

"There must be a manic running loose in Schenectady," Alice said wearily.

Changing the subject, so Agnes wouldn't think of the murders, Jerome mentioned General Electric's innovations on television. "Dr. Ernst Alexanderson hopes to give a television demonstration soon."

"Radio's just fine for me," Agnes said, rather stubbornly, sipping coffee. "These days everyone wants a radio. I prefer the newspaper. How else would we get news around here?"

"Remember what Dr. Alexanderson and his wife went through four years ago?"

"Yes, poor little Verner. At least he was found, unharmed, in Watertown, wasn't it?"

Jerome nodded, got up and looked through a series of newspaper clippings in a cabinet. He handed the clipping to Agnes who nodded in remembrance.

Schenectady Gazette
May 4, 1923

Verner Alexanderson, the kidnapped Schenectady boy for whom a nationwide search was conducted, was found yesterday in a shack near Watertown. He was reunited with his mother and father, the eminent scientist, Dr. Ernst Alexanderson of General Electric.

Agnes handed the clipping back to her husband just as the phone rang. Finishing her coffee, she pushed back her chair and entered the hallway. As though afraid to answer it, she was relieved when she heard her sister's voice. Before she could say anything, Alice bluntly told her about the murder of Theresa Hayes, in Cucumber Alley, last night.

Agnes told her sister she already knew, having read about it in the morning paper. She mentioned they'd stop by later, to support Rodney and suggested eating out this evening if they wished. She replaced the handset on the candlestick phone and returned to the kitchen.

"Two murders in two days, Agnes," Jerome said thoughtfully.

"Well, I didn't know Miss Hayes too well, except when I'd see her at the library. I don't think there was any love lost between that young woman and my sister."

Jerome looked at his wife. "Your sister has a problem getting along with a lot of people," he remarked dryly. "Didn't she have a run-in with Mrs. Bradshaw not too long ago?"

Agnes made light of it. "Yes, some silly nonsense. More coffee, dear?"

Jerome declined. He walked out of the kitchen and up the stairs, to dress for the day.

As Agnes started to clean the breakfast dishes, the phone rang again from in the hallway. She had already been shocked by her sister's call, so she didn't think she'd receive anything more appalling. Entering the hallway, she picked up the handset reluctantly. It was a colleague from the college, a Latin teacher. Agnes stiffened. She said, her voice rather hoarse, "I can hear you," and continued listening intently.

In their brownstone house on North Church Street, the Banks were also having breakfast.

Russell sat at the head of the kitchen table, finishing a plate of scrambled eggs that his daughter-in-law prepared for him. Steven sat across from his father, not awake, finishing his coffee and cigarette. A piece of toast was on a plate before him, although he hadn't touched it yet. Wilma poured coffee and sat next to her husband. A comparative silence followed as no one felt much like talking, too early for small talk, none of them quite fully awake. Steven reached over for the paper at the same time the phone rang from in the hallway. They looked at each other, wondering who'd be calling at such an early hour on a Saturday.

Reluctantly, Steven rose, butted his cigarette in an ashtray and went to the hallway to answer the phone. Admittedly, he was not in the mood for talking to anyone. He was therefore relieved yet surprised to hear his friend Rodney Longworth on the other end. He and Rodney spent much time together, especially as they participated in the summer tennis leagues at Central Park in the city. But this was only February and by the excitable tone of his voice, Steven could tell it was indeed something quite different, if not alarming.

"Rodney, what's up?" Steven asked his friend. "Something wrong?"

Rodney was upset but was attempting to collect himself. He told Steven that Theresa's body had been found early this morning by a policeman on patrol in Cucumber Alley, stabbed, near the Mohawk River. Steven froze and leaned against the wall for support. At the same time, Wilma entered the hallway and from the hard look on her husband's face, she could tell something was extremely wrong.

"Wilma and I will come over, Rodney," Steven told him. "I want to be sure you're okay."

Rodney assured him he was managing. "What time will you be here?"

Steven looked at Wilma. "Is noon good for you, Rodney?"

Rodney welcomed Steven and Wilma to stopover. After hanging up the handset on the candlestick phone, Steven looked at his wife, a disturbed and aggrieved expression on his face, and told her the devastating news.

"Murdered?' Wilma gasped, clearly horrified. "Like Mrs. Bradshaw!"

Russell entered at that moment, carrying the newspaper. He looked gravely at his son and daughter-in-law, at a loss for words. He merely showed them the front-page article on the murder of Miss Theresa Hayes.

"Dad, what do you make it?" Steven asked his father, following him into the living room. "Do you think there's a madman loose here in the village, preying on women? This makes the second murder in two days. First, Mrs. Bradshaw and now Theresa."

Russell nodded but said nothing. He was completely withdrawn, almost pale. Steven had never seen his father looked like that before. Russell looked closely at his son and daughter-in-law as they read the article on the front page of the *Schenectady Gazette*. He lit a cigarette, threw the match carelessly into an ashtray on an end table, and realized his son was speaking to him.

"Wilma, and I plan to visit Rodney at twelve today. Do you want to come with us?"

Russell Banks looked away, as though the subject of the murders of Mrs. Bradshaw and Miss Hayes was too much for him. Steven understood how he'd be upset but he took it so personally, as though the victims meant something more to him. He finished his cigarette, crushed it in the ashtray, and was about to light another when he addressed his son and daughter-in-law.

"No, I think I will contact Mrs. Hayes first," he told him. "She must be devastated by this news." He paused, looking again at his son and daughter-in-law. He lit the cigarette in his hand as though stalling for time. "I have a notion whoever killed Miss Hayes was killed by someone she knew. The paper didn't mention robbery or assault. She was easily identified, according to the information given, by her purse."

"The same for Mrs. Bradshaw," Wilma pointed out.

"So, what are you saying, Dad?" Steven asked him, impatiently.

"Well, I'm not an expert, of course," Russell said, taking his time, troubled by the murders of the two women. He drew heavily on his cigarette thoughtfully. "I wouldn't doubt if the murderer is someone within this very neighborhood. Someone in the village we call home."

Rodney was tired and overwhelmed. He had never experienced such a horrendous shock in his young life. After dressing and preparing for the day, he told his parents that before noon rolled around and Steven and Wilma stopped by, he wanted to see Mrs. Hayes himself, to express his condolences. His parents started to protest as they planned to visit her this evening, and naturally expected him to join them, but he insisted. He had picked up the phone, asking the operator to call Mrs. Flora Hayes, and was soon connected. Mrs. Hayes thanked Rodney and invited him to stop by within the half-hour, as the police would soon be at her home again to meet with her.

Outside in the chilly air, the wind had subsided, but the snow made walking difficult. Rodney wore his winter coat along with his cap and found the crisp air invigorated him, giving him some much-needed energy. On Washington Avenue, walking north toward State Street, he thought of Theresa, the girl he loved and contemplated marriage. She had her strange ways, of course, and could be difficult at times but he still cared deeply for her. He passed a man walking his dog and two women heading toward the trolley stop. They were talking animatedly between themselves, and Rodney wondered how they could act like nothing was wrong. Didn't they know about the recent murders?

He reached Mrs. Hayes's house, another charming and well-preserved brownstone. He knocked snow off his shoes and rang the bell. After a minute or so, he heard someone in the hallway, and slowly the front door opened. Mrs. Hayes smiled weakly upon seeing him.

"Rodney, dear. Thank you for stopping by. Please come in."

She had been crying, her eyes bloodshot, a handkerchief in her hands. She moved aside permitting Rodney to enter the hallway. She led him to the cozy living room, well-furnished with chintz-covered armchairs and a Victorian sofa. A fireplace on the far wall highlighted the room, although there was no fire lit. There was a chill in the air and as he sat in an armchair, he wished she'd turn up the thermostat. A large radio console was against the wall near the sofa and was tuned to radio station WGY, relaying the news and the local weather report. Mrs. Hayes offered him coffee or tea, which he declined. She sat zombie-like in the armchair near Rodney and soon enough began to cry, softly at first, then quite heavily, as though with his presence she'd, at last, be able to unload all the pent-up emotions she had experienced upon learning about her daughter's murder. She dried her eyes and looked up at Rodney.

"Rodney, dear, what could have happened to poor Theresa? She was always careful on her way home. And why was she in Cucumber Alley late at night?"

Rodney looked at her carefully. Mrs. Hayes was attractive in her own style, with a rather fine figure, and brown hair and eyes. Even in mourning, there was still a certain dignity and grace. Rodney wasn't sure her age, but figured she must be about fifty, but thought she could pass for forty-five or so. He waited for her to compose herself before replying.

"I don't know what happened, Mrs. Hayes. I'm just in as much shock as you are. My parents saw Theresa in the library yesterday, but they didn't mention anything out of the ordinary."

Mrs. Hayes nodded. "The police have been here already and questioned me. I couldn't tell them anything. An inspector will be speaking with me again, although I've told them everything I know." She paused, irritated. "I wish I knew what Theresa was up to. She got herself killed and for something she shouldn't have been involved with."

Rodney loosened his tie and looked at Mrs. Hayes in amazement. "Why do you say that Mrs. Hayes? Do you mean bootlegging or drugs? That she was involved with gangsters?"

Mrs. Hayes shook her head irritably. "No, no, nothing like that, Rodney. But you knew Theresa as well as I did. She could be stubborn. I don't know if she was up to something I wasn't aware of." She hesitated. "Do *you* know anything about Theresa that I don't, Rodney?"

Rodney was taken aback. Just what did she mean by that? What a strange thing to ask, as though he and Theresa had deep and forlorn secrets that they kept from her. He wasn't sure what she was implying and took his time in answering her forward and rather awkward question.

"No, Mrs. Hayes, I don't know any secrets that Theresa may have had. If she did, she never shared them with me." Looking at her closely, he could tell that answer didn't quite satisfy her, as though she expected him to relate something that would solve her daughter's murder and have it done with.

Mrs. Hayes mentioned she'd arrange Theresa's wake and burial in time although she couldn't concentrate on those endeavors now. Observing her, Rodney couldn't shake the thought that there was something more, of which he wasn't aware. Something else that bothered her, regarding her daughter. She then started to cry again, wiping away tears. She looked up at Rodney and smiled briefly.

"You'd have made a fine son-in-law, Rodney, dear. I'm so sorry for this tragedy."

"If you need my parents and I, you can call us or visit anytime."

Mrs. Hayes thanked Rodney for coming, signaling an end to the visit, to which he was rather glad. She saw him to the front door.

"Thank you again, Rodney, dear. I'll look forward to your parent's visit later today."

Rodney wished her well and eagerly left the house, stepping out onto the snowy sidewalk. It seemed colder than when he had first arrived, as though his visit to Mrs. Hayes more than the weather created a chill inside him. He avoided a woman and her unruly dog and a man and woman walking steadily north, toward State Street. Snow showers stung his face and hit his shoulders while walking the short distance south on Washington Avenue to his parent's house.

He then thought back to the woman he just visited. He had a strange conviction that there was much more disturbing Mrs. Hayes than just Theresa's murder. Something that, for whatever reasons, she was keeping to herself, telling no one and bearing the burden alone. It seemed more than just bereavement, something that lay not only in the past but in the present, too.

CHAPTER THREE

M onday morning brought the police to the Hotel Van Curler. It was unusual to see law enforcement inside the luxurious hotel, but Mr. Lennox did his best to accommodate them, by answering their questions patiently and thoroughly and then directing them to other employees, including Rodney.

Rodney came out from the back room, where his desk was located and was introduced to Inspector James and his colleague Sergeant Eberhart by Mr. Lennox. Rodney invited them to sit in front of his desk. Upon returning to his swivel chair and stalling for time by moving the candlestick phone from one side of the desk to the other, he looked up and asked them what he could do for them. He hoped it wouldn't be too long.

Inspector James, a middle-aged man, with piercing green eyes and a distinguished manner, spoke first. "Mr. Lennox mentioned you were the last employee to see Mrs. Bradshaw before she left. Can you tell us anything that can help with the investigation?"

Rodney shook his head. "I wish I could, Inspector. I hardly knew Mrs. Bradshaw, except when she was here working. She was always friendly and pleasant, a good worker." He paused. "Are you also looking into the death of Miss Theresa Hayes?"

This time Sergeant Eberhart spoke. A serious-faced older man, with a fine head of white hair and vivid blue eyes, he looked at Rodney as though he had seen it all as a policeman and was used to difficult cases. He cleared his throat before speaking.

"Yes, we're also investigating the death of Miss Hayes. Were you acquainted with her?"

Rodney nodded. "She was my companion."

Sergeant Eberhart nodded. "Do you know why she or Mrs. Bradshaw went to Cucumber Alley late in the evening?"

Rodney shook his head. "Theresa worked the evening shift at the Nott Memorial Library. I called there to speak with her, but Mrs. Fillmore told me she couldn't be found."

"Mrs. Fillmore?" The Sergeant asked patiently.

"The night librarian. She told me she couldn't find her anywhere."

"And what about Mrs. Bradshaw? She had an appointment after her shift ended?"

"No, she mentioned there was a radio program she wanted to listen to, so she went straight home." He hesitated. "Is there a mass murderer here in Schenectady, preying on women?"

"We don't know yet, Mr. Longworth," the Sergeant said seriously, closing his notebook in which he had been writing. He stood to leave, along with the Inspector. Rodney showed them to the lobby and the front entrance, thanking them for stopping by. The Inspector mentioned they'd speak to the library staff at the Nott Memorial, including Mrs. Fillmore. He added they'd be in touch soon. As Rodney was about to return to his office, he saw Mr. Lennox hastily making his way toward him. He seemed confused and overwhelmed.

"You got rid of them?" Without waiting for an answer, he continued. "Good. The last thing we need here is police officers. Did they say they'd return?"

Rodney mentioned they'd come back shortly, although they didn't give an exact date and time. Mr. Lennox grumbled something incomprehensible and trudged off toward the elevators. Looking after him, Rodney wondered if all he thought about was business. What about poor Mrs. Bradshaw? And Theresa, too?

Returning to his office, agitated, and disturbed by this entire ordeal, he sat at his desk and glanced at his watch. Noontime. With the snowy weather, he'd eat lunch at the hotel restaurant but oddly didn't feel he had an appetite. Too much happening in too short a period. Two murders in two days, in his neighborhood? He thought over the events as he knew them.

The terrible tragedies that had befallen people close to him; first, the murder of Mrs. Bradshaw, a good-hearted elderly woman, without an enemy in the world. She loved Schenectady and the stockade district, and the hotel considered her part of the family. Who would have wanted to kill her? Did she stumble onto something she shouldn't have? And as a result, she needed to be silenced? But what could she have seen in Cucumber Alley? Such a nondescript place, nothing outstanding about it. It was a dead-end alley. Her body was found there, just at the base of the river, covered in snow. Like Theresa, too.

Rodney lit a cigarette and blew smoke angrily. Damn girl, he thought miserably. Theresa had her fair share of enemies, which she readily admitted. Always butting in where she shouldn't, finding information on people, using it to her advantage. She never told him anything in particular but more than once he saw her with a satisfied smile, gleaming as though she had just won a million dollars. When asked about her almost euphoric state, she'd tell Rodney she was happy just to be with him and that she loved him so. Rodney puffed furiously at his cigarette. No, it was more than that. Theresa had been up to something. Her mother was right, that her daughter knew things she shouldn't, and how clever of Mrs. Hayes to pick up on that. But it certainly didn't involve him. He deserved better than Theresa, he thought in hindsight. What did he want with a girl like that anyway? He had seen her display of temper with others, even with his parents. Her mother was just the opposite.

Rodney puffed thoughtfully at his cigarette. He wondered if he ever really knew Theresa. There were plenty of times that she'd upset him, talking about his mother, whom she didn't like. She tried his patience more than once, but when you're in love, you overlook things, don't you? But was it really love, he thought bitterly? Marriage to her would have been a disaster. That was out of the picture now, he thought wryly. Theresa, that insufferable young woman, never to interfere in his life or the lives of anyone else again. There were plenty of girls around, Rodney thought brightly.

Another desk clerk, Olive Mae, a new employee, and recent Union graduate, was certainly an attractive person and always cast smiles at him. He'd chat her up a bit. And it'd help to forget about Theresa, too.

In the mid-afternoon hours, Wilma Banks was stocking shelves and assisting customers at the United Cigar Store on Jay Street. Not the greatest job, she admitted grudgingly, but it was close to home. She thought the store name was misleading. There were more than cigars and cigarettes on sale at the United Cigar Store, a full stock of perfumes, cosmetics, gifts, books, newspapers, and magazines. She suggested to her boss a name change, but that'd come from the higher-ups, so there was nothing much she could do about it. She admitted to herself, she hated the store name.

Wilma glanced at herself in a counter mirror, used for customers purchasing cosmetics. Her brown hair was tastefully arranged in the bob style, although it was falling loose from the clip at the back of her neck. She fidgeted with it, fixing it, before noticing her downcast eyes and overall somber pallor. She wasn't a beauty, which she certainly knew, but she had a certain grace and style that Steven and even her father-in-law appreciated, and to Wilma that was what mattered most. Her gray dress and string of pearls accentuated her slim figure. She craved a cup of coffee and a cigarette. Looking at her watch, her break time was fast approaching, for which she was glad.

Her mind flew to Theresa Hayes, who was murdered in Cucumber Alley, along with Mrs. Stella Bradshaw. She shook her head doubtfully. What were they doing in Cucumber Alley so late at night? Having a rendezvous with someone? Theresa possibly, but Mrs. Bradshaw? Wilma thought that highly unlikely. But then Theresa was involved with Rodney unless she was keeping something secret from him. How Rodney ended up with her Wilma couldn't figure.

Wilma assisted an elderly man wanting a box of cigars and a middle-aged woman wanting two packs of Lucky Strikes. What could have happened to Mrs. Bradshaw and Theresa Hayes? She, Steven, and Mr. Banks lived on North Church Street, close to Cucumber Alley. Could it have been random? Suppose she, Wilma, was out walking and passed by Cucumber Alley around the same time? Would she have also been a victim of violence?

Wilma looked out the store window onto Jay Street, a charming pedestrian thoroughfare, lined with boutiques, florists, cafes, and bookshops. Glancing upward, she noticed the sun trying to break through, although it seemed like the clouds were winning over. She grimaced as she realized another cold and dreary day was in store. The bell on the door clanged signaling a new customer. Wilma turned and saw Mrs. Edna Grey, smiling and shaking snow off her coat.

"Hello, Mrs. Banks," Mrs. Grey said pleasantly. "Nasty weather, isn't it? Hope we'd have that February-thaw as they always say, but no such luck this year." She sighed, looking around the cramped yet fully stocked store. "I'm looking for my favorite lipstick, Mrs. Banks. I know it's usually cheaper here than at Carl's."

Wilma smiled. Certainly, a friendly woman, Mrs. Edna Grey was a regular customer and always cheerful. Sizing her up, Wilma thought she looked matronly. No flapper fashion for her, but her face, along with her coat, red cloche hat and red paisley scarf were pleasant, although Wilma couldn't help noticing the lines around her eyes. She also noticed her red paisley scarf, identical to the one she wore. Paisley designs were certainly all the rage, she thought brightly.

"Yes, Mrs. Grey, it's currently in stock. It's over here." She led the older woman to the end of the cosmetic counter, where a variety of lipsticks, perfumes, and eye shadow were on display. Mrs. Grey choose her favorite and upon making the purchase, thanked Wilma and was about to turn toward the exit when she glanced at the morning edition of the *Schenectady Gazette* along with several other local papers on display near the front door. As Wilma observed her, the local headlines made her squirm, and she thought the woman would faint. For a moment, she thought of asking if she'd like to sit down or want a glass of water, but Mrs. Grey recovered her dignity and forced a tired smile.

"Sorry, dear. I just noticed the article on the front page about poor Mrs. Bradshaw and now Miss Hayes. It's so frightening." She took out a handkerchief, dabbed at her eyes, and looked mistily at Wilma. "It's shocking and in our own neighborhood."

Wilma came out from behind the counter. "I understand, Mrs. Grey. But the police will find whoever is responsible. Don't worry yourself sick."

Mrs. Grey looked up and smiled. "Thank you, Mrs. Banks."

Wilma smiled. "Please call me Wilma, Mrs. Grey. You're a special customer here and part of our community." She gave her a reassuring smile. "How are your classes this semester?"

"Just fine, dear. Mrs. Brennan enjoys teaching Latin and increased enrollments for a Friday evening class. The college hasn't had Friday evening classes until recently, thanks to Mrs. Brennan. Isn't that something?"

Wilma commented that it certainly was something, then thought privately how one conniving, selfish, money-hungry woman could single-handedly convince a college administration to offer courses on Friday evenings when most professors and students would prefer to be home with families or doing other things. Wilma had little patience for Mrs. Brennan or her arrogant sister, Mrs. Longworth. Fortunately, her encounters with them were exceedingly rare. She wondered how Rodney managed to contend with his mother and aunt. He certainly didn't display any of their characteristics. He was more like his father, down-to-earth and sincere. Wilma knew they were loaded, with the Brennan's mansion in the General Electric Realty Plot and the Longworth's handsome brownstone on Washington Avenue, the best street in the stockade village. Wilma realized Mrs. Grey was talking to her and she blinked several times, rather embarrassed.

"Are you all right, dear?" Mrs. Grey asked her suddenly.

"Oh yes, I'm fine, Mrs. Grey. Will you be needing anything else?"

"No, I'm fine, dear. How are your husband, Steven, and Mr. Banks, your father-in-law?"

Hating idle small talk, Wilma commented her husband and father-in-law were both well and enjoying their careers, and hoped it'd end there. She thought Mrs. Grey showed a touch of envy, knowing both Mr. Banks and his son were prospering, the one as a bank manager and the other as an engineer at the General Electric plant.

"Do you still live on North Church Street?" she asked Wilma.

Wilma nodded but wanted to say of course you know that what a silly question. "If you need us for anything, Mrs. Grey, call or stop by. We're close to Washington Avenue."

Mrs. Grey nodded, then shuddered slightly. "Cucumber Alley is off Washington Avenue, you know. There must be a killer running loose in the area. Wilma, I'm so frightened."

"Let's think positive and continue with courage," Wilma told her soothingly.

Approaching the door to leave, Mrs. Grey turned to Wilma, a strange expression on her lined face. "Continue with courage? What an interesting adage, my dear." She paused, then spoke as though a newfound strength welled up in her. "Yes, that is something I intend to do. How correct you are, Wilma. Continue with courage!"

She smiled at Wilma, pushed her red cloche hat lower on her head, bundled her red paisley scarf tighter around her neck, opened the door to a cold gust of air, and stepped onto Jay Street, leaving Wilma staring after her.

The General Electric plant, the lifeblood of Schenectady, stood proudly and majestically at the end of Washington Avenue. Although located in the heart of the Electric City and certainly its largest employer, it seemed a city by itself. The imposing and rather intimidating large neon sign of the company name, winking on and off as though to emphasize its grandeur and stature, the splendor of its many buildings, and the reputation of such a distinguished place of scientific research and discovery, was renown not only in Schenectady but around the country and the world. Analysts predicted more prosperity through 1927 and into the coming year.

In an office on the third floor of the main building, Jerome Brennan was busy at his desk, preparing to assist in a laboratory, and collaborating with fellow researchers on numerous projects. He collected a notebook and pen, preparing to join his colleagues. Looking at his wall calendar, he realized he did not turn the page to February. Irritably, he got up and removed the calendar off the wall, turned the page that showed a farm in a winter scene, and the emblazoned words FEBRUARY 1927 in large letters on the top. He had noted a meeting he had scheduled for next week on the January page, so he crossed it off and rewrote it on the same date in February. Unusual for Jerome, always meticulous to detail.

So, it's February already, Jerome thought wryly. But he didn't complain. Last year, 1926, was Mr. Brennan's most profitable. He received a promotion to the front rank of researchers, dutifully moved into his own office, and was responsible for his division's daily operations. His degree in Economics and Science from Union College enabled him to secure employment at General Electric. Many years later, he was still reaping the benefits of a prosperous career with a growing and prestigious company.

Jerome collected his notebook and was out of his office, in the hallway, heading for the stairs when he encountered Steven Banks, also making his way hastily in the same direction.

"Hello, Steve," Jerome said good-naturedly.

"Hi Jerome," Steven Banks said and smiled.

They were on a first-name basis, not usual for business, but as they had worked together on numerous projects and served on the same committees, their friendship developed into an amicable one. Jerome was also acquainted with Steven's father, Russell Banks and he and Agnes often dropped by their brownstone on North Church Street. He and Agnes returned the invitation, having them for dinner or a barbecue during the summer months.

"Heading for the meeting?" Jerome asked him.

Steven nodded. "Hopefully, it won't be a long one this time."

Before entering the meeting room with the other researchers and engineers, Jerome asked Steven what he thought of the recent murders in Cucumber Alley. Steven stood still at the bottom of the stairs and shook his head.

"Honestly, I don't know. Wilma, Dad, and I have discussed it. Mrs. Bradshaw was a nice lady. I can't imagine who'd want to kill her. Theresa is something different."

"People certainly have secrets," Jerome said, absently, as though thinking to himself.

Steven looked at him. "Secrets? What do you mean?"

Jerome blinked several times. "Oh, nothing. Just wondering about Mrs. Bradshaw. And Miss Hayes, too." He paused, glancing into the meeting room as it was soon to begin. "We need to be careful, too, Steven. There's a killer loose in the village."

They then entered the large meeting room, sitting together at the long table, with other executives and researchers, listening to the discussion of upcoming discoveries, including the possibility of broadcast television. The executives wholeheartedly agreed that discovery would put General Electric and Schenectady on the map for further prosperity and innovation. Steven concurred with the others but noticed Jerome was aloof and didn't seem to be paying much attention to his surroundings.

"Just be alert, Steven," Jerome whispered. "No one is safe."

Steven was about to ask what he was getting at, but the meeting continued, a long monotonous discussion, preventing him from speaking to him any further.

Rodney walked along State Street, brushing past the after-work crowd, his hands in his pockets, his cap low on his head. Oblivious to the snow showers hitting his face and shoulders and the bone-chilling air, he trudged along despite the weather, hoping he didn't appear aggrieved and depressed. But as he looked into a store window and saw a reflection of himself, his downcast eyes, his sullen expression, he knew his emotions were evident on his face.

It was after five o'clock and already dark. The evening rush hour was in full swing, trollies were crowded going up and down State Street, while a brave policeman directed cars and pedestrians. Horns honked, traffic snarled, the usual routine made even more arduous in February when people rushed home to dinner and a warm house.

But Rodney didn't feel like going straight home. Before leaving the hotel, he called his mother to tell her he wanted to shop for a new sweater at Carl's or Woolworth's, which was just an excuse. He needed to clear his mind. Too much happening in too short a period.

He looked to his right and noticed the recently opened Proctor's Theater, busy even on a Monday evening. He had read that the current feature *Rio Rita*, another great Ziegfeld musical, was a Broadway hit and had made it to Schenectady. He wondered if Mr. Ziegfeld was in town. He continued up State Street, aimlessly, as though he was exploring it for the first time. Passing H.S. Barney's department store, the window displays showed mannequins highlighting current fashions, including the latest cloche hats for women. In another window, he noticed a box-shaped appliance, called a television. In its experimental stage, H.S. Barney's predicted its use in the future, with its origins right here in Schenectady. Like many people, Rodney didn't quite understand television, as his parents had recently purchased a radio console. They also bought a new phonograph player, and Rodney enjoyed playing 78 records of Duke Ellington, Bessie Smith, and Ruth Etting over and over. Jazz was the bee's knees!

Further up State Street, he noticed a stationary store. Upon entering, he saw a booklet on aviation, highlighting the career of Mr. Charles Lindbergh. With his single-engine, single-seated *Spirit of St Louis* airplane, he planned to leave Roosevelt Field on Long Island this spring and fly to Paris. Rodney marveled at people's innovative escapades.

As he was about to exit the store, he almost collided with a tall, solidly built middle-aged man, who appeared in a hurry to leave. Rodney was about to give him a curt greeting when he recognized Mr. Russell Banks.

"Hello, Mr. Banks."

"Well, hello, Rodney. Good to see you. How are you doing after Theresa's sudden death? Terrible thing to have happened. Murdered in Cucumber Alley? It was dreadful, just dreadful."

No beating around the bush with him, no subtlety, Rodney thought irritably, certainly an impertinence to be so blunt. Fortunately, the store wasn't crowded so he doubted anyone overheard his callous remarks. He noticed his rugged face, bushy eyebrows, the expensive Fedora hat, well-dressed in a long winter coat. He appeared nervous and even out of breath. He, too, was preoccupied with the recent murders in Cucumber Alley. It certainly had been front-page news and broadcast extensively on WGY daily.

Rodney composed himself and managed to produce an appropriate answer. "I'm fine, Mr. Banks, thanks for asking. Steve and Wilma were nice to stop by afterward."

"If there's anything we can do, Rodney, just let us know," Mr. Banks said, and Rodney had the impression he didn't mean it and couldn't wait to take leave of him. He glanced at his watch. "I must get going. Steven and Wilma are preparing dinner. Good evening."

"Good evening, Mr. Banks," Rodney said, watching his bulky frame go through the door and out onto the sidewalk. He noticed he wasn't carrying a bag, so he didn't make a purchase. Certainly, an odd fellow, Mr. Banks, like he was up to something he didn't want anyone else to know about.

Rodney then turned from the newspaper section, approached the clerk, asked for a pack of Lucky Strikes, and having paid the fifteen cents, proceeded to the front door and outside. The frigid air made him feel better and after an hour of aimless walking, he decided to go home.

Walking north on State, heading toward Washington Avenue, he crossed with a sizeable crowd. He'd ask Olive Mae, the new girl at the hotel if she'd like to go to the theater sometime soon. She sure was a fine young woman, so pretty, too. Rodney was so entranced about Olive Mae that he almost stepped into the path of an oncoming trolley.

"Rodney, dear, be careful!" a firm female voice exclaimed by his side.

Rodney turned to his right and saw Mrs. Edna Grey beside him. He was shaken by the experience and Mrs. Grey, recognizing his disturbance, pulled him aside, away from the crowd, and tried to console him.

"Just relax, Rodney dear. You almost had a close shave. You must be more careful in the heavy traffic, especially this time of the evening."

Rodney smiled gratefully. Mrs. Grey was friendly and caring, rather ugly to the extreme, he thought, although she must have been pretty at one time. Certainly, an ungainly appearance, she looked strong. Her long, gray winter coat was large and billowy, her red paisley scarf was wrapped around her neck as though choking her and her red cloche hat was low on her head, shielding her face from the stinging snow and ice pellets. She asked him if he was all right. Rodney, embarrassed, straightened his cap and bundled his coat around him.

"Yes, I'm fine, Mrs. Grey," he said, shivering slightly, seeing his frozen breath in the chilly evening air. "Just a little shook up. I didn't see the trolley."

Mrs. Grey nodded. "Was that Mr. Banks I saw you talking with at the stationery store?"

Nosy old woman, Rodney thought. Where was she that she noticed his conversation with Mr. Banks? As though reading his mind, Mrs. Grey smiled.

"I was out shopping and passed by that stationary store. Lovely window displays."

Rodney didn't know what to say so he decided to say nothing. Pulling himself together, he thanked Mrs. Grey again for her help and was about to leave this good-hearted yet interfering woman, when she suddenly spoke, rather sharply, stopping him in his tracks. Looking at her, it seemed as though she had just thought of something, albeit of no importance.

"I didn't know Miss Hayes too well, of course, except when I'd see her at the library, but she told me she discovered something important about them." She stopped, as though Rodney knew what she was referring to.

The older woman nodded, moving slightly to allow people to pass. "That's why I wondered about your speaking to him just now. Did Miss Hayes say anything about them?"

Before Rodney had a chance to speak, as he had no idea what she meant, she rambled on. "Miss Hayes mentioned she found something out about the Banks, said she needed proof or something like that. She must've gotten the proof and that's why she was killed, so she couldn't reveal anything. It must've been Mr. Banks, his son or daughter-in-law she was referring to. Don't you understand now, Rodney?"

CHAPTER FOUR

A week passed without incident. The residents of the stockade village attempted to go about their lives as normally as possible, although most considered that difficult to do. Increased patrols were set up, city policemen and state troopers kept vigil not only in Cucumber Alley but the area surrounding it including Washington Avenue and the Hotel Van Curler. Volunteer groups of residents kept watch over the area, taking turns walking and driving around the village at regular intervals, especially in the evenings and overnight. The police continued questioning people who lived near Cucumber Alley, including homes on Washington Avenue. Union College even stepped-up patrols, enforcing their security to monitor not only the campus but the surrounding areas, including Union Street and the General Electric Realty Plot.

Despite February being over, the weather turned sharply colder with more snow in the forecast and most residents were hunkered down by nightfall. Although many claimed the bitter cold kept them safely at home, their preoccupation with the two murdered women in their neighborhood was foremost on their minds.

In her warm and cozy brownstone on Washington Avenue, Mrs. Flora Hayes, having just finished a light dinner, settled in her favorite armchair in her comfortable living room, near the fireplace where flames danced brilliantly, emitting a fine glow and plenty of warmth. A cup of tea and a pack of cigarettes were on the end table to her right and in her lap were the latest issues of her favorite magazines: *The Saturday Evening Post*, *True Story* and *Photoplay*. Casual reading, Flora knew, sipping her tea, but given the recent tumultuous event of her daughter's murder, she needed some escapism, and reading about film stars and other modern stories was just the ticket. She opened *Photoplay* and noticed an article about her favorite actress Mary Pickford and her husband Douglas Fairbanks. She was about to start reading when to her extreme annoyance, the doorbell rang. Who in the world would be calling on such a cold evening, Flora thought irritably? She put the magazines on the end table and slowly and reluctantly got up, entered the hallway, and peered out the narrow window near the front door. To her chagrin, she saw Mrs. Brennan and Mrs. Longworth on her doorstep. Realizing she couldn't leave them outside in the cold, and surmising they saw the lights on in her living room, she reluctantly unlocked the front door. Forcing a smile, she greeted Agnes and Alice as though glad to see them and invited them inside.

The sisters eagerly entered, stomping their snowy shoes on the doormat. Agnes handed her fur coat, reddish-paisley scarf, and cloche hat to Flora. Alice took off her elegant fur coat, cashmere scarf, and sleek cloche hat. After depositing them on a hallway chair, the sisters followed her down the hallway to the living room. Agnes and Alice sat on the sofa, admiring the warm and comfortable room, remarking that Flora looked genuinely well and refreshed given the recent ordeal. Flora sized them up quickly. Agnes Brennan was serene as though nothing could disturb her placid life, her brown hair tastefully arranged, her gray dress simple yet appropriate. Alice Longworth looked well-composed as usual, with her short bob hair, her blue dress exuding a quiet elegance. Flora smiled and hid her annoyance and wondered what this visit was all about.

"We wanted to stop by earlier, Flora," Alice said. "I hope we're not intruding. Agnes suggested calling first, but since you're practically next door, we thought we'd just stop by. Of course, Mr. Longworth and I came here as did my sister and brother-in-law previously, but my sister and I came to express our most heartfelt condolences. I didn't know Theresa well, although she and Rodney were fond of each other. And I'm glad Rodney came here to see you, too."

And how you resented that, Flora thought contemptuously. She knew this arrogant, rich woman sitting before her couldn't stand Theresa and that she wanted nothing more than to break up any marriage plans she and Rodney may have contemplated.

"How are you holding up, Flora?" Agnes asked.

Flora smiled at Agnes Brennan. Of the two sisters, Agnes was the most tolerable.

"I'm fine, Agnes. Would you care for tea? I always like tea in the evenings."

Agnes smiled. "No, thank you, dear. We're concerned about these murders here in the village, especially since you live so close to Cucumber Alley."

Alice agreed. "We live here on Washington Avenue, too. I'm afraid to walk around in the evening anymore. If I must go anywhere, my husband Simon comes with me."

"I have my Friday evening class," Agnes mentioned. "I don't know if the college will continue it or cancel because of the recent murders."

"Same with my volunteer work at the library," Alice said. "I heard the other day the college is considering eliminating evening hours." She paused. "I wonder about the Banks."

"What about the Banks?" Flora said, surprised.

"That hodgepodge they call a home," Alice said distastefully. "His wife divorced him, and his married son and daughter-in-law live there.

I've heard Wilma Banks is wild, a flapper as they're called. She smokes, drinks, and acts luridly, in public."

"Well, they seem pleasant enough," Flora said, hoping to change the subject.

"Yes, to you indeed," Alice offered, with a slight lift of her eyebrows. "You and Mr. Banks were an item some years ago, weren't you?"

"Alice, please," her sister interjected, saving Flora from responding. "We're not here to intrude on Flora's private life. Besides, it isn't our business."

Alice smiled wanly. "Forgive me, Flora dear. I meant nothing by it. Mr. Banks seems a nice man. And there's nothing wrong with gentlemanly company for a fine woman of your prestige and character."

She sounded so sincere that Flora was momentarily at a loss for words. "Thank you, Alice. Mr. Banks is a friend, someone I've known for many years." She paused. "The police don't have any leads. They've no idea what happened."

Agnes and Alice glanced at each other. Alice cleared her throat and smoothed a wrinkle in her dress. She looked at Flora with understanding.

"Perhaps Mrs. Grey knows more than she tells. She's a busybody, you know."

Flora agreed with her. "I know, but she's baked bread and cakes and brought them here. She's been most kind." She paused, an awkward silence. "How is Rodney, Alice? You and Mr. Longworth must be so proud of him."

Alice smiled. "Mr. Longworth and I love Rodney very much. He means the world to us."

"And poor Mrs. Bradshaw," Flora said. "I didn't know her too well, but I don't know why she'd be in Cucumber Alley at night."

Neither Agnes nor Alice could explain why Mrs. Bradshaw was in Cucumber Alley that night. They commented they didn't know her well either, but their encounters with the elderly woman were always pleasant. Who'd want to kill a nice elderly lady like Mrs. Bradshaw?

Agnes steered the conversation toward more pleasant topics, such as the church rummage sale next month, plays at Proctor's Theater, and shopping at Carl's, H.S. Barney's, and Woolworth's. The ladies chatted pleasantly for an hour until Agnes mentioned they needed to leave. Gratefully, Flora led them to the hallway, not asking them to stay longer, and handed them their belongings.

"Please take care, Flora dear," Alice said, putting on her coat, scarf, and cloche hat. "Mr. Longworth, Rodney, and I aren't far away, so if you need us, just call."

Flora thanked Alice then looked at Agnes as she shrugged into her fur coat, placed her cloche hat on her head and the red-paisley scarf around her neck. She waved goodbye and closed the door. She could tolerate Agnes, but not her sister, Alice.

As she was ensconced in the armchair in the living room, getting ready to read about Mary Pickford and Douglas Fairbanks in *Photoplay*, a strange thought struck her. She put the magazine on her lap thoughtfully. The scarf Agnes placed around her neck just now, reddish-paisley colored, but it seemed…No, impossible, absurd. Agnes would notice. She imagined it, her mind too cluttered, thinking of the recent murders.

Flora started to read about Mary Pickford, but her mind was too far off. She stared at the fire, deep in thought. It seemed to her as though the paisley scarf she just saw was stained with the brilliant yet unmistakable color of blood.

Earlier in the evening, Rodney called Steven and Wilma at their home on North Church Street and asked if they'd want to meet for coffee.

Steven suggested something a bit stronger, a speakeasy off Union Street, but at the moment Rodney wasn't in the mood for liquor, especially the illegal kind. Puffing away at a cigarette, he told him he'd meet them at a coffee shop on State Street, near Proctor's Theater, in about twenty minutes.

As he gathered his coat and cap from the hallway closet, he entered the living room to see his father reading the evening paper and listening to the radio. He looked up upon seeing Rodney.

"Where are you going on such a chilly night?" Simon asked his son.

Rodney put on his coat and his cap. "I'm meeting Steven and Wilma at a coffee shop near Proctor's. It's good to talk with them."

At the same time, the front door opened, and Alice entered, her face flushed from the cold. She smiled upon seeing her son and graciously entered the living room, as though the queen had just arrived at the palace, decorously and nonchalantly removing her fur coat and cloche hat, and casually draping them on an armchair. She approached her husband, kissed him on the cheek, and then settled on the sofa, content to spend the evening at home. Glancing up at Rodney, she realized he was going out. Like his father, Alice asked him where he was going on such a chilly night.

"I'm meeting Steven and Wilma at a coffee shop," Rodney explained again. The bad part about living at home, he thought grudgingly.

"Be careful, dear," his mother told him. "Your Aunt Agnes and I just came from visiting Mrs. Hayes. It's awfully cold and icy, too."

Rodney assured his parents he'd be careful. He'd take the trolley instead of walking. He paused before heading for the door.

"How is Mrs. Hayes?" he asked his mother.

Alice picked up the front page of the evening edition of the *Schenectady Gazette* that Simon had left on the coffee table. She glanced at the headlines and then addressed her son.

"She seems fine, dear. It's been a shock, of course. She appreciated your visit after Theresa died. She's a good soul, Mrs. Hayes."

Simon agreed, folding the last section of the paper, and placing it also on the coffee table. "Perhaps we should invite her to dinner some evening," he suggested.

"Well, I'm not much of a cook, dear," Alice said sweetly, trying to discourage the idea of Mrs. Hayes eating at their house.

Rodney told his parents he wouldn't be too long, then eagerly left the house and caught the first trolley on Washington Avenue. It looped around the stockade until it came to the city center, entering State Street and the business district. He got off in front of H.S. Barney's and crossed at the light to the coffee shop near Proctor's Theater. Upon entering, he noticed Steven and Wilma were already there, sitting comfortably at a corner table, enjoying coffee, pastries, and cigarettes. Steven motioned to Rodney, pulling out a chair and signaling a waitress for more coffee.

"And a chocolate eclair for my friend here," he added with a smile.

Taking off his coat and cap and leaving them on an empty chair, Rodney sat next to Steven and across from Wilma. From his expression alone, the Banks could tell he was extremely preoccupied and distressed. The waitress soon returned with the coffee and the eclair, but Rodney found he didn't have much of an appetite. Wilma asked him how he was holding up.

"The police haven't made any progress in Theresa's murder," Rodney said, sipping the hot coffee. "It's almost two weeks and no arrests have been made. And the same for Mrs. Bradshaw."

Steven tried to console his friend. "Relax, Rodney. Patrols have been set up all over the stockade. You must've seen them. You can't walk anywhere without a policeman nearby."

Wilma puffed on her cigarette. "Especially Cucumber Alley. Curiously, I looked down that way the other day and I saw at least two policemen, on guard."

Steven cast an irritable look at his wife. Blowing smoke from his cigarette angrily, he asked her why she'd even go near Cucumber Alley in the first place. "It's dangerous, Wilma, don't you know that?"

Wilma sipped her coffee, puffed on her cigarette again, and nibbled at her pastry. "Well, I just wanted to see what was going on. With all the ruckus, there must be something happening in Cucumber Alley."

Rodney finished one cigarette and immediately lit another, puffing intensely while sipping the coffee. His fears had gotten the worst of him, and chain-smoking was clearly an indication that he was in a nervous state.

"I don't know what to think anymore," he told Steven and Wilma. "I miss Theresa. I was in love with her. But if she had another side, I wasn't aware of it. Somebody killed her in that alley, and I want to know who and why."

Rodney looked at Steven and Wilma and decided to tell them what Mrs. Grey told him last week when he saw her on State Street. Wilma clearly expressed indignation.

"What's she talking about, Rodney? We don't have any secrets!"

"She said Theresa found out something about us?" Steven asked, surprised. "I'd like to know what she meant. She's just making it up, Rodney. She's a foolish woman. I'm surprised the college lets her teach there."

Wilma nodded. "Mrs. Grey can be difficult. She was in the United Cigar Store recently and her whole demeanor was uncouth, to say the least."

"I wouldn't believe a thing she says," Steven added, smoking furiously, clearly agitated.

"What about Mrs. Bradshaw?" Rodney continued. "What was she doing in Cucumber Alley, so late at night?" He paused thoughtfully, as Steven and Wilma also were thinking back to the elderly woman they hardly knew. But then something came back to Rodney, clearly and vividly as though it had just taken place.

"I remember a few times Theresa came to the hotel to meet me," he told them, between puffs on his cigarette. "I was getting ready to leave. She'd wait for me in the lobby. From a distance, I noticed she had been conversing with Mrs. Bradshaw. I didn't think anything about it."

"You think Theresa told her something she shouldn't?" Wilma asked.

Rodney shrugged. "I don't know. But she could be sneaky, clever, and manipulative."

"Untrustworthy, too," Steven added, finishing his coffee.

What would she have told Mrs. Bradshaw?" Rodney stammered. "I don't think Mrs. Bradshaw would've listened much less believed anything Theresa told her. She had more sense than that. She must've realized Theresa was a gossiper."

"Mrs. Bradshaw knew you were involved with her," Steven said. "She took what she told her at face value. She tried to find out if whatever she told her was the truth."

Rodney's face was troubled. "As I've thought before, marriage to Theresa might have been the wrong thing to do. But I still want to know what really happened." He hesitated. "I've thought of hiring a private investigator."

"For what?" Steven showed surprised. "That's what the police are for, Rodney. It does take time, you know. We've already been questioned by the police. They're speaking to everyone who lives near Cucumber Alley."

Rodney shook his head, stubbornly. "The city police drag their feet. A private investigator can uncover leads and find answers quicker."

"Do you have any idea who you'd contact?" Wilma asked him.

"No, it's just a thought. I might look in the city directory."

An awkward silence ensued. They continued to discuss who could have killed Theresa and Mrs. Bradshaw. They discounted Mrs. Grey, as being too old and rather feeble, although she looked strong. Mrs. Brennan, Rodney's aunt, and Mr. Brennan, Rodney's uncle, were also eliminated, as they wouldn't have had the gumption to commit murder. They hardly knew Theresa and barely knew Mrs. Bradshaw. His own parents, Rodney also discounted. Wilma and Steven were aghast that he'd even contemplate his parents committing murder. Rodney admitted he knew his mother wasn't fond of Theresa, but that didn't mean she'd kill her. He added he didn't think Theresa thought highly of his mother, either. And his father was the soul of goodness. He'd never lift a finger to hurt anyone.

"That leaves Mrs. Hayes," Rodney concluded.

"Mrs. Hayes killed her own daughter?" Wilma asked, clearly surprised. She too began to smoke furiously, chain-smoking until her pack was almost depleted and she had to ask Steven for another. "Unless Theresa wasn't really her daughter."

Steven eliminated Mrs. Hayes. "Of course, she was her daughter, Wilma. What are you getting at? Regarding Mrs. Bradshaw, Mrs. Hayes didn't know her. None of us did, really."

Another uncomfortable silence passed between them. An unspoken horror lay dormant, as though they wondered if one of the three of them could have committed the murders of Theresa and Mrs. Bradshaw. Rodney cleared his throat and hesitantly mentioned Mr. Banks. Steven put down his coffee and cigarette and vehemently defended his father.

"Dad wouldn't hurt anyone. He had no reason to kill Theresa or Mrs. Bradshaw."

"Well, I guess that leaves us," Wilma said, puffing away on her cigarette.

They looked at her in disbelief, that she would think of that much less say it.

"I suppose it's true," Wilma continued. "Unless it's a madman running around the stockade district, preying on innocent women."

"Maybe Theresa wasn't all that innocent," Rodney said slowly.

"Do you think she had something on someone, Rodney?" Wilma asked him.

"Like what?" he asked, clearly frustrated

"Blackmail," Wilma practically whispered. "For money, Rodney, what else?"

"Who could she have been extorting? Mrs. Bradshaw?"

The waitress soon appeared, filling their cups with more coffee, and leaving the check. Steven tried changing the subject, by talking about plays at Proctor's, tennis at Central Park over the summer, and future trips to New York City. He then glanced at his watch and noticed the time. He mentioned they needed to leave, as morning came early, and another workday would be upon them. Wilma put on her dark gray coat, red paisley scarf, and pretty cloche hat while Rodney and Steven settled the bill at the cashier. They then put on their coats and caps, left the busy coffee shop, and stepped out onto a fresh snowfall on State Street. The wind had picked up, but Rodney found the fresh air invigorating. Steven and Wilma mentioned they'd catch the trolley, but Rodney preferred to walk. He assured them he was fine; the fresh air would do him good. Crossing State Street at the light, he walked briskly until he came to Washington Avenue, taking a right. His parent's wonderful brownstone house was within sight.

His thoughts returned to Steven and Wilma. They were in as much of the dark as he regarding the murders. Unless they were hiding something, as Mrs. Grey insinuated. Funny, too, how Steven tried changing the subject when his wife mentioned blackmail.

As he approached his parent's house, something else gnawed at his mind. Not the coffee, not the cigarettes, certainly not the eclair. Something he saw just now, casual, but unmistakable. He racked his brain, deep in thought. It was Wilma's red paisley scarf. Well, there were plenty of red paisley scarves, so what difference did it make? Certainly, nothing unusual.

Arriving home, he greeted his parents but couldn't shake the thought permeating his mind. Hadn't he seen a red paisley scarf somewhere before?

Tuesday, March the first dawned cloudy and cold, with intermittent snow showers and gusty winds. Rodney found his time at the Hotel Van Curler even more difficult than he had anticipated. The ornate crystal chandelier in the lobby, the exquisite restaurant, and the grandiose staircase leading up to the luxurious rooms, helped to alleviate his troubled mind. On good days, the tranquility of the hotel was timeless. He immersed himself in his work, hoping to diminish the chaotic thoughts swirling in his mind. He had spoken with Olive Mae and made plans to meet her this weekend at a dance hall off State Street. And why not, he thought, putting on his coat and cap, turning off the banker's lamp on his desk, and butting a cigarette in an ashtray. He couldn't mourn Theresa forever, although he still missed her terribly.

It was close to five-thirty when he left for the day and as he got off the trolley and approached his parent's house, it was closer to six. Before turning the key in the lock and opening the door, he sensed something was different. He was no sooner inside, his coat and cap left on the hallway chair when he heard the unmistakable sound of strangers. He turned toward the sound of the voices and entering the living room saw his parents on the sofa, and across from them sat Inspector James and Sergeant Eberhart of the Schenectady Police. He greeted the policemen politely, not imaging he'd see them again and at home, too. He smiled at his parents and sat next to his mother on the sofa.

"Hello, Mr. Longworth," Inspector James said professionally if not pleasantly. "My partner and I spoke to you at the hotel but we're here to speak to your parents about Miss Hayes and Mrs. Bradshaw. And we'd like to speak to you again, too."

"There is very little we can tell you, Inspector," Simon told him, finishing a cigarette. Sergeant Eberhart turned to him, pen in hand, ready to take notes.

"How well did you know Mrs. Bradshaw?"

"Not well at all, I'm afraid," Alice offered before her husband could speak. "I used to see her at the market and our church. And when I'd stop by the hotel to see Rodney. She was always pleasant and cordial."

"Do you know if she had enemies, Mrs. Longworth?"

Alice showed surprised. She batted her eyelashes and extinguished a cigarette in the ashtray on the coffee table with a well-manicured hand.

"I'm afraid I can't help you with Mrs. Bradshaw. Rodney can provide more insight into her character."

The policemen turned to Rodney, who felt as though he wanted to be just about any place now than in his own house. Why his mother made that comment he didn't know and wished she hadn't, as he didn't know Mrs. Bradshaw and told exactly that to the policemen previously. What more did they expect of him?

"Nothing untoward in her behavior that you can recall?"

Rodney shook his head. "A few times when Theresa came to the hotel, I saw her speaking with Mrs. Bradshaw. I have no idea what they were talking about."

Sergeant Eberhart thanked Rodney for that information. "We're trying to determine if there is a connection between these murders. We've spoken to Mrs. Hayes, but she couldn't provide us with any relevant information on her daughter or Mrs. Bradshaw."

"Would you tell us about that evening at the hotel, Mr. Longworth?" Inspector James asked. He looked at Rodney, then at Alice and Simon, figuring they knew more than they were willing to tell. Usually the case with rich people in comfortable homes such as this.

"I was working with Mrs. Bradshaw," Rodney said. He wanted to remind the inspector he had already told him that when questioned previously. "She left at eleven and I left at around eleven-thirty. I mentioned already that she wanted to go straight home, as there was a radio serial she wanted to listen to."

"She lived by herself, did she?"

"Yes, on Front Street, not far from here," Alice said. "Her husband died many years ago and she didn't have children."

"And she had worked at the hotel since it opened two years ago?"

Rodney nodded. "Yes, she and I almost started at the same time. I was hired as an assistant manager. She was hired as a desk clerk."

"She walked home alone, Mr. Longworth?"

Again, Rodney nodded, suddenly feeling uncomfortable. He had already supplied this information and didn't understand the reasons for this second interrogation. He loosened his tie and unbuttoned the top of his vest.

"She'd walk up Washington and passed Cucumber Alley."

"And when Miss Hayes was murdered, Mr. Longworth? Where were you?"

"At the hotel, as I believe I already explained." He fought hard to keep the irritation out of his voice. "We thought of going to a dance hall that night, but with the snowstorm, I didn't think it was a clever idea. My mother volunteers at the Nott Memorial Library and my father and I were waiting for her to return."

"Yes, it was Friday, February eighteenth," Alice put in.

"And what time did you arrive home, Mrs. Longworth?"

"Rather later than usual," Alice admitted. "My sister, Mrs. Jerome Brennan, teaches a Latin class on Friday evenings, so after my library shift was over, I walked over to the building where she teaches and sat in on the rest of the class. Afterward, she and I conversed with a few students in Latin and French and before we knew it, it was ten-thirty. We then left the building, with the three or four students, and we caught the trolley home." She hesitated. "I didn't see Theresa in the library after I started shelving books and periodicals. Mrs. Fillmore, the evening librarian, couldn't find her anywhere. Her shift hadn't ended yet, but she had just disappeared."

Sergeant Eberhart was busy scribbling in his notebook. He looked up at Simon.

"Do you have anything to add, Dr. Longworth?"

Simon had lit another cigarette and casually blew smoke, as though he was bored by the whole ordeal. "No, I can't say I do. I saw Miss Hayes at the library earlier in the day, as my wife did when I asked for the latest issue of a particular journal. After that, I left to return home. I prepared dinner for Rodney and my brother-in-law."

After a few more questions about Theresa's character and that of Mrs. Bradshaw, Inspector James and Sergeant Eberhart stood to leave. They thanked the Longworths for their time and reiterated that if they could remember anything that could help to solve these murders, to please contact them at police headquarters. Rodney showed them to the door. Upon returning to the living room, he saw his parents still seated comfortably, as though nothing out of the ordinary had just taken place.

Alice was immersed in the evening paper and Simon had turned on the radio to hear the evening news report. Rodney threw himself in an armchair, sighed deeply, and lit a cigarette, exhaling a long trail of smoke. He took off his tie angrily, unbuttoned his vest, removed his shoes, and sat fuming. Realizing his parents were practically ignoring him, he told them he was retiring to his room. Alice looked up from the paper.

"Already, dear? It's early, but you're tired, aren't you?"

"Mother, do you own a red paisley scarf?"

Alice had bent her head back down to the paper but then looked up sharply. Even Simon, intent on the evening radio report, looked at his son strangely.

"A red paisley scarf," Alice thought. "No, dear, you're thinking of Aunt Agnes. She loves paisley designs." She hesitated. "Why do you ask?"

"No reason." He was sounding nervous, and he knew it. "Good night, Mother, Dad."

Before Alice or Simon could say anything else, Rodney gathered his shoes and tie and butted his cigarette in an ashtray. He walked out of the living room, to the hallway, and up the stairs to his bedroom, leaving his parents to stare after him.

Chamber of Commerce
Schenectady Lights and Hauls the World
Population 100,000
Welcome

Russell Banks looked at the message on the large billboard as he drove his Mercedes-Benz north on Central Avenue, heading into the city. Schenectady was certainly growing, he thought pleasantly. Experimenting with the new medium of television, General Electric was more lucrative than ever. Thinking of his successful banking position and his keen stock market investments, Mr. Banks was grateful for his profitable expenditures. The future was assured, he smiled contentedly.

Mr. Banks glanced at Mrs. Flora Hayes, in the passenger seat. They had come from a restaurant in Albany, where they enjoyed a delicious dinner at a reputable steak restaurant. They had also enjoyed each other's company, as they had on previous occasions. An excursion, driving down to Albany when there were plenty of fine restaurants locally, but Mr. Banks insisted and Mrs. Hayes relented, eager to get out of the house.

Mrs. Hayes glanced at Mr. Banks as he drove into Schenectady. A handsome man, she thought, although sinister looking in some respects. And he was only five years older than me, she thought positively. Certainly well-dressed, his black hair slicked back from his prominent forehead, his dark eyes alluring. His clothes spoke of money and class. She knew his banking position paid well, he had excellent health and very few worries. His son and daughter-in-law kept him company after his divorce. Like Theresa kept me company, Flora thought. But that's another story, which she tried to put behind her.

Mr. Banks admired Mrs. Hayes, an attractive divorcee of fifty, pretty and fashionable, with a good figure and expressive brown eyes. Her brunette hair, worn in the bobbed style, her gray dress, simple yet appropriate along with a lovely string of pearls accentuated her fine appearance.

They reached the intersection of State Street and Nott Terrace. A busy evening as Proctor's Theater was still showing the new Ziegfeld musical.

Flora asked if he liked to see the play, either this evening or another night this week. Reviews were excellent and she loved musical theater.

"It may be too late for this evening," Russell said, looking at the theater from the car.

He parked on Clinton Street and Flora eagerly got out, leaving Russell to catch up with her until they came to the theater. As Russell suspected, the evening performance had already started, although there were still several patrons in the lobby, hoping to secure tickets.

Once in the ornate lobby, Flora approached the ticket vendor to ask for a schedule. The helpful young woman handed her a brochure, told her tickets were sold out for tonight and tomorrow night, but the weekend still had seating available. Flora thanked her for the brochure and had no sooner turned from the counter when she was suddenly hailed.

"Why, Mrs. Hayes, what a surprise to see you here!"

It was Mrs. Edna Grey standing in her path. A large, overbearing but friendly older woman, Flora shrunk back as though afraid of being stepped on. She forced a smile and greeted Mrs. Grey pleasantly. She noticed her friend, Mrs. Norris, whom she had met on previous occasions was also with her. She smiled at Flora and greeted her pleasantly.

"How are you holding up, Mrs. Hayes?" Mrs. Grey asked her, sincerely. "I feel so sorry for your loss. Theresa was a wonderful girl, always helpful at the library."

At that moment, Russell approached the women and greeted Mrs. Grey and Mrs. Norris. Mrs. Grey eyed Mr. Banks curiously, realizing he was with Mrs. Hayes and had obviously been spending time with her. Flora sensed her insinuation and was hard-pressed to tell her to mind her own business. Mrs. Grey introduced Mrs. Norris to Mr. Banks and after greetings were exchanged, an uncomfortable silence ensued until Flora was brave enough to break it.

"It was nice seeing you again, Mrs. Grey. Please stop over some time and you as well, Mrs. Norris. The coffee at my house is always warm."

Mrs. Grey smiled and thanked her kindly for her invitation, then with Mrs. Norris they approached the vendor to inquire about tickets for later in the week. Flora eyed Russell and nodded toward the exit, as though she couldn't get there fast enough.

Once on State Street, the wind had picked up and light snow was falling. Russell had to keep pace with her on walking back to the car. He could tell she was obviously perturbed but was it just because she encountered Mrs. Grey and Mrs. Norris?

Flora waited for him to unlock the car doors and once inside, sat brooding, fidgeting with her pocketbook, retrieving a new pack of cigarettes, opening the wrapper, and putting one to her lips. Russell took his lighter from his inner coat pocket and lit it for her. Opening the window, exhaling a great puff of smoke, Flora was clearly agitated.

"Do you want to tell me what's wrong?" Russell asked. He had yet to start the car.

"Let's just get going, Russell," Flora said, curtly.

Starting the engine and pulling slowly onto Clinton Street, he crossed at the light onto State, finally reaching Washington Avenue. At the light, he turned right and found a spot directly in front of Flora's brownstone, close to Cucumber Alley. She quickly opened the door, jumped out, and without waiting for Russell, reached her front door and entered. Russell was still getting out of the driver's side, looked over the top of the car roof, and realized his companion was already inside. He found her in the kitchen, where she had put on the kettle for tea. She was smoking furiously, pacing back and forth. He waited for her to tell him what was troubling her, although he already had an idea.

"That woman bothers me," Flora said between puffs. "She knows too much."

Russell had taken off his coat and sat at the kitchen table. He didn't tell her to stop pacing or to calm down. He looked at her and his face and tone were grave.

"I wouldn't worry about Mrs. Grey, Flora. We can handle her."

She approached the stove as the water started to boil. Filling a cup with the hot liquid, she stirred it absently, her mind far off.

"I don't think anyone should know, do you, Flora?" he asked, meeting her eyes.

Flora had turned from the stove, sipping the hot tea. "No, no, I don't."

CHAPTER FIVE

It was Wednesday morning, sunny but cold, with no snow in the forecast, at least not for the rest of the day. Plenty of snow remained on the sidewalks and driveways, however, and men worked feverishly to clear paths for pedestrians and cars to maneuver.

The snow had a minor impact at the Hotel Van Curler, bustling with activity, as conventions were taking place and numerous guests checked in. Governor Smith planned to visit Schenectady soon and would eat lunch at the hotel. Certainly, an occasion when a head of state was at the hotel.

None of this activity had much effect on Rodney Longworth. At the moment, he was attending a meeting of the hotel management, including Mr. Lennox, who repeated the bad publicity of the murder of Mrs. Bradshaw. Rodney still thought it sounded like he was more concerned for the hotel's name than finding the person responsible for her death. They had all been questioned by the police, without any success. As the meeting continued Mr. Lennox mentioned the hotel considering air conditioning to attract more clients. He also reiterated the expense as air conditioning was costly, especially for a large hotel.

Listening to Mr. Lennox rattle on and on, Rodney wondered about Theresa's murder while also curious about these new inventions for 1927. Mr. Lennox mentioned the notion of watching shows on a screen. He discussed that while television may be technically feasible in the future, commercially, and financially for the hotel it was an impossibility. He concluded guests surely wouldn't want to stare into a box while in their rooms and that it'd be a waste of the hotel's money, of which the majority of those present agreed. After about an hour, the meeting adjourned, and Rodney gladly returned to his office on the first floor.

Seated behind his desk, he ran his fingers through his hair, lit a cigarette and exhaled deeply. His thoughts returned to Theresa and Mrs. Bradshaw. He mentioned to Steven and Wilma his decision to contact a private investigator. He wouldn't make calls from the hotel, as the switchboard operator would place them. And he knew the operator was nosy and would wonder why he was calling a private investigator.

But someone had to find the underlying cause of the recent murders, he thought impatiently. The police haven't found anything helpful. Despite Theresa's faults and reputation, he loved her still and couldn't accept her untimely fate. He puffed on his cigarette moodily, then left his office for the front desk. He noticed Olive Mae, busy checking in guests. He waited for her to finish before speaking to her.

"Do we have a city directory, Olive Mae?"

Olive Mae smiled at Rodney, a pretty girl, with wholesome looks, deep green eyes, and a fair complexion, just enough make-up, an attractive figure, and a sleek gray dress highlighted with a string of pearls. Her appearance was pleasing and pleasant.

"Sure, Rodney, it's right here," she said and reached underneath the counter. She handed him the 1927 Schenectady City Directory.

Rodney took the city directory. "Have the police questioned you, too?"

Olive Mae nodded. "I didn't know Theresa. I only saw Mrs. Bradshaw a few times. But we never worked the same shift, so there wasn't much I could tell them." She looked at Rodney closely and could tell he was preoccupied. "Is everything okay, Rodney?"

Rodney puffed on his cigarette and deposited ash in an ashtray on the counter. "I'm fine, just a little tired." He paused, uncertainly. "Well, I have to get back to my desk." He turned to leave when Olive Mae stopped him.

"You know your mother is coming here for lunch today, don't you?"

She made it sound like an intrusion, as though Alice would check up on her son, which knowing his mother, Rodney concluded was most likely accurate. He then remembered his mother telling him at breakfast she'd be coming to the hotel for lunch, with his aunt and Mrs. Grey, as they usually did every few weeks.

Rodney nodded. "My mother, my aunt, and Mrs. Grey get together often." He paused. "When they're here, will you let me know?"

Olive Mae told Rodney she'd let him when they arrived, which wasn't until closer to noontime. Upon returning to his desk, he placed the city directory in front of him, an imposing, large book, with endless pages of listings. He admitted he had few reasons to consult such a book. He opened it randomly but then thumbed to the I section and found private investigators. He skimmed through the listings and noticed several in and around Schenectady. One listing caught his eye. He read the advertisement carefully.

SLOANE SHEPPARD, PRIVATE INVESTIGATOR
Criminal, Civil and Personal Investigations –
Reports Rendered Daily
Confidentiality Assured – Office Phone Main 2107
11 North Pearl Street, Albany, N.Y.

He jotted down the number and address but then realized it was in Albany. That'd mean he'd have to travel to Albany, and take time off during the weekday, as he was sure this Mr. Sheppard didn't work weekends. Strange he'd advertise in the Schenectady City Directory, but then Rodney assumed his work covered the entire Albany and Schenectady areas. He glanced again at the listings. There were investigators here in Schenectady, so he should stick with someone local. On the other hand, an investigator from Albany may not be familiar with the case or the local scene and could offer a fresh insight. Local investigators could be influenced by the city police and the newspaper. He should call this Mr. Sheppard. Albany wasn't far away. He glanced at his watch. He'd wait until later in the day when he left work. There was a payphone on State Street he could use. He jotted down the names and phone numbers of a few Schenectady private investigators as well as this Mr. Sheppard, in case he didn't pan out.

Closing the city directory, he sat at his desk, lost in thought. Just what would he expect a private investigator to uncover, anyway? Maybe he should just leave it to the city police. Certainly, Mrs. Hayes wasn't hiring a private investigator to investigate Theresa's murder, not to his knowledge, so why should he?

His reverie was broken by a knock on his office door. It was Olive Mae, letting him know his mother, aunt, and Mrs. Edna Grey were settled in the restaurant and were about to order lunch.

The ladies were seated comfortably in the main restaurant. Leaving their coats with the cloakroom attendant, they entered the elegant restaurant and upon taking menus from the waiter, reviewed the opulent lunch choices. It was a busy lunchtime scene: the murmur of conversations, the clatter of dishes, waiters rushing about, carrying trays, and taking orders. The room was filling up quickly, regular patrons included General Electric staff, nearby office workers as well as faculty from Union College. Some patrons had bags and parcels on the floor, the result of shopping at Schenectady's high-end department stores.

Agnes, Alice, and Edna were carefully reviewing the menu, undecided at first, chatting among themselves. Agnes looked pleasant and serene, her face showing the least bit of make-up, her blue dress stylish. As always, Alice was dressed lavishly, a green dress along with a pearl broach highlighted her appearance. Edna Grey, on the other hand, was sensibly but not fashionably dressed in a low-waisted dress of dark gray, no make-up, her gray hair worn back from her forehead, in an unbecoming bob.

The waiter busily scribbled down their choices on a pad while another filled their coffee cups. After they left their table, Edna asked Agnes about her Friday evening Latin class.

"Well, it's the best so far," she admitted, confidently. "The students are wonderful. And how is your Friday evening class coming along?"

"Well, my students may not be as exuberant as yours," Mrs. Grey said and smiled.

Alice sipped her coffee, changing the subject. "Terrible about these murders. It's too dreadful. Simon accompanies me when he's available. I'm too afraid to walk around alone."

Edna agreed. "Usually, I go to the market with Mrs. Norris. The police said there's a madman loose in the village. We have to be careful."

Agnes demurred, not as concerned as her sister or Edna Grey. "We mustn't get hysterical, ladies. We're safe in the village. We know where we're going all the time."

"So did Mrs. Bradshaw and Miss Hayes," Alice said, accepting a plate from the waiter.

"The police don't have any leads," Edna said, also taking a plate from the waiter. She began to cut a piece of grilled chicken. "It's almost a month now."

"It's frightening," Alice remarked. "And what were they doing in Cucumber Alley so late at night? Hardly anyone goes there anyway, especially at night."

"Unless they met someone," Edna suggested. She put oil and vinegar on her salad. "I thought highly of Mrs. Bradshaw. Such a nice lady."

"I didn't know her too well, of course," Alice said, enjoying her meal. "But she seemed pleasant enough. Although Miss Hayes was quite different."

Agnes looked at her sister. "Weren't she and Rodney practically engaged?"

Alice frowned. "They were contemplating marriage. Although neither Simon nor I encouraged it. Rodney is old enough to make his own mistakes, of course."

"Mrs. Hayes is pleasant," Edna commented. "I saw her last night with Mr. Bank at Proctor's Theater."

Alice showed surprised. "Mr. Banks and Mrs. Hayes at the theater together? What a disgrace. She hasn't wasted time in mourning for her daughter."

"You can't expect her to mope the rest of her life," Agnes said sensibly. "Mr. Banks seems like a genuinely nice man. I don't know him too well, though."

"He may have secrets," Edna commented, causing the sisters to stop eating and look at her. "And I imagine Mrs. Hayes has, too."

Neither Agnes nor Alice commented on her surprising remark. Instead, Agnes cleared her throat, sipped her coffee, and asked the waiter for another napkin.

"We all have our secrets, Edna," she said. "There are things better left unsaid, never to be made known. No one else's business."

Alice nodded. "Some people are nosy. I know I appear to meddle, but I don't pry. There's a difference, you know."

Edna nodded. "Theresa was meddlesome. I know she was unpleasant to many faculty and even students. I don't know why they kept her there."

"It was just her personality," Agnes offered, spearing a tomato in her salad. "Her mother is lovely. In her daughter's case, the apple certainly fell far from the tree."

At that moment, Rodney approached their table and greeted his mother, aunt, and Mrs. Grey. He noted how well they looked, and the fine meal they were enjoying, as well as the other patrons, packed around them in the busy restaurant.

"Why don't you join us, dear?" Alice asked her son.

Rodney declined. "I can't, Mother. Some other time. I have too much to do." Which he knew wasn't true, but he didn't feel in the least like joining these gossipy women, including his mother and aunt, in nothing more than idle chit-chat.

"Well, suit yourself, dear," Alice said, sipping coffee.

"Such a lovely hotel, Rodney," Agnes said, looking around as though she had never been there before. "And so busy, too."

"Governor Smith is expected later this week," Rodney told them.

Conversation then ensued about Governor Smith running for the presidency in 1928 and the political climate of the country. Rodney couldn't wait to take leave of them and was glad when Mrs. Grey cleared her throat and mentioned the time.

"I need to go to the Nott Memorial Library to research for my science class."

Rodney signaled the waiter to bring their check. He then told them he'd collect their coats from the cloakroom and meet them in the front entrance. Settling the bill at the cashier, Alice, Agnes, and Edna met Rodney in the hotel foyer. He handed his mother her fur coat but wasn't sure which of the remaining two belonged to whom.

"Well, we both must like red paisley scarves," Mrs. Grey laughed, taking her coat, red cloche hat, and red paisley scarf from Rodney.

Agnes shook her head, taking her coat from her nephew. "I don't believe that's my scarf, Rodney dear. That one is mine." She pointed to the scarf in Edna's hand.

Edna frowned, startled, holding her red cloche hat, coat and the red paisley scarf. "I'm sorry, Agnes, but I know my scarf. Mine doesn't have little red marks on it."

"Funny, those marks look like dried blood," Alice commented, putting on her fur coat, and placing her cloche hat delicately on her head. "How did you get blood on your scarf, Agnes?"

Agnes had it around her neck. "It does look like dried blood, doesn't it?" Her tone implied she wasn't aware of it before.

Alice looked at the red paisley scarf around Edna's neck and noticed those red marks didn't appear on hers, although the two scarves were identical in design. "Has it been like that for long?"

Alice shook her head, nonchalantly. "I haven't noticed it before."

The ladies wished Rodney well and Alice told her son she'd see him this evening when he arrived home. He watched as they walked down the stairs and out onto Washington Avenue to catch the trolley.

Dried blood, he thought, and now three red paisley scarves: Wilma, Aunt Agnes, and Mrs. Grey. Was it really blood on her scarf? Wouldn't she have noticed it before? She seemed so casual about it, as though she didn't care.

On the way back to his office, Rodney wondered if the conversation he just heard was somehow connected to the murders of Theresa and Mrs. Bradshaw.

Dr. Simon Longworth extinguished a cigarette in the ashtray on the coffee table in the living room of his home on Washington Avenue. He had been listening to the news on the radio while drafting an article for *Scientific American*, to be published in an upcoming issue. He put his notebook aside, rubbed his tired eyes, and listened to the news report.

Economic prosperity for Schenectady continues as General Electric, the city's top employer, makes headlines with new innovations, including the future of television broadcasting. Wall Street sees an increase in buying, investors believe stocks will continue growing, and borrowing to invest more is occurring daily...

Simon listened thoughtfully to the radio and believed it was an opportune time to invest, with the stock market gaining rapidly. Mr. Banks would assist him in his investments. Glancing at the windows overlooking Washington Avenue, he decided he'd go to the Schenectady Trust Company to speak with him, then walk over to Carl's and H.S. Barney's.

He got up and looked at himself in the hallway mirror. Not too bad for seventy, he thought, trim and professional in gray slacks, dress shirt, and tie. Like his wife, Simon believed in presenting his best, especially in public. With his coat on and his Fedora low on his head, he closed and locked the door and despite the chilly air, decided to walk, letting a trolley pass him by. Alice had gone for lunch with her sister and Mrs. Grey at the Hotel Van Curler, so he decided a long brisk walk was the best remedy to clear his mind.

It was mid-afternoon and although March already, it was still gloomy with intermittent sunshine. With his footsteps crunching in the snow, Simon wondered why the sidewalks in the stockade village weren't better maintained. Of course, with all the snow, it was hard to keep up with it. Rodney would shovel the steps and the sidewalk in front of their house, but the rest of the area could certainly use a thorough scraping.

Arriving at the corner of Washington and State Street, Simon felt invigorated in the chilly air. He walked past Woolworth's, H.S. Barney's, and Carl's, marveling at the fabulous window displays. He walked another block down State Street until he came to the Schenectady Trust Company. He hadn't been to the bank in a while, but upon entering, he could tell it was a scene of almost chaotic activity. Banks officials were busy on telephones, advising clients on stock options, savings accounts, bonds, and other money matters. Clerks made deposits and withdrawals for customers, patiently waiting their turn in line.

At the far end of the busy lobby, was the office of the manager, Mr. Russell Banks. Simon was greeted pleasantly by a young woman, who inquired if she could be of assistance. Simon thanked her and said he wished to speak to Mr. Banks. She glanced at his closed office door, and told Simon he was still with a client, if he cared to wait. Simon nodded and sat in one of the chairs outside Mr. Banks's office. After what seemed an interminable amount of time, the office door finally opened, and out stepped Mr. Banks, followed by a middle-aged woman, carrying a portfolio. She thanked him for his time and walked to the main lobby, while Russell turned and recognized Simon, in the waiting area. He greeted him amicably and ushered him into his office.

"Good to see you, Mr. Longworth," he said, returning to his desk. He moved the candlestick phone and a few papers around. "How can I help you today?"

"I'd like information on investments," Simon said, unbuttoning his coat. "Now is the best time to invest, according to what I've heard on the radio."

Russell agreed. He extracted from a drawer, numerous brochures on stock options, what stocks were worth investing and the bank's current borrowing rates. He explained many clients preferred to borrow to buy stocks, which had proven advantageous for them and as predicted will continue to do so. Simon put on his spectacles, accepted the brochures from Russell and read through them carefully. Although he was interested, he was unable to reach a sound decision. Russell suggested several options, but Simon shook his head.

"Sorry, Mr. Banks, I guess I can't think too clearly lately. I've been too preoccupied with the murders. Living close to Cucumber Alley doesn't help much, either."

Russell nodded, his black hair slicked back, as usual, his brown eyes attentive and as he listened to Simon, sympathetic to his concerns. He asked him how he, Mrs. Longworth, and Rodney were holding up, given the recent events.

"Rodney's more frustrated now than anything else. He thinks the police are dragging their feet with the investigation. They have no leads at all."

Russell lit a cigarette, offered one to Simon, held out his lighter, and then the men sat back, seeming to relax, although both were extremely perplexed. After a moment, Russell exhaled a cloud of smoke and asked Simon what he thought happened to Miss Hayes and Mrs. Bradshaw.

Simon shrugged. "Your guess is as good as mine. I hardly knew Mrs. Bradshaw and Theresa I knew only from the library."

Russell took his time in replying. "If the police haven't uncovered any leads, it's safe to assume there's a madman loose in the stockade village. It may not be safe to walk at night, especially for women."

Simon agreed. "But there must be something more, something we're not seeing!"

Russell looked at him across the desk with raised eyebrows. "Like what?"

Simon puffed at his cigarette, before crushing it out in frustration in the ashtray on Russell's desk. He got up and walked over to the windows, overlooking North Center Street, in the rear of the bank. He took his time in replying.

"I think there's more than it just being a madman," he said, facing him. "I think the killer is someone we know."

Russell also extinguished his cigarette in the ashtray. "I agree with you. I thought that after Theresa was killed. I didn't know Mrs. Bradshaw."

Simon paced the area near the windows. "Certainly not Mrs. Grey or Mrs. Hayes."

Russell's eyebrows went up again. "I hardly think Mrs. Grey capable of murder. Certainly not Mrs. Hayes. Mrs. Grey has brought food over for Flora during this difficult time."

Simon nodded and then as though exasperated from his thoughts, thanked Russell for his time and was almost to the door when Mr. Banks stopped him.

"Mr. Longworth, who do you suspect?"

His hand on the doorknob, deep in thought, Simon shook his head. "I don't know."

"What about your brother-in-law or sister-in-law? I'm sure that's far from your mind. Didn't they have issues with both Theresa and Mrs. Bradshaw in the past?"

Simon was appalled. Agnes or Jerome cold-blooded killers? Was that even remotely possible? How could he even suggest Agnes or Jerome capable of murder?

"I think they did have some sort of problem with Mrs. Bradshaw, years ago. As far as Theresa is concerned, I don't think Jerome really knew her. A lot of people had issues with Miss Hayes. Agnes saw her at the library, of course." He stopped speaking, as he realized his sister-in-law could very well have had issues with meddling, conniving Theresa Hayes, but if she did, he wasn't aware of them.

Russell stood and joined Simon at the door. "My best to your wife and son. And if I can help you with your investments, please let me know. I've assisted several city residents to get the most of current stocks and now is certainly the time to invest. The stock market isn't showing any signs of slowing down."

Simon smiled wryly. "I heard it on the radio this morning." He hesitated, as though about to say something else, then changed his mind. "Thanks, Mr. Banks, for your help. I'll review these brochures and get back to you."

Russell joined him at the door, where they shook hands. As though he couldn't wait to leave, Simon abruptly opened the door, walked steadily through the lobby and out the front doors. Bewildered by his behavior, Russell remained in the doorway of his office, looking after him, then returned to his desk to finish his work.

Rodney stood at the end of Cucumber Alley, overlooking the Mohawk River. It was close to five-thirty and darkness had fallen over the city. He had left work early and instead of going straight home, decided to investigate Cucumber Alley.

He had been wanting to come here since the murders but kept putting it off. It was a quiet, desolate area, not well-traveled. What happened to the police and the community members? Of course, it was still early. They came more toward the later hours.

He stood with his hands in his pockets, feeling foolish, not understanding the unexpected fate of Theresa and Mrs. Bradshaw. He shivered at the chilly air blowing off the water. It was still cold, as early March tended to be in Schenectady, so he pulled his cap lower on his head and his scarf closer around his neck. Standing in the near darkness, with little light from the few houses nearby, he wondered what brought Theresa and Mrs. Bradshaw here and who killed them.

Theresa must have known information about someone or something. She could have told that information to Mrs. Bradshaw, as he saw them chatting away when Theresa came to the hotel. But what did Theresa know? Or did Mrs. Bradshaw know something and related it to Theresa?

He stood still and looked around. Easy to kill someone here, no one around to hear a scream or see a struggle. Looking at the river, he marveled at the calmness of the water and the soothing effect it had, although the reality of the murders set in and wiped away any serenity he felt.

The killer must have stood right here, he considered, and stabbed them both, leaving them for dead. He remained planted in front of the base of the river, staring out onto the water, deep in troubled thoughts.

Realizing there was nothing here to accomplish, he turned and walked quickly toward Washington Avenue. Taking a right, toward his parent's brownstone, he was relieved there were more lights, pedestrians, cars, traffic, and trollies, in fact, more of life than in bleak and dismal Cucumber Alley.

He didn't notice Wilma Banks, standing at the farthest side of Cucumber Alley, wearing her fur coat, red paisley scarf, and cloche hat, smoking, and staring after Rodney, with a hard-set look on her face.

CHAPTER SIX

Alice stood at the stove, humming a tune while preparing break-fast. It was quarter past eight on Thursday morning. She glanced out the window. Another chilly day, but at least the sun was trying to come out. She planned to shop at Carl's and H.S. Barney's today and later work at the library. She cooked oatmeal, one of Rodney's favorites. Putting the lid on the pot and lowering the burner, she was saving the rest for her son, who was still in bed.

She looked at Simon as he sat at the kitchen table, reviewing the morning paper. He was always absorbed in reading, she thought irritably, as though he were an ostrich, burying his head in the sand, shutting out problems, not wishing to discuss them. She filled his coffee cup, left the pot on the table, and then absently sat down, putting sugar in her cup, along with cream, but not drinking it. Simon looked away from the paper at his wife and noticed her forlorn expression, her tired eyes, her sullen face. He asked what was wrong.

"I'm concerned for Rodney," Alice explained, wearily. "He's taking these murders badly. I don't know what else to do for him. He's pre-occupied all the time."

Simon folded the paper and put it on the table. "We should talk to him. It isn't healthy to keep it bottled up all the time."

Just then they heard Rodney come down the stairs. Upon entering the kitchen, unshaven, clearly disheveled from a poor night's sleep, he blinked a few times, pulled his robe tighter, and greeted his parents, sleepily. He sat next to his father, yawning, not quite awake.

"Rodney, dear, I thought you would've stayed in bed longer," his mother said, tenderly. "Isn't today your late day?"

Rodney yawned again, scratched the stubble on his face, and ran his fingers through his tousled hair. "I have some calls to make this morning."

Simon and Alice looked at him questioningly, waiting for him to explain. Alice poured coffee and placing a cup in front of him, asked who he wanted to call so early in the morning.

"Usually, you enjoy sleeping late when you don't have to go in early," she said again. She looked at her son across from her and then at her husband, trying to find answers to her son's peculiar behavior. "Would you like me to fix your oatmeal, dear? I'll sprinkle nutmeg, just how you like it."

Rodney shook his head. "I'm not really hungry." He paused, realizing his parents were staring at him, obviously waiting for him to explain his early morning appearance.

He sipped the coffee and boldly told his parents he planned to contact private investigators to investigate Theresa's murder. He continued drinking his coffee and did not offer anything more.

Alice and Simon started to speak at once, but Simon authoritatively cleared his throat and addressed his son, trying to keep the annoyance from his voice.

"Rodney, why do you want to contact a private investigator? What's wrong with the police? They're doing their job, it takes time, you know.

Murder investigations can last weeks, even months. I have confidence the police will find the underlying cause of these murders."

Alice agreed, putting the coffee cup to her lips. "It'll be expensive, dear. Besides, shouldn't Mrs. Hayes do that? It was her daughter."

"Do you have names you plan to contact?" Simon asked before he had a chance to reply. "Someone here in Schenectady? You're wasting your time, Rodney. And your money, too."

"I have a list of names," Rodney managed to say before his parents could interject anything further. "I think it's a good idea. It's been a month and no leads." Before his father could protest, he continued. "I want to hire someone from Albany, who isn't familiar with the case. He might offer a fresh insight and find the underlying cause of it."

"Albany?" Alice questioned. "I'd imagine there are plenty of detectives here in Schenectady, dear. Wouldn't that mean you'd have to go there to meet him?" She made it seem as though Albany was a thousand miles away from Schenectady.

"The trolley will take me there," Rodney said, sipping the coffee and finding the caffeine gave him renewed strength. "If the private investigator I contact agrees to meet with me, that's what I plan to do."

An awkward silence followed, broken only by the sound of the grandfathers clock in the hallway, chiming the half-hour. Rodney and his parents continued sitting at the breakfast table although no one felt much like talking any further. Simon mentioned he needed to finish an article he planned to submit to *Scientific American* while Alice announced her shopping plans for later. Rodney lit a cigarette while sipping another cup of coffee, thoughtfully, wondering if he'd have luck contacting private investigators. Alice started to straighten the kitchen while Simon excused himself and entered the living room, taking up his notebook and pen.

"I'll be placing calls this morning, Mother," Rodney told her, getting up from the table, extinguishing his cigarette in an ashtray, and bringing his cup to the counter. "I may be using the line for a while, just so you know."

Alice was wiping the dishes. "If that's what you want, dear. I do agree with your father. The police will find out what's going on."

But Rodney was not to be deterred. He hurried upstairs to his bedroom. Once there, he reached for his wallet on his desk and took out the list of private investigators he found from the city directory. He glanced at his alarm clock and noticed it was just after nine o'clock. Offices should be open by now. First, he'd prepare for the day, as he still had to report to the hotel.

He entered the bathroom and filled the sink with water to shave. He stroked his face and neck with the razor angrily, nicking himself, his thoughts too preoccupied to concentrate on shaving. Nothing would stop him, not even his parents. There was a pattern to the murders in Cucumber Alley. And a private investigator would help him learn the truth.

Inspector James and Sergeant Eberhart of the Schenectady City Police paused before the brownstone house on North Church Street. The inspector glanced at the list of names in a notebook and nodded to his colleague. He rang the doorbell and waited patiently. After a moment, a stocky middle-aged man, still in robe and slippers, came to the door.

"Good morning, Mr. Banks," Inspector James said. "I'm Inspector James and this is my partner, Sergeant Eberhart. I know you, your son, and daughter-in-law have been questioned by the police regarding the recent murders. My partner and I are continuing our investigation."

Russell wondered why they'd come so early, rather an impertinence. Lucky for them to catch us at home he thought grudgingly. He planned to go to the bank later in the morning, Wilma had the day off and Steven was going to General Electric this afternoon. Reluctantly, he stood aside and allowed the policemen to enter.

"Russ, who is it?" Wilma said, entering the hallway, also in her robe and slippers. She stopped when she saw two gentlemen she didn't know. She looked at her father-in-law questioningly.

"This is Inspector James and that's Sergeant Eberhart of the city police, Wilma," Russell said, as though making a social introduction. "This is my daughter-in-law, Wilma. My son, Steven, is having breakfast in the kitchen."

"We've already spoken to the police," she said boldly. "I don't believe there's anything more we can tell you."

Standing in the hallway, feeling foolish, Russell closed the door and invited the policemen to the kitchen, where Steven was at the table, finishing his breakfast and pouring more coffee. His back was to the doorway, so he didn't know who was the unexpected company until Wilma brought them to his attention.

"We've already spoken to the police," Steven reiterated his wife's statement. He also tried to hide his annoyance at such an early call. "Usually, I'm on my way to work at this time but I'm going in this afternoon." His tone implied he'd prefer not to speak to them under any conditions.

Russell invited them to sit at the table, while Wilma offered them coffee, which they refused. Inspector James came directly to the point.

"As you know, there have been two murders recently, Mrs. Stella Bradshaw, and Miss Theresa Hayes. We're speaking to people who live near Cucumber Alley and the vicinity."

Sergeant Eberhart took a small notebook out from his jacket. "Any more information you can provide? I understand you knew Miss Hayes well."

Wilma cleared her throat and spoke first. "As I already told the policemen who were here, I didn't know Mrs. Bradshaw, although she didn't live far from us. I used to see her walking to the hotel, where she worked. We exchanged a few words every so often. She seemed pleasant enough."

"And Miss Hayes?"

Wilma lit a cigarette and deposited the match in an ashtray on the table. She took her time in replying. "Miss Hayes was another matter, Sergeant."

Steven cleared his throat. "She was jealous of my wife, especially after Wilma and I announced our engagement. She tried to interfere in our marriage several times."

"How long have you been married, Mr. Banks?"

"Three years. Theresa tried to break us up."

Inspector James wondered where this was going. "By doing what, Mr. Banks?"

"By spreading malicious gossip. News travels around this community quickly and at the college where she worked, too."

The inspector nodded. "Do you know anyone who'd want to harm either Miss Hayes or Mrs. Bradshaw?"

"I can't speak about Mrs. Bradshaw," Steven answered. "But Theresa had her share of enemies. She wasn't well-liked on the campus, either."

Wilma knocked ash from her cigarette into the ashtray. "What were they doing in Cucumber Alley so late at night?"

Sergeant Eberhart closed his notebook. "Possibly they were there to extort someone with incriminating information. Mr. Rodney Longworth mentioned he saw Miss Hayes speaking to Mrs. Bradshaw a few times at the hotel, but he didn't know what they were discussing."

"I can see Theresa as a blackmailer," Wilma said. "But not Mrs. Bradshaw."

"How well do you know your neighbors, Mr. Banks?" the Inspector asked Russell.

Taken aback, Russell cleared his throat. "I've known most of the people who live on this street and around Washington Avenue, including the Longworths for many years. Mrs. Longworth's sister, Mrs. Brennan and her husband, on Union Street, are pleasant people."

Steven agreed. "I work with Mr. Brennan at General Electric. He's an intelligent man, devoted to his research."

"Mrs. Brennan teaches at the college," the Inspector noted. "As does Mrs. Edna Grey."

"Mrs. Brennan teaches Latin," Russell said. "And Mrs. Grey teaches science, part-time."

"You don't suspect the Brennans or Mrs. Grey of murder," Steven said, incredulously. "There must be a madman running loose here in Schenectady. What else could it be?"

"Rodney Longworth was Theresa's boyfriend," Wilma offered. "Although what he saw in her, I could never understand. I don't think his parents cared for her very much."

"Do you suspect the Longworths of murder, Inspector?" Steven asked.

"With murder, everyone is a suspect," the Sergeant remarked dryly.

"Are we under suspicion as well?" Wilma asked bluntly, causing Steven to look at her with anger. Even Russell stared at his daughter-in-law with contempt.

"Until these murders have been cleared up," the Inspector said, "everyone is a suspect."

More questioning followed, as to their whereabouts the evenings Mrs. Bradshaw and Miss Hayes were murdered. Russell verified they were together both evenings. The snowstorm kept them from going out. He had joined Steven and Wilma in the living room, listening to the latest headlines and reading the evening newspaper.

Inspector James and Sergeant Eberhart rose and thanked the Banks for their time. Russell saw them to the door. Upon returning to the kitchen, he noticed Steven and Wilma still at the table in a silence so thick Russell thought he could've cut it with a knife.

"I'll be in the living room, listening to the radio," he announced, uneasily.

"I'll join you, Dad," Steven said., rising from his chair. "I like hearing what's going on in the world. WGY always has an excellent news report in the mornings."

Father and son entered the living room, leaving Wilma alone at the kitchen table, meditatively sipping her coffee and smoking anxiously. Since it was her day off, she'd shop at Carl's, Woolworth's or H.S. Barney's. Perhaps another walk to Cucumber Alley, too.

In the Brennan's home on Union Street, breakfast was also in progress. Agnes and Jerome had coffee, cigarettes, and the morning paper on the kitchen table, along with the radio console on in the living room. After she retrieved the morning paper on the doorstep, she left her fur coat and red-stained paisley scarf on an empty chair in the kitchen. She finished her second cup of coffee when the doorbell suddenly rang. Not used to company so early in the morning, Jerome, still in his robe and slippers, rather sleepily, went to the hallway to see who'd be calling. He opened the door and saw Mrs. Flora Hayes.

"Good morning," Flora said pleasantly, carrying a small basket. "I promised Agnes to bake some muffins, so I wanted to bring them to her."

Jerome smiled. "Please come in, Flora. Agnes is in the kitchen, having breakfast."

Flora entered and then turned to Jerome. "I hope I'm not too early. It's my day off so I wanted to catch her before she left for the college."

She followed him down the hallway to the large kitchen, where Agnes, also still in her housecoat and slippers, was at the table, drinking coffee. Flora greeted her and removed her cloche hat and fur coat, leaving them on an empty chair. Agnes smiled and admired her navy-blue dress along with a fine string of pearls, looking pretty and quite feminine.

Accepting a cup of coffee, Flora admitted to herself she preferred the company of Mrs. Brennan to Mrs. Longworth. Flora found Alice Longworth extremely egoistic while Agnes was more down-to-earth and genuine. Not that she wore out her doorstep, of course. But after Theresa's death, it was valuable to have people to visit. And Agnes Brennan was friendly and welcoming.

"Today's my day off," Flora explained to Agnes, putting sugar in her coffee. "I wanted to stop by before you left for the college. I baked some blueberry muffins. Hope you like them."

Agnes had opened the basket and extracted a plate full of muffins. She unwrapped the foil and exclaimed that they looked heavenly. She rewrapped them and was about to ask Flora if there were any further leads regarding Theresa's death when the doorbell unexpectedly rang again.

Jerome, Agnes, and Flora looked at each other, wondering who'd be coming here, again so early. Agnes thought it might be her sister but knew she had called her last evening. Alice mentioned she wasn't in the mood for visiting today. This time Agnes went to the door, leaving Jerome and Flora at the kitchen table. She returned with Inspector James and Sergeant Eberhart.

Inspector James and Sergeant Eberhart refused coffee, sat at the remaining chairs and as with the Banks, came straight to the point, first addressing Flora, expressing gratitude that she was there for them to speak to her as well as the Brennans.

"We're continuing our investigation into your daughter's murder," the Inspector said, "as well as the murder of Mrs. Stella Bradshaw."

Agnes cleared her throat. "Mrs. Bradshaw was a wonderful lady. Quiet, friendly, she kept mostly to herself. She was involved with our church and the community center. I know she'd enjoy lunching at the Hotel Van Curler with my sister and I on occasion, and with Mrs. Grey, too." She paused. "Other than that, I can't help you, Inspector. If she was involved with something illegal, I was unaware of it. Although I do find it difficult to believe anyone would want to kill her."

"Illegal, Mrs. Brennan? What makes you think that?"

"Well, with those speakeasies, the illegal liquor here in the city, and the drug smuggling. She may have been accosted by a bootlegger."

Jerome looked at his wife incredulously. "That doesn't explain what she was doing in Cucumber Alley that night."

"Maybe she was there to meet someone," Flora suggested. "The same for my daughter. I waited for her that night, but she never came home. If she was up to something, I wasn't aware of it." She paused. "My daughter had a secretive nature. She mostly kept things to herself."

The Inspector nodded. "You are divorced, Mrs. Hayes? Your daughter lived with you?"

Flora fidgeted in the chair. "Yes, my husband and I are divorced. I live on Washington Avenue, close to the Longworths and Mrs. Grey."

"Do you maintain communication with your ex-husband?"

"No, we parted and haven't spoken in years."

"How long ago was your divorce?"

"Inspector, I don't see the need for these questions."

"Please answer the question, Mrs. Hayes."

"It was over twenty years ago."

Sergeant Eberhart wrote in his small notebook. He looked up and addressed Agnes.

"Did you see Miss Hayes often, Mrs. Brennan?"

Agnes nodded. "Only at the Nott Memorial Library."

Sergeant Eberhart was busy taking notes. "And you, Mr. Brennan? Did you have any dealings with Miss Hayes or Mrs. Bradshaw?"

"I didn't have reason to go to the library. General Electric maintains its own library. As for Mrs. Bradshaw, I'll reiterate what my wife said earlier. She was quiet and friendly."

Further questioning about Mrs. Bradshaw, Theresa and the surrounding community produced little results. Inspector James thanked them for their time and with Sergeant Eberhart, walked down the hallway, Jerome showing them to the door. Upon returning to the kitchen, he found his wife and Flora talking about the church rummage sale, as though a normal conversation would naturally ensue after a visit from the police.

"Well, I must be going," Flora said, finishing her coffee. "It's always nice to see you, Agnes, and you too, Jerome. This weekend we can have dinner."

Agnes commented that she'd cook a sumptuous meal and then joined her friend at the front door. Returning to the kitchen, she found Jerome pouring more coffee, still at the table, and smoking in what appeared extreme agitation.

"We've spoken to the police already Why do they keep prying?"

Agnes sat across from him and stifled a yawn. "I'm glad he didn't notice my red scarf." She glanced at her fur coat and the red-stained paisley scarf on a kitchen chair. "Blood stains, how ridiculous! I'll wash it and there'll be no more talk of blood stains."

"But that doesn't solve the murders," her husband said gravely.

Agnes sipped her coffee. "For Rodney's sake, dear, it's best not to say anything more. So, we won't."

At Union College, Mrs. Edna Grey was busy grading exams. She was in the main academic building, seated at the teacher's desk in an empty classroom on the second floor. She glanced out the large windows overlooking the front campus. Gusty winds rattled the windowpanes, bringing a definite chill to the classroom. She was getting ready to leave for lunch when she saw two men in the doorway. Realizing they were not students, she cleared her throat and asked if she could assist them.

"Mrs. Grey, I'm Inspector James and this is my partner Sergeant Eberhart of the Schenectady Police. The secretary downstairs mentioned we'd find you here. We'd like to speak to you about Miss Hayes and Mrs. Bradshaw."

Mrs. Grey nodded solemnly. "Yes, of course, please sit down." She motioned to the student desks, in front of the teacher's desk.

"We're interviewing everyone who knew Miss Hayes and Mrs. Bradshaw," the Inspector said. "We know you were already questioned by the police after the murders. They've questioned people who live on Washington Avenue and the vicinity. My partner and I are continuing the investigation. You were one of the last people to see Miss Hayes the evening she disappeared."

Mrs. Grey nodded. "Yes, I saw her as did Mrs. Fillmore, Mrs. Longworth, and Mrs. Brennan. Dr. Longworth saw her, too."

Sergeant Eberhart cleared his throat, looking at Mrs. Grey carefully. A tall, gaunt older woman, certainly matronly, nosy for sure, precise, inquisitive but helpful. Severe looking in a black dress, gray hair worn tightly back from her forehead with a clip and rather thick spectacles, behind which her dark eyes looked at them suspiciously.

"Thank you, Mrs. Grey. We've spoken to those you mentioned. The police already spoke to Mrs. Fillmore. Can you offer any insight as to what happened to Miss Hayes?"

Mrs. Grey moved the stack of exams from one side of the desk to the other. "I'm sorry, but I wish I could help you. I saw Miss Hayes briefly that evening before heading over to my class. She handed me the latest nursing journals, which I reviewed while in the library, as she reminded me current periodicals don't circulate. I returned them to her afterward and then came here."

"And how long was that?"

She thought for a moment. "About twenty minutes or so, I'm not sure."

"Were you acquainted with Mrs. Bradshaw?"

"Only briefly. I used to see her on Washington Avenue, shopping on State Street, and around the village. She seemed pleasant enough. She was active in the community center."

Inspector James nodded. "Your whereabouts the evening these murders occurred?"

Mrs. Grey wrinkled her face, causing more lines to appear underneath her eyes. "Well, Thursday evening, I was at home, writing my lesson plans for the next evening's class. I spoke with my friend, Mrs. Norris on the phone and listened to a program on the radio before going to bed. I read for a while before falling asleep. Friday evening, I was here teaching a class."

Sergeant Eberhart wrote in his notebook. "Have you always worked here at Union?"

"I'm a retired nurse," Mrs. Grey said. "I've taught here part-time for several years."

"Do you have reason to go to Cucumber Alley?"

"Oh, my goodness, no, Inspector. I don't know the people who live there. It's a rather lonely spot. I don't like it at all."

"Do you have any idea who'd want to harm Mrs. Bradshaw or Miss Hayes?"

"Miss Hayes could be difficult with students and faculty. As I mentioned, I hardly knew Mrs. Bradshaw." She spoke with an air of finality, as though she was finished speaking and didn't care to offer anything further.

"Are you a widow, Mrs. Grey?"

Mrs. Grey was unused to personal questions. "Yes, my husband died many years ago. I have no children." She paused. "Have you spoken to Mr. Banks and his son and daughter-in-law?"

Inspector James was surprised. "Yes, we've spoken to the Banks. Do you know them?"

Mrs. Grey wrinkled her eyes. "I wouldn't say I know them, but they have plenty of secrets, Inspector. Mr. Banks may know more about Miss Hayes than he lets on."

"What do you mean, Mrs. Grey?"

"The Banks are not to be trusted. I don't particularly care for his daughter-in-law, rather a foul-mouthed flapper. She smokes, drinks, and goes to speakeasies with her husband." She paused. "Is there anything more I can help you with, Inspector?"

Sergeant Eberhart asked for her address and phone number, which Mrs. Grey reluctantly provided. She commented she lived on Washington Avenue, not far from Cucumber Alley.

Inspector James realized he could not get anything more from Mrs. Grey. Most likely she didn't know anything else. Or perhaps she was hiding something she didn't want to reveal. He didn't understand her observations on the Banks but decided not to press her any further, at least not now. The policemen got up from the student desks, thanking her for her time.

"We may be in touch again, Mrs. Grey," the Inspector said, turning back to look at her as he reached the doorway.

"Oh yes, please let me know if I can be of further assistance."

Mrs. Grey sat at the desk in the empty classroom, wondering what more, if anything, could happen in Cucumber Alley.

CHAPTER SEVEN

Sloane Sheppard finished with the documents on his desk and placed them in a folder. A simple matter of divorce, with both parties not contesting, easily resolved within a reasonable amount of time. He had handled many such cases previously. He placed the folder in the top drawer and then turned his eyes to other papers that needed his attention. He completed his morning assignments and with a glance at his calendar, realized there were no further appointments for the late morning. It came as no surprise that as soon as he decided to take an early lunch and had just put on his jacket, that the phone rang once again.

At thirty-seven and already established in his profession, Sloane Sheppard was a respected name in private investigations in Albany and the surrounding area. A trained investigator as well as a librarian, Sloane received a master's degree in Library Science from the State Teachers' College. His services were highly sought after, and his business was prospering.

He had attended to several calls already from established clients and assumed it was someone calling back, with more questions. Realizing his lunchtime would be shortened, reluctantly he answered and listened to the high-pitched voice at the other end.

"Hello, Mr. Sheppard? Is this Mr. Sloane Sheppard?"

"Yes, this is Sloane Sheppard."

A young male voice, Sloane guessed, would undoubtedly ask him to resolve family issues or divorce. It didn't sound like a local call, as the connection was rather poor. He was about to advise him to place the call again, but the voice spoke, almost shrilly.

"Mr. Sheppard, my name is Rodney Longworth. I'm from Schenectady. My companion was murdered, and I need your help."

True to his nature and profession, Sloane was not surprised or alarmed. He waited for Mr. Rodney Longworth to continue.

"My companion was murdered in Cucumber Alley," Rodney explained, as though Sloane knew all about Cucumber Alley and the stockade village. "And so was Mrs. Bradshaw. The police haven't found any leads and it's been almost a month. Can you help me, Mr. Sheppard?"

Sloane found his voice. "Thank you for contacting me, Mr. Longworth. I assume you're in Schenectady. Isn't it more advantageous to contact an investigator locally? I'm in Albany."

Rodney said rather curtly he knew he was in Albany. "But I saw the listing in the Schenectady city directory, so I assumed you handled cases here, too."

Sloane grimaced slightly. He had me on that one, he thought. "Yes, I've handled a few cases in Schenectady, but the bulk of my work is here in Albany."

Rodney explained he had contacted several investigators in Schenectady, all of whom were not interested or refused to take on new clients. He reiterated that the city police had no leads and the investigation had stalled. He explained in more detail about Theresa Hayes, his companion, where she was employed and the manner of her death. He also mentioned Mrs. Stella Bradshaw, who also met the same fate. Sloane listened carefully while Rodney spoke, making a few notes.

"Mr. Longworth, I understand your concern, but the city police handle murder investigations. I've had little contact with the Schenectady Police."

"Mr. Sheppard, please, I really need your help. I don't know what to do! Mrs. Bradshaw and Theresa were stabbed in Cucumber Alley and the entire village is on alert. People are afraid to walk around, especially at night. Murders don't happen in the stockade village."

Murders can happen anywhere, Sloane thought grimly. He remembered reading in the *Albany Evening News* about the recent murders of two women in Schenectady, although it was several weeks ago. He realized the young man speaking to him was extremely agitated and rightly so, but he wasn't sure if he could be of help to him.

"Please, Mr. Sheppard, may I make an appointment to speak with you? I don't mind coming to Albany to see you."

Sloane asked him more about himself. Rodney explained he was employed at the Hotel Van Curler as an assistant manager and a graduate of Union College, class of 1921. He lived in the stockade village with his parents.

Sloane deduced Rodney Longworth to be about twenty-seven and intelligent, articulate, perhaps from a comfortable family financially. He flipped his calendar book to next week and noticed that Monday, the seventh was free in the afternoon. He mentioned this to Rodney who eagerly said he'd be available Monday afternoon.

"Let's say three o'clock on Monday the seventh," Sloane said, noting it on his calendar. He asked Rodney to spell his last name and for his phone number. He gave him the address on South Pearl Street, in the Home Savings Bank Building, tenth floor. After a few more details, the call was finished.

Rodney replaced the handset on the candlestick phone, leaned against the wall, and heaved a sigh of relief. He'd speak to Mr. Sloane Sheppard Monday afternoon. He'd tell Mr. Lennox he'd need to take the afternoon off. He'd find the underlying cause of Theresa's murder no matter what.

After ending the call with Sloane, Rodney entered the living room to join his parents. The radio console was on, tuned to WGY as always, with popular tunes of the day a soft background. His father was busy writing in a notebook while his mother was reading the morning paper. They looked up as he entered.

"Any luck, dear?" Alice asked her son.

Rodney explained how he contacted Mr. Sloane Sheppard. "He doesn't have contacts in Schenectady, although he's handled cases here before."

"Mr. Sheppard," Simon said thoughtfully. "I'm afraid I don't know the name."

"Neither do I," Alice said disapprovingly. "What do you hope to accomplish, Rodney? Private investigators are quite expensive. Have you considered the cost of retaining him?"

Rodney loosened his tie. "Well, no, actually I didn't even think of the expense. I called a few investigators here in Schenectady, but no one wanted to take on new clients." He paused. "Mr. Sheppard would offer a fresh perspective. So far, the police here have learned nothing."

"What time do you work today?" Simon asked him.

"At three o'clock," Rodney responded. "I'll be on the late shift."

"I don't like you to walk alone at night, Rodney," his mother said anxiously. She put the paper on the coffee table. "There must be a madman running loose here. What else could it be?"

"When do you plan to see this Mr. Sheppard?" Simon asked, putting aside his notebook.

"Monday afternoon," Rodney answered. "I'll take the afternoon off and ride the trolley to downtown Albany." Before his parents could ask, he told them Mr. Sheppard was in the Home Savings Bank Building on South Pearl Street.

"I still think you're wasting your time and money," Alice said again with strong disapproval. "Do you expect this Mr. Sheppard to come to Schenectady often, Rodney? Would it be at his expense or yours? You must find these things out, dear, before you agree to hire him."

There ensued a strange silence, as though Rodney and his parents were reluctant to speak further about Mr. Sheppard or the recent murders. His mother picked up the paper again and his father returned to his journal writing, leaving Rodney a few moments of quiet reflection.

Was he about to waste his time and money in hiring a private investigator? Surely, it wouldn't cost that much, or would it? He admitted he didn't know the first thing about private detectives, or the cost involved. He then realized his father was speaking to him.

"...the Home Savings Bank Building recently opened," Simon was saying, remembering the hoopla about Albany's newest office building. "I'm sure it's beautiful inside."

Rodney commented he remembered hearing on the radio about the grand opening of Albany's newest and tallest office building. Simon continued making small talk, but Rodney hardly heard him. Even though it was still cold out, he felt as though he were suffocating in the living room, in his shirt, tie, and vest. Alice handed him the front section of the *Schenectady Gazette*, and he looked at the headlines, absently, too preoccupied, and troubled.

His mind was fixated on his appointment with Mr. Sheppard. What did he hope to gain? The truth, he thought grimly. The truth about the murders of Theresa and Mrs. Bradshaw.

On Saturday, Agnes called Flora and invited her to dinner that evening and decided to ask her sister and brother-in-law to attend, too. While Flora balked at the idea of spending the evening with Alice Longworth, she told Agnes she'd be glad to come and, if she didn't mind, she'd asked Russell Banks to join her. Agnes told her Mr. Banks was welcome and looked forward to seeing them around six o'clock. Upstairs, in her boudoir, she dressed modestly for her dinner guests, in a gray dress and a choker of pearls, just enough lipstick, and perfume, as was her custom.

Joining her husband in the kitchen, she saw Jerome getting the food ready. Lamb, au gratin potatoes, vegetables, and Agnes's homemade chocolate cake for dessert. As usual, Jerome was in a shirt and tie. Like his wife, he dressed for his guests and looked forward to their arrival.

"Alice doesn't spend enough time in the kitchen," Agnes commented to her husband, peeling potatoes, and lighting the gas stove. "Her casseroles are good, I will admit."

Jerome smiled. "Yours are excellent too, dear. I'm glad you asked Flora to have dinner with us. I haven't seen Russell Banks for a while."

"I think they're an item," Agnes said, with a twinkle in her eye.

"Well, why not," Jerome said. "After Theresa's murder, I imagine Russell's good company for her."

Agnes put the tray of potatoes in the oven. "I agree with you, but some may find that rather appalling. After all, her daughter hasn't been dead awfully long."

"Did you ask Rodney to come tonight, too?"

"No, Alice said he was going out with a new girl from the hotel. They plan to go to a speakeasy in the city."

"I suppose the Banks will join them," Jerome said, lighting a cigarette and sitting at the kitchen table. "Steven Banks is an intelligent young man, but he likes to drink. His wife does, too."

Agnes turned from the stove. "Wilma Banks is a flapper, dear. Theresa Hayes was a flapper, too; smoking, drinking, dancing all night at dance halls." She paused thoughtfully. "Quite different when Alice and I were that age."

She returned to the counter, to finish preparing the meal. Within a half hour, the doorbell rang, and Jerome welcomed Alice and Simon. They took off their coats and handing them to Jerome, headed for the kitchen, where Agnes was still busy at the stove.

"Hello, dear," Alice called pleasantly. She looked fresh and pleasant in an olive-green dress with a lovely string of pearls, her hair fixed neatly, her lipstick and rogue highlighting her pretty face. She approached her sister to see what she was cooking. "Agnes, you are the best cook ever!"

Alice told her sister she'd help to set the table in the dining room. Meanwhile, Jerome and Simon had settled in the living room, where the radio broadcast the evening news. Further reports on the murders of Miss Theresa Hayes and Mrs. Stella Bradshaw concluded the killer was still at large, somewhere in the stockade village and may strike again, without warning.

"I'm concerned when Agnes teaches Friday evenings," Jerome said to his brother-in-law.

Simon agreed. "I go with Alice to the library when she volunteers in the evenings. It gives me a chance to use the reference books."

The doorbell soon rang again, and Jerome entered the hallway, opening the front door to allow Flora and Russell to enter. They exchanged greetings and as with the Longworths, left their coats with Jerome, who dutifully hung them up in the closet. Russell and Flora followed him to the living room, where they greeted Simon and sat on the sofa. Jerome suggested to Flora if she wanted to join his wife and sister-in-law in the kitchen, but Flora told him she preferred to stay here, where the fire was lit, and it was warm and pleasant.

Agnes then entered, greeted Flora and Russell warmly, and offered them a glass of wine or ginger ale. She also announced that dinner was being served. Obediently, they followed her along the hallway to the opulent dining room, where Alice was busy placing the food on the table. She smiled upon seeing Flora and Russell.

"Please sit where you'd like," Agnes said, the perfect hostess. She sat next to her husband, who immediately began passing around the meal choices. He also served the wine and Agnes lit candles in the center of the table.

"This wine is delicious," Flora said, sipping the liquor. "How did you get it?"

Jerome smiled. "Well, let's just say, it pays to know people."

A round of laughs ensued and the atmosphere and conversations at the table were light and appealing. Everyone ate plenty and enjoyed their meal. Afterward, Flora helped Agnes and Alice serve coffee and the delicious chocolate layer cake, while the gentlemen relaxed with cigarettes and finished their wine.

"My goodness, Agnes, this cake is the best," Russell exclaimed, digging into the layer cake. "Or as the young people would say the cat's meow!"

Simon also agreed. "The best, Agnes."

Only Alice seemed to stiffen a little. "It's good but too much sugar for my tastes."

"You have such a lovely home, Agnes," Flora said, looking around the dining room.

Agnes thought Flora looked attractive. Her black dress, with a string of pearls, accentuated her fine figure, her brown hair tastefully arranged. She wondered if she and Russell would marry.

"Thank you, dear," she said graciously. "We enjoy living here in the Realty Plot. After all, Jerome is important to General Electric."

"As Simon was during his time there," Alice said, putting the coffee cup to her lips.

"Do you think they'll solve the murders?" Flora asked, rather awkwardly.

Everyone looked at her, wondering why she'd casually mention such an unpleasant topic. As though sensing the rebuke, Flora apologized for mentioning such an unpleasant topic.

"No need to apologize, Flora," Jerome said, good-naturedly. "We can't turn our backs to it. There's a murderer loose somewhere in Schenectady."

Russell nodded. "We have to be careful. Especially around Washington Avenue."

"I'd like to know what Theresa was doing in Cucumber Alley so late at night," Flora said as though thinking out loud. "I waited for her to come home during the snowstorm and instead she went to Cucumber Alley."

Agnes cut a slice of the rich cake, put it on a plate and handed it to her husband. "You can't blame yourself, Flora. The police will arrive at a satisfactory conclusion soon enough."

This remark was met with skepticism. Even Jerome commented that the police investigation had gotten nowhere, and it had been several weeks.

"The police questioned us again recently," Agnes said, taking a bite of the cake. "Fortunately, they didn't notice my red paisley scarf."

Alice looked up at her sister. "What about your scarf, Agnes?"

She shook her head. "Remember those red marks? We thought they were blood."

"I noticed those red marks when you stopped by my house recently," Flora commented.

"How did you get red marks on your scarf?" Russell asked curiously.

"I don't know. We had lunch with Mrs. Grey at the hotel and as we were leaving, we saw the red marks, which looked like dried blood. Mrs. Grey and I have the same scarf."

"My daughter-in-law, too," Russell said, causing everyone to look at him with interest.

"You bought it at Barney's," Alice said to her sister, trying to be helpful.

"Maybe you took Mrs. Grey's scarf by mistake," Simon offered.

"That's what I thought," Agnes said. "But she said hers didn't have the red marks on it."

There followed a rather long and awkward silence, as though Agnes, Jerome, Alice, Simon, Flora, and Russell were reluctant to speak further, their minds churning over the recent murders and the unexplained red marks on a red paisley scarf.

"Rodney wants to hire a private investigator," Alice announced breaking the silence and then regretted it. Her husband glared at her, and she realized she should've kept quiet. "He wants to clear up Theresa's death once and for all."

"A private investigator?" Flora asked. "I have confidence the police will figure out who's responsible. I imagine it'd cost him quite a lot to retain an investigator."

"Well, he's thinking about it," Alice said awkwardly, hoping to change the subject.

Simon then cleared the air by asking his brother-in-law about General Electric, what was new in research. Russell commented that Steven and Jerome worked together often and their input in electronics was astounding. Jerome wiped his mouth with a napkin and addressed his guests.

"There's talk of television," Jerome said. "Broadcasting would be named WGY Television. By early 1928, they hope to have the first daily programs."

Even Flora was impressed. "I never heard of television. What will they think of next?"

Simon smiled. "At General Electric, there's always something in the works."

Agnes offered more coffee and cake. Jerome had seconds as did Russell and the ladies enjoyed a second cup of Agnes's delicious coffee. The gentlemen then entered the living room, to listen to the radio, smoke and discuss politics. The ladies cleared the table, with Agnes and Alice placing the dishes on the counter and Flora collecting the dinner napkins.

"Did Russell mention that his daughter-in-law has a red paisley scarf?" Alice asked Flora.

Busy at the counter, helping Agnes clear plates and set the cups and glasses to wash, she turned to look at Alice. Just what was she insinuating now?

"Yes, I believe he did mention it," Flora said, trying hard to keep the irritation out of her voice. She looked at Agnes, busy at the sink. "What do you think those red marks are from?"

Jerome entered and mentioned they were interested in playing bridge. He invited the ladies to join them in the living room, where he'd set up the bridge table.

"We'll be there shortly, dear," Agnes called, from the sink. She invited Flora to join the men, as she would finish with the rest of the plates and cups.

"Perhaps Russell has information," Alice said, looking at Flora. "Maybe he could tell us more about Theresa. He does seem to know quite a lot, doesn't he?"

Sandwiched between Jay Street and Clinton Street in downtown Schenectady, in a narrow pedestrian walkway, a small, nondescript former garage stood next to an office building and a shoe repair store. While busy during business hours, the walkway was quiet in the evening, except for revelers destined for the garage, known to most people, police included, as *Madison's*, a speakeasy with quite a notorious reputation. It was to this establishment of inebriation that Rodney, Olive Mae, Steven, and Wilma were headed, that Saturday evening.

Walking on the snowy sidewalk, Rodney chatted amicably with Olive Mae and felt fortunate to have her company. He missed Theresa terribly, but Olive Mae was certainly appealing, in every sense. Steven and Wilma also chatted with them, glad to have the weekend to spend time with friends. They entered Jay Street and then turned left onto the walkway. Rodney found it eerily quiet, but then speakeasies didn't flaunt their business. Steven was well known and received cordially by the doorman, who ushered him, Wilma, Rodney, and Olive Mae into the club.

Once inside, it was a scene of mad frivolity. A band was playing the latest tunes and the dance floor was full. Crowds stood about, laughing, talking, smoking, and drinking. The long bar was busy, as Rodney assumed, and they had to wait to order their drinks. Wilma found a corner table and after securing their beverages, they made their way past numerous drunken patrons, settling in chairs, near the dance floor. Steven and Wilma had ordered gin, while Rodney had a beer, Olive Mae a glass of white wine. She admitted she wasn't much for drinking.

It wasn't long before Wilma and Steven were on the dance floor, frolicking to the latest tunes, including an elaborate exhibition of the Charleston and the Lindy Hop. Rodney and Olive Mae enjoyed a slower fox trot. Rodney noticed Wilma and Steven had returned to the table after dancing quite flamboyantly and after the fox trot finished, he and Olive Mae joined them.

"Well, I can't remember when I've had so much fun," Steven exclaimed, clearly in a state of advanced intoxication. He laughed, rather loudly. "We should have another go at it, Wilma."

Finishing her gin and lighting a cigarette, she told her husband to sit this one out, to rest up before the next Lindy Hop. Rodney noticed the club was crowded, with more patrons coming in. He wondered where all the people would fit as it wasn't that big a place. He finished his beer and asked Olive Mae if she wanted another glass of wine.

"No, Rodney, I'm fine. Maybe we can get going soon."

Rodney glanced at his watch and saw it past midnight. He didn't realize the time and agreed it was getting late. By the time they returned to Washington Avenue, it would be closer to two. Olive Mae lived on North Ferry Street, two blocks from Washington. He insisted on walking her there, so that she wouldn't go alone. He motioned to Steven it was time to leave, but Steven, clearly drunk with a cigarette dangling from his mouth, ignored him. He was laughing and talking with people at the next table, Wilma also enjoying their company and mingling in.

After a half hour, Steven and Wilma decided to leave, although Rodney wondered if he'd be able to make it home. Wilma suggested calling a cab, but the Banks lived on North Church Street, not too far away and Steven didn't want to spend money for a cab.

Once outside, it had grown colder, and Rodney pulled his scarf around his neck and his cap lower on his head. He lit a cigarette, exhaling a fine trail of smoke, while he and Olive Mae waited patiently for Steven and Wilma, who were still inside, chatting with the doorman, while collecting their coats and hats.

"Here we are, buddy," Steven said, loudly, lighting another cigarette, almost slipping on the snowy walkway, laughing drunkenly. Wilma helped him to Jay Street, where they walked north on Liberty Street. Although Rodney counted Steven as a friend, he did not approve of his drinking habit. While walking with Olive Mae, he decided not to frequent a speakeasy again, at least not with Steven and Wilma. He had been to *Madison's* before, with Theresa, but never found it as rowdy as it was this evening. They came to the corner of Liberty and Union and took a right, toward North Church Street. Rodney mentioned to Steven and Wilma that he'd walk Olive Mae home, on North Ferry Street.

"Okay, old pal," Steven slurred. "Thanks for a good night, Roddy!"

Rodney saw a red paisley scarf caught in the brisk wind, flapping across Wilma's face. Irritably, she pushed it back down, and resumed helping her husband. Another red paisley scarf, he thought, watching them walk up North Church Street. They saw Wilma help Steven stagger across Union Street. They could hear Steven talking loudly and laughing from where he and Olive Mae stood on the corner. Shaking his head, Rodney turned to Olive Mae, almost apologetically.

"I didn't realize Steven drank so much," he told her, finishing his cigarette.

Olive Mae smiled. "Don't worry, Rodney. Let's just get going before we get murdered."

Rodney had taken another cigarette out of the pack from his coat packet and was about to light it when he looked sharply at Olive Mae. "We're not going to be murdered!"

Olive Mae shivered slightly, obviously from fright as well as the cold. "There's a murderer loose here in the stockade, Rodney. I don't like being out so late at night."

Inwardly he agreed with her. They walked to North Ferry Street, finally arriving at the house Olive Mae lived in with her mother and younger brother. She thanked Rodney for a nice evening, depositing a kiss on his cheek.

"Are you sure you'll be okay walking home, Rodney?" she asked, concerned.

"Yes, I'll be fine," he assured her, puffing heavily on his cigarette.

Rodney watched as she entered the house, locking the door behind her. He then turned toward Front Street, the shortest way to Washington Avenue. Turning left, he made his way up Front Street until he came to the corner of Washington and Cucumber Alley. Washington Avenue, usually full of pedestrians, cars, and trollies, was now extremely quiet, but then he didn't expect it to be busy, not in the overnight hours. He then looked down Cucumber Alley.

Rather eerily serene in the dark, he thought. It must have been like this when Theresa came here and Mrs. Bradshaw, too. He expected to see someone lurking around, a furtive shape in the distance. His mind couldn't stop thinking of the red paisley scarf. Was it Wilma who was in Cucumber Alley? Maybe Aunt Agnes or Mrs. Grey? But why would they want to kill Mrs. Bradshaw or Theresa? Of the three, he could eliminate his aunt and Mrs. Grey. That left Wilma. She was foolish and enough of a flapper to do something stupid.

Suddenly he noticed a figure near the river. Squinting toward the end of the alley he stood planted on Washington Avenue, but his curiosity got the best of him, and he decided to investigate. With a fresh cigarette to steady his nerves, Rodney set off down Cucumber Alley, puffing heavily, not sure why he was walking in this desolate, poorly lit alley toward the river at one in the morning and why he didn't hightail it home.

Arriving at the end of the alley, looking around, he saw no one, and realizing he was foolish to have ventured to such a remote spot in the first place, he decided to retreat. He had no sooner turned to walk back up Cucumber Alley when something hit him squarely on the back of the head. His mind registered red somewhere before he hit the ground and lost consciousness.

CHAPTER EIGHT

Alice was dreaming of springtime, when the cherry blossoms bloomed so magnificently, and the air was fresh and clean. She was picking apples and putting them happily in a basket, joining her husband and son. It was a pleasant dream and quite relaxing. From somewhere far off she heard a bell ringing. She kept dreaming of the golden spring weather, so warm and comforting but the bell persisted. Realizing it was not in her dream, she was awake and listened. She heard the sound again, but then knew it was the doorbell. She glanced over at her husband, snoring lightly in the next bed. She called his name and not getting a response, got up and shook him gently.

"Simon, I think there's someone ringing the doorbell!"

Simon, not quite awake, listened and then heard for himself what was clearly the doorbell, stridently ringing, through the quiet house. He looked at his wife in concern, reached for his robe, got up quickly and hurried downstairs, his wife trailing after him.

Turning on the hallway light, Simon then opened the front door and saw Rodney with a policeman. It was obvious there had been some sort of trouble. Rodney looked ill, his face and eyes were drawn, his whole semblance untidy and even scruffy. Simon noticed his pants and jacket were marked with dirt. Momentarily speechless, he looked at his son and then at the policeman and then back to Rodney.

"Rodney!" Alice exclaimed in great distress, from behind Simon. She moved past her husband and helped her son enter the house. The policeman followed. They walked down the hallway to the living room, where Alice turned on the lights. She helped him take off his coat. He handed her his cap and then sat down wearily on the sofa.

"What happened?" she asked, still in shock. She looked at the policeman who stood next to Simon. "Please tell us what happened!"

Rodney was not fit to talk so he merely looked at the policeman, a youngish officer with a firm manner, who cleared his throat and address Simon and Alice.

"I was on patrol and found him lying in Cucumber Alley."

"What!" Alice almost screamed, looking at Rodney in a mixture of pain and anger.

Simon also looked at his son, waiting to hear more details and then saving his wrath for when the policeman left. He told the officer to continue.

"Apparently, he had come from a speakeasy off Jay Street, having said goodnight to his date on North Ferry Street. He told me he decided to explore something he saw moving in Cucumber Alley. He was attacked from behind and lost consciousness."

"Are you all right now?" his father asked him, patiently.

Rodney was still in considerable pain and feeling rather embarrassed. He simply looked at his father and nodded, too weak to speak.

"He refused medical attention," the officer continued. "I was going to take him to Ellis Hospital, but he came around and told me he was feeling all right, although there's a small bump on the back of his head."

Alice quickly looked at the back of her son's head and then went to the kitchen and the icebox. She returned with a dishtowel filled with ice, which she placed on the back of Rodney's head. She sat next to him, holding the rag in place.

"I don't know any more than what he told me," the officer said. "I contacted the station to send another car to patrol the area, to be on the lookout, but so far nothing's been found." He paused, looking first at Rodney, still in some pain. He then looked at Alice and Simon. "There's a killer loose in this area of the city and he could've been another victim. I recommend your son not explore areas by himself. Until we catch whoever is responsible, the streets aren't safe at night."

"Thank you for bringing him here, Officer," Simon said gratefully.

"He was in no condition to walk the short distance. My patrol car is parked on Washington Avenue. He told me he has a key to your front door, but he was too weak to open it, so I rang the bell." He hesitated, with a wry smile. "Sorry for waking you up."

"No apology needed, Officer," Alice said. "I'm grateful you found Rodney and brought him home." She heard the grandfather's clock in the hallway strike two o'clock. Simon walked the officer back to the door and thanked him again for his help.

Upon returning to the living room, he noticed Alice still holding the dishtowel to the back of his head, with Rodney leaning forward, as though he would be sick. Patiently, he sat down in an armchair, waiting for his son to look up. When he did, he spoke to him directly and forcefully.

"Rodney, what the hell did you think you were doing, walking around Cucumber Alley late at night? You could've gotten killed!"

Rodney tried to formulate words. "Sorry, Dad, I don't know what came over me."

"Let's not be too hard on Rodney," Alice said, patiently. She continued applying the ice to the back of his head. "A good night's sleep will be the best thing for Rodney, poor dear."

Simon was clearly agitated. Whatever made his son decide to walk down Cucumber Alley, knowing full well two murders had already taken place there recently, late at night? It was apparent the killer was still at large, as Rodney was attacked, but mercifully did not perish.

"I won't do it again, Dad," Rodney said. "I saw something and wanted to investigate."

"That's enough for now, dear," Alice said soothingly. "You'll feel better in the morning. Let me help you up the stairs."

Simon remained in the living room, smoking meditatively. He realized his son could have been another victim. He saw something in Cucumber Alley, but what? He wondered why the killer didn't use a knife, like he or she had done previously. He extinguished his cigarette, turned off the lights and then went upstairs to bed.

In his bedroom, after his mother helped him into bed, Rodney knew it'd be a long day, but it was Sunday, and he could rest before returning to work tomorrow. He fell asleep rather quickly, still troubled and wondering what exactly he saw earlier in Cucumber Alley.

Good morning and welcome to WGY news for Monday, March 7, 1927. Here are stories we are reporting this morning. In this year of discovery, Dr. Ernst Alexanderson of General Electric intends to give a lecture on the future of television at the General Electric facility and is also planning the first demonstration of television broadcast reception at his General Electric Realty Plot home on Adams Road in Schenectady..

Rodney was listening to the news on the radio and eating breakfast at the kitchen table with his parents. Simon was up early, made the coffee and gotten breakfast ready for when Alice and Rodney came downstairs. He enjoyed listening to the morning news and had turned the radio console on in the living room loud enough so they could hear it from the kitchen. He smiled upon hearing the latest General Electric news and marveled about the newest scientific innovations. He served bacon and eggs to his wife and son, then joined them, with a cup of coffee.

"Dr. Alexanderson has put our city on the map," he said, obviously pleased.

"I don't care about that at the moment, dear," Alice said to her husband, wistfully. "My concern is for Rodney." She looked at her son with worry.

"I'm much better now, Mother," Rodney told her, lighting his first morning cigarette. "It's just a bump. I'll be fine, so don't worry."

Simon and Alice continued looking at their son with concern, unsure what to do next. At this point, Rodney was feeling better, although he was rather annoyed that his parents were treating him like an invalid.

"Are you still working half a day today, Rodney?" Alice asked him.

He realized he had forgotten to remind his parents that he planned to go to Albany this afternoon. He was surprised his father remembered. Reluctantly, he nodded.

"Yes, I plan to see Mr. Sheppard this afternoon. I'll take the trolley to Albany."

Alice again voiced her disapproval. "Do you want me to go with you, dear? I don't like for you to travel to Albany alone. Especially after what happened to you. Are you sure the bump on your head is better?"

Rodney smiled weakly, enjoying his coffee and cigarette. "Yes, Mother, I'm feeling much better. Perhaps Mr. Sheppard can help with the investigation. After all, I was attacked and could've been killed."

"You should've thought of that before venturing down Cucumber Alley," his mother said.

Simon picked up the morning paper and started to flip the pages. He came to the police bulletin on the third page and read about the attack in Cucumber Alley on Mr. Rodney Longworth of Washington Avenue. He mentioned it to his wife and son.

"Newspapers contact the police for local reports," Alice said. "They certainly work fast."

"Now everyone will know," Simon said, putting the paper back down on the table irritably.

"Dad, it isn't the end of the world," Rodney said, trying to calm his father. "I doubt if Steven or Wilma even read the paper."

"They'll wonder why you were in Cucumber Alley so late at night," his father retorted.

"Your father has a point, dear," Alice said. "People will talk. There's always gossip."

Hoping to change the subject, Rodney asked his parents what they planned to do today. Alice commented she planned to go to the church, to work on the bulletin and then shop at Woolworth and Carl's. Simon mentioned he was typing up an article for *Scientific American* before sending it off to the publisher.

Rodney crushed his cigarette in an ashtray and shook his head. He heard the grandfathers clock strike seven o'clock. "I'd better get dressed for work. I have to be there at nine." He got up from the table and dashed upstairs.

Alice listened while Simon mentioned shopping on State Street, but her mind was too preoccupied. She hoped that by meeting with this private investigator he wasn't putting himself in any more danger.

Rodney left the Hotel Van Curler in an agitated state. It was almost twelve-thirty and he planned to leave at noon. Last minute inquiries tied him up, including booking a conference for the end of the month and taking dinner reservations. As he expected, many at the hotel read in the morning paper about the attack in Cucumber Alley, including Olive Mae, who expressed her concern over his wellbeing. She told him she'd help him if he needed it.

"Thanks, Olive Mae," he said, putting on his coat and cap. "I'll be in tomorrow for the late shift. You work then too, don't you?"

Olive Mae smiled and told him that she was scheduled for the late shift on Tuesday. He said goodbye to her, and fortunately, she didn't ask where he was going on his half-day, which Rodney thought was considerate and sensible. Other girls would quiz him to no end. He stepped out onto Washington Avenue in a snow shower.

Crossing Washington at the light with State Street, he walked down State until he came to the trolley stop. Usually, during the daytime, trolleys were not as plentiful as in the morning and evening rush hours, but he'd have to wait regardless. He was gasping for a cigarette, but when he felt his pockets, he didn't find his pack. Cursing himself for having left it in his desk drawer, and not wanting to return to the hotel, he walked further along State Street until he came to a store selling newspapers and other sundries. He entered and bought two packs of Lucky Strikes, handing the woman behind the counter thirty cents. He then returned outside to wait for the trolley.

He didn't have long to wait. When it pulled up to the curb, he climbed aboard, deposited the nickel, and found a seat in the back. It'd be a long trolley ride to downtown Albany, but he had plenty of time. His appointment with Mr. Sheppard was at three o'clock. Glancing at his watch, he saw it was a little after one. He tried to relax, looking out the window as the trolley progressed down State Street, eventually entering Albany city limits.

It had been a while since he visited Albany, and like a tourist, he marveled at the imposing architecture of the State Education Building and the State Capitol. The trolley stopped at a red light at the top of State Street hill, then turned left, arriving at the intersection of State Street and South Pearl Street. Rodney exited and crossed with a sizeable crowd to the other side of North Pearl Street. He walked hastily until he came to the Home Savings Bank building. He stood a moment hesitantly, finding the courage to enter. The ornate lobby with a high ceiling resonated with opulence and sophistication and Rodney was favorably impressed with the city's newest office building. He entered an elevator and asked the attendant for the tenth floor. Several other people got off on lower floors, so Rodney had to wait for what seemed an interminable amount of time until the car slowly reached floor ten. The attendant opened the gate and Rodney got off. The elevator shot upward, and Rodney was rather bewildered, as he was the only person to get off and, looking around at the quiet lobby, he was unsure where to go. He looked down a hallway and noticed a law office and then in the opposite direction, he saw another door, near the exit for the stairs. Approaching it, he read the small sign posted on the wall to the right of the door: *Sloane Sheppard, Private Investigator.* Gathering his strength, he knocked on the door. He pulled his jacket tighter around him and the cap lower on his head, feeling rather nervous. He couldn't wait to light a cigarette. Hopefully, Mr. Sheppard wouldn't mind if he smoked. Within a minute, the door opened, and Mr. Sloane Sheppard stood before him.

"Hello, Mr. Sheppard. I'm Rodney Longworth. I have an appointment with you today. I realize I'm rather early."

Sloane smiled and stood back allowing Rodney to enter. "I was just finishing with a client."

The client, a rather heavy-set middle-aged woman seeking grounds to divorce her unfaithful husband, glared at Rodney as though she distrusted the entire human race, and bid farewell to Mr. Sheppard. Sloane invited Rodney to sit in the chair before his desk, while he returned to the other side, shuffling papers, putting them in a folder and then looked at Rodney. He had taken off his coat and cap and looked imploringly at the man behind the desk.

"What can I do for you, Mr. Longworth?" Sloane asked him.

A commanding presence, Rodney thought, his jet-black hair, center-parted and worn back from his forehead. His piercing brown eyes gave the impression of fortitude and perseverance, as though he had fought for his clients and his own personal turmoil over the years and resulted virtuously. Rodney thought he was somewhere in his thirties. He admired his professional appearance, certainly handsome, even intimidating; his vest matched his pleated slacks, and his pristine white shirt and his pin-stripe tie were appropriate to his overall appearance. He realized he was taking a while to answer. He then cleared his throat and spoke rather urgently.

"Mr. Sheppard, I really need your help. My companion was murdered in Cucumber Alley and the police haven't found anything! I was attacked early Sunday morning in the same alley. There's a killer running around the village, and no one is safe!"

Used to overwrought clients, Sloane asked him to start at the beginning. Rodney told him in detail about the murders of Theresa and Mrs. Bradshaw in Cucumber Alley. He explained how Theresa had worked at the Nott Memorial Library at Union College. He reiterated how he was knocked unconscious. Sloane had taken a few notes and then looked at Rodney carefully.

A nice-looking young man, articulate if not a little high-strung, especially after surviving an attack, a good head on his shoulders, obviously from a good family. Sloane was cautious before committing himself.

"Certainly, you've spoken to investigators in Schenectady?"

Rodney nodded. "Nobody wanted to help. They were biased since they were familiar with the case and from Schenectady. You're from Albany and could offer a unique perspective."

"Have the police spoken to you?"

"Several times. They questioned me at the hotel since I was the last employee to see Mrs. Bradshaw. She was a widow and didn't have relatives. The police questioned me again, at home, with my parents." He paused. "Theresa was my companion and we contemplated marriage, although we weren't engaged. I don't know if she was involved with something or knew information about someone. She didn't share a lot of things with me."

"And you thought of marrying her?" Sloane asked.

Rodney shrugged. "She was a good person, but if she had secrets, I wasn't aware of them."

Sloane nodded. He could tell Rodney Longworth was one of the good guys, used to bad luck, having people disrupt his peace of mind and wellbeing. He knew those disturbances extremely well from his own personal and professional life.

"Will you help me, Mr. Sheppard? Someone killed Theresa and I want to know who!"

Sloane sighed and then rubbed his eyes. He lit a cigarette, which appeared a sign for Rodney to extract his own pack from his pocket and eagerly light one, from the lighter Sloane held out for him. Sloane noticed he seemed more relaxed.

"Is there anything else you'd want to tell me, Mr. Longworth?"

"Everyone calls me Rodney, so you can too." He puffed heavily on his cigarette, finding it made him less nervous. He then went into more detail about his parents, his mother's library work and his father's retirement from General Electric. His Aunt Agnes, a Latin teacher at Union College and his Uncle Jerome, a researcher at General Electric also lived nearby and stayed connected often, along with Mr. Banks and his son, Steven and his daughter-in-law, Wilma. He also mentioned their friends, Mrs. Edna Grey and Mrs. Flora Hayes, Theresa's mother. He explained in detail how he came upon Cucumber Alley so late at night after an evening out with Olive Mae and Steven and Wilma Banks and how he was knocked unconscious.

Sloane looked at his desk calendar. He had a busy March with clients, mostly divorces, and court cases at the end of the month. Rodney looked at him pleadingly, almost desperate for assistance. Sloane then explained his fees and how he'd want to receive compensation.

"First, I'd like to speak to the Schenectady police in charge of this case," Sloane added.

Rodney mentioned Inspector James and Sergeant Eberhart of the Schenectady City Police. Sloane wasn't sure if he knew them, but he'd call and get as much information as possible. He then smiled encouragingly at Rodney.

"When is the best time to speak to your parents? And your aunt and uncle?"

Rodney's face beamed. "They're home during the day, most of the time. Mother volunteers at the library, although given the recent murders I don't know if she'll continue. Aunt Agnes teaches during the day and on Friday nights. Uncle Jerome works at General Electric during the day, but they're home most evenings." He gave Sloane his home address and phone number as well as the phone number for the Hotel Van Curler.

"Thank you, Mr. Sheppard," Rodney said, standing and putting on his coat and cap. He extinguished his cigarette in the ashtray on Sloane's desk, already overflowing with cigarette butts.

Sloane accompanied him to the door. "I'll do what I can, Rodney. I'll be in touch with you soon after I speak to Inspector James. Perhaps this week I'll meet with your parents."

He walked him to the lobby and the elevators. "Just be careful, Rodney. If there's a killer loose in the neighborhood, you don't want to be another victim."

Rodney nodded, rather tiredly. The elevator then arrived, the doors opened, and the attendant lifted the gate. Rodney shook hands with Sloane and then stepped in, the car clanging downward toward the lobby.

Upon returning to his office, Sloane closed the door, and sat behind his desk, deep in thought. An intelligent young man, this Rodney Longworth and a perceptive one, too.

His mind returned to the murders in Cucumber Alley, and the attempt on Rodney Longworth's life. He made a note on his calendar for tomorrow morning. First thing upon arriving, he wrote in large letters, without hesitation, and as a start on this case, he'd speak to Inspector James of the Schenectady Police Department.

CHAPTER NINE

True to his word, upon arriving at his office Tuesday morning, Sloane settled at his desk, grabbed the candlestick phone, and asked the operator to connect him to the Schenectady Police Department. At this hour of the morning, the circuits were busy, so Sloane had to wait for the operator to call him back once she could put the call through. In the meantime, he lit a cigarette and sipped the coffee that Lois, a secretary at the law office down the hall, brought for him. Sloane maintained a one-man operation, without an assistant and preferred to work by himself. Although there were days, he admitted, when the paperwork became cumbersome, and he could have benefitted from a secretary. He reviewed the notes he wrote when he met with Rodney yesterday.

He wasn't too familiar with Schenectady and wondered about Cucumber Alley. Certainly, a strange name, must have a history behind it. He knew of the stockade village, a reputable neighborhood, oblivious to crime. What relation was there between the murdered women? And why were they in Cucumber Alley so late at night to begin with?

He looked at his calendar for the week, deciding when he'd be free to venture to Schenectady, when the phone trilled loudly in the quiet office. He picked up the handset and heard the operator's voice, telling him she was connecting him to the Schenectady Police Department.

"Schenectady Police," said a crisp sounding young officer.

Sloane introduced himself and explained he wished to speak to Inspector James regarding the Cucumber Alley murders. The officer asked Sloane his name and after writing it down, mentioned the inspector had just come out of the interrogation room. He asked Inspector James if he were free to take a call. Upon hearing who was calling, the inspector grabbed the candlestick phone, with enough cord trailing behind him, and entered his office. Soon enough another phone rang nearby, and the young officer quickly answered it. Closing the door and sitting behind his desk, he greeted Sloane as though speaking to an old friend.

"Hello, Mr. Sheppard. I do remember you from many years ago. You had handled a divorce case that turned to murder here in Schenectady, about eight or nine years ago."

Sloane acknowledged that case. "Thank you, Inspector. I wasn't sure if I knew you. We worked on that case together. Quite an interesting one, too."

The inspector mentioned details of that case so long ago and then asked Sloane how he could assist him. Sloane mentioned he was working for Mr. Rodney Longworth of Schenectady, who asked him to investigate the murder of his companion, Miss Theresa Hayes and his attack on Sunday morning in Cucumber Alley.

"We've questioned Mr. Longworth and his parents," Inspector James said stodgily. "We have few leads so far, including who was responsible for his attack over the weekend."

"What about the first woman who was killed, Mrs. Bradshaw?"

"She was stabbed in Cucumber Alley. The next evening Miss Hayes was murdered there as well. Is Mr. Longworth hiring you to look into both murders?"

"He didn't specify Mrs. Bradshaw, but his companion and his attack. There may be a connection and the murders may have been committed by the same person."

Inspector James referred to a folder, with notes on the case. "We've questioned everyone who lives in and near Cucumber Alley; his aunt, uncle and friends and associates."

"What leads have you followed so far, Inspector?"

Inspector James reiterated that their leads were few. "There were no witnesses to the murders, at least none uncovered so far, and the fact that they occurred so late at night, during a snowstorm both times, made it difficult to ascertain what exactly happened. The snow obliterated footprints from the previous night, so that too was a dead end." He paused. "Mr. Sheppard, after speaking with Mr. Longworth, what are your thoughts on this case?"

Sloane hesitated. "I need to know the relationship between Mrs. Bradshaw and Miss Hayes. Were they related; did they get along, how did they know each other?"

The inspector coughed slightly. "No, they weren't related. They didn't work together, so I don't know if they got along. Mr. Longworth works at the Hotel Van Curler, so Miss Hayes would stop there often. According to Mr. Longworth, he saw Miss Hayes chatting with Mrs. Bradshaw from a distance, but he had no idea what they were discussing." He paused. "We've had patrols in the area and continue to do so. Volunteers from the neighborhood also patrol. The village is a highly regarded area of the city and crime is unusual in that area."

The inspector was silent, holding onto the handset. He remembered Mr. Sloane Sheppard well, his probing and inquiring and finally resolving the murder years ago. He thought him rather obstinate to a point, determined, resolute to finding the solution to the case.

"This may be just the beginning," Sloane told him gravely. "If the killer has struck twice, there may well be another crime soon. Rodney Longworth could have been a victim, too."

He looked at his calendar. He had a few appointments tomorrow afternoon, but he could move them to Friday, after contacting his clients. He asked the inspector if he were available tomorrow, Wednesday. The inspector did likewise with his calendar and told Sloane that he'd be available in the morning if that was feasible for him. It was then arranged that Sloane would come to the Schenectady Police Department tomorrow morning at ten o'clock.

After ending the call, Inspector James pushed the candlestick phone to the edge of his desk and sat reflecting on the conversation he just had with Mr. Sloane Sheppard. Sergeant Eberhart entered at that moment, carrying a file loaded with papers. He asked his colleague if there was something wrong. From his expression alone, he could tell there was an issue of importance.

"I've just spoken with Mr. Sheppard in Albany," he told him. "Remember how he helped us with a murder case some years ago? He'll be here tomorrow about the recent murders."

The sergeant showed surprise. "He's getting involved with Schenectady again?"

Inspector James smiled wryly. "He was hired by Mr. Rodney Longworth to look into the murder of Miss Hayes. And his attack on Saturday evening. Mr. Sheppard has decided to investigate the Cucumber Alley murders."

"Not much we can do about that if he's working for Mr. Longworth." Sergeant Eberhart paused. "So, what's bothering you?"

The inspector opened a desk drawer and took out a few reports. "It's what Mr. Sheppard *thinks* that disturbs me. I remember how meticulous he was on that murder investigation." He hesitated. "We've been superficial with the Cucumber Alley murders."

"He said that to you?" Eberhart said incredulously.

The inspector shook his head. "He didn't have to. He implied there may be more. From our last dealing with him, I can tell you his instinct may be right."

At four o'clock, Steven Banks came out of General Electric and waited for the trolley. It was cloudy and cold, with gusty winds and intermittent snow showers. He pulled the collar up around his neck, his scarf tighter and his cap low, shielding his eyes. Making its way up to Washington Avenue, he saw a trolley in the distance and soon enough, it stopped in front of the General Electric building. Upon depositing a nickel in the slot and finding a seat in the front, he marveled how he didn't need a car, the trolley picked him up right in front of the premises. The bee's knees!

Although he could have ridden the trolley down Washington to North Church Street, arriving home before his father and wife, he got off at the corner of Washington and State, crossed at the light and stood before the Hotel Van Curler. After reading about Rodney's attack in yesterday's paper, he called him last night to inquire what happened. Rodney invited him to stop in to see him since Tuesday was his late shift and before the dinner hour, he'd have time to chat.

Quickly he climbed the steps, two at a time and arrived at the main door, which was held open for him by the doorman. He was always impressed with the Hotel Van Curler. A beautiful and spacious lobby, a huge mirror on a wall across from the registration desk and an ornate crystal chandelier gave the hotel its charm and sophistication. The restaurant, the spacious rooms and the courtyard out back contributed to the Van Curler's popularity and prestige.

He looked around for Rodney and saw him speaking to a couple with their small children. As he finished, he turned and noticed Steven. He was glad to see him, although Steven could tell he looked rather drained from his ordeal.

"I stopped by to see how you are," Steven said, with concern.

"Let's go to my office," Rodney said, and led the way, behind the registration desk.

Rodney's office was a small, rather cramped room, with a manager's desk, and two chairs in front. There was a filing cabinet in one corner and a small table in another, on which reposed a stack of files and other important papers, along with an adding machine.

Steven pulled out his cigarettes, offered one to Rodney, and lit it for him. The young men relaxed for a moment before speaking. Steven explained how his father and Wilma were extremely alarmed by what they read in the morning paper.

Rodney exhaled smoke slowly, leaned back on his chair and waited to answer. "I was attacked in Cucumber Alley. I was hit over the head and lost consciousness."

Steven was at a loss for words. "What the hell were you doing there so late at night? You left us and walked Olive Mae home, didn't you?"

"You sound like my father," Rodney said. He put his feet up on the desk, ran his fingers through his hair and drew heavily on his cigarette. "I did walk Olive Mae home and just before heading up Washington, I passed Cucumber Alley and thought I saw something."

"Wilma and I thought you went straight home," Steven said, rather angrily. "That was a pretty stupid thing to do. There's a madman running loose around here. What were you trying to do, get yourself killed or something?"

"Please, I heard all the wrath from my parents. I was attacked from behind although…"

Steven looked at him through a haze of smoke. "Although what?"

Rodney paused, deep in thought. "The color red was somewhere."

"The color red? What are you talking about?"

Rodney hesitated. "I thought I saw red or something like that just before I was struck from behind. I don't know what it could've been. Maybe a red light."

"There are no traffic lights in Cucumber Alley," Steven told him. "Maybe you think you saw red, but it was just before you blacked out."

"Maybe," Rodney said, doubtfully.

He extinguished his cigarette, unbuttoned the top of his vest, and loosened his tie. He glanced at his watch and saw it was nearly five-thirty, so he should make the rounds of the hotel, to safeguard any potential issues that may crop up. Although he got home late in the evening, he rather enjoyed the evening shift, when he was the only manager on duty and Mr. Lennox was nowhere around.

"Didn't you say you saw Theresa chatting with Mrs. Bradshaw?" Steven asked him.

"They weren't friends, but when Theresa would came here to see me, I saw her talking with Mrs. Bradshaw from a distance, but I had no idea about what. It didn't occur to me to ask her what they were discussing."

"Don't be hard on yourself," Steven said. "You didn't know anything was happening or the extent of Theresa's evil ways."

Rodney gave a tired sigh. "It could've been nothing, you know."

"But then they were killed in Cucumber Alley," Steven pointed out.

"I hired a private detective from Albany," Rodney mentioned bluntly. "His name is Mr. Sloane Sheppard. He'll find the underlying cause of this mess."

Steven choked on his cigarette. "A private detective? What made you decide to do that?"

"Because the police in this city take their sweet time in doing things. We could all be dead and buried by the time they find out—if they ever do—who killed Theresa and Mrs. Bradshaw."

"What do your parents think of your hiring a private investigator?"

Rodney hesitated. "Well, they weren't keen on it. But I'm doing the right thing."

"I don't know the name. Have you met with him?"

Rodney explained how he had taken half a day yesterday and met with Sloane in his office in downtown Albany. Steven was impressed and whistled, the cigarette dangling from his lips.

"You sure move fast." He glanced at his watch. "Sorry, Rodney, I should get going."

They got up and shook hands, Rodney accompanying his friend to the lobby.

"I'll see you later, Rodney," Steven said, pulling his cap lower on his head before heading out. "And be careful. I don't want to read in the paper that you've become a murder victim, too."

He then turned toward the main door which the doorman opened for him, allowing him to exit onto Washington Avenue. Straightening his tie and buttoning the top of his vest, Rodney returned to the registration desk, to assist new guests checking in and to try to forget at least for the time being the horrendous murders that occurred in Cucumber Alley.

Mrs. Edna Grey was settled comfortably in an armchair in her living room, the current issues of *Love Stories*, *Vanity Fair* and *Ladies Home Journal* on her lap. She enjoyed nothing more than relaxing with a cup of tea and her favorite magazines. The radio was tuned to WGY, playing popular music and Mrs. Grey loved Duke Ellington and Bessie Smith. A fire was burning silently in the fireplace. She was engrossed in a story when the doorbell suddenly rang. She saw it was just six-thirty by the clock on the mantel above the fireplace. A quick glance out the windows reminded her it was still winter and dark out. She wasn't expecting any visitors and wondered who'd be calling on such a cold evening.

Upon reaching the front door, she saw her friend, Mrs. Norris, from the side window. She opened the door and exclaimed her surprise by this unexpected visit. She welcomed her into the living room and invited her to sit by the fire, where it was warm and rather charming. Mrs. Norris took off her coat and cloche hat and although Mrs. Grey said she'd hang them up for her, she insisted she'd hold onto them, as she wasn't planning to stay too long. Mrs. Grey sat down, put the magazines on the end table, and then looked up at Mrs. Norris. She could tell something was bothering her friend.

"Marion, dear, what brings you out on such a chilly night?"

Mrs. Norris smiled wanly. "Well, I'm afraid to stay home alone, Edna, especially evenings. Suppose someone tried to break in? I live alone, you know."

"As do I, my dear. We must not be afraid. We must be strong."

Mrs. Norris admired the charming living room. It was simple yet pleasant and well-decorated, with an ornate fireplace, several pictures of landscapes on the walls, a long sofa, and two old-fashioned armchairs. Mrs. Grey offered her coffee or tea, but Mrs. Norris shook her head. She came to the point of her visit.

"Did you read about poor Rodney Longworth in the paper, Edna?"

Slowly, Mrs. Grey nodded. "Rodney could've been killed."

"It didn't say why he was in Cucumber Alley so late at night."

Mrs. Grey sipped her tea. "Well, Rodney should've known better than to go there alone, especially at night. Like so many young people today, he can be stubborn."

Mrs. Norris agreed. "I'm afraid today's generation is unlike ours, Edna."

Mrs. Grey continued drinking her tea. "Steven Banks is a wild young man and his wife, Wilma, too. Those flappers are totally unbecoming. Theresa Hayes was a flapper, too."

Mrs. Norris shook her head. "Suppose someone is attacking innocent women?"

"There, there, Marion, dear," Mrs. Grey said, trying to console her friend. "There've been patrols all over the village. I see the police cars go by and the villagers who've volunteered to walk around at night. I feel entirely safe, and you should, too."

Mrs. Norris nodded slowly, still unconvinced. To change the subject, Mrs. Grey mentioned the upcoming church rummage sale and the latest gossip about a few members of the congregation. Mrs. Norris commented about so-and-so's daughter and another member's unruly children, making church services difficult. Mrs. Grey agreed and then they lapsed into an uncomfortable and strange silence. It was almost seven-thirty before Mrs. Norris decided to leave. She expressed her fear again to her friend, but Mrs. Grey tried to ally her doubts.

"Would you go with me, Edna? I'm afraid to walk alone."

"Of course, dear. Why don't we take a walk? Do us both good."

"In this chilly weather and at night, Edna?"

Mrs. Grey smiled. "I've been home most of the day. And it isn't too late for a walk. There'll be plenty of people on Washington Avenue. Besides, Marion, you don't live far."

Mrs. Grey went to the hallway closet and returned with her long coat, red paisley scarf, and red cloche hat. Mrs. Norris commented how lovely she looked in the red scarf and red hat.

"Thank you, dear. Mrs. Brennan and Mrs. Banks have red scarves, too. Funny, isn't it?"

Mrs. Norris joined her at the front door and once outside on the steps, Mrs. Grey closed and locked it. They turned to walk south on Washington Avenue, toward Mrs. Norris's house, which was only a short distance away.

The wind and snow showers had subsided, making for a chilly but pleasant evening. Several neighbors walked past, greeting the women amicably, stopping to chat briefly before continuing on their way. Dim light from the streetlamps reflected off the snowy sidewalk, creating a rather favorable atmosphere for strolling. They came to the southern end of Washington Avenue before it bisected Front Street, parallel to Cucumber Alley.

"What a deserted place," Mrs. Norris said, shivering slightly.

Mrs. Grey agreed. "The patrols start later in the evening. Let's walk down the alley and look out toward the river. I always find it so peaceful. I haven't been there since before this nightmare began."

Mrs. Norris thought she was mad. "Walk down Cucumber Alley? Edna, it's dangerous!"

"Come along, dear," Mrs. Grey said, more in control of her nerves than her friend. "It'll help to calm our fears, Marion. Nothing will happen, I promise."

Reluctantly, Mrs. Norris joined her friend in walking down Cucumber Alley, past the few brownstones at the beginning and the empty wide lot just before the river. There were few lights in the area and one dim overhead light from a telephone pole which reflected off the river. It was calm and peaceful, and silent.

"See, dear, there's nothing to fear," Mrs. Grey said pleasantly, looking toward the river.

But Mrs. Norris wasn't listening. She was looking at something not far from them, lying at the base of the river, adjacent to a small landing at the end of the alley. She pointed it out to Mrs. Grey, who also couldn't make out the object. They moved to look closer. Mrs. Norris gave a startled cry, and then a scream. Mrs. Grey shuddered and grabbed her friend to turn away from the horrendous sight.

On the landing just before the river's edge, was the lifeless body of a man. The embankment where he lay was saturated with blood. He had been stabbed, repeatedly, and left for dead.

CHAPTER TEN

Wednesday morning Alice was at the Nott Memorial Library for an early shift. She mentioned to the library dean she preferred mornings over her usual late afternoons since a murderer was loose in the city. The dean acquiesced although reluctantly and rearranged the schedule to accommodate Alice's request.

She was busy sorting books that needed shelving and chatting with Mrs. Fillmore, the librarian. They commented on the recent murders, Rodney's mishap and the police investigation that had stalled. Alice mentioned how her son hired a private investigator to investigate Theresa's murder. Mrs. Fillmore showed surprise.

"A private investigator? Whatever on earth for? That's what the police are for."

Alice agreed. "We told him that, but he was rather stubborn about it. Soon enough this Mr. Sheppard will be here to speak to us."

"Mr. Sheppard? From Albany? I've heard of him. He's got quite a good reputation. I've seen his name in the paper dealing with various inquiries."

As she spoke, she opened the morning edition of the *Schenectady Gazette* and glanced through the pages, including the local news.

She had no sooner turned a page when she gave a sharp cry, causing Alice to look up from the book cart and ask if something was wrong. Mrs. Fillmore's face had gone ashen white, her usual calm composure replaced with fear and apprehension. She barely spoke to Alice who could tell something was obviously wrong.

"Here, Mrs. Longworth, in the paper," she stammered, her face clearly horrified.

Alice had no idea what she was referring to. She and Simon didn't have the chance to read the morning paper and left it on the kitchen table for Rodney when he came downstairs, although she knew he wasn't fond of reading the paper early in the morning.

"What is it, Mrs. Fillmore? Has something happened?"

The look on the other's face was enough to make Alice realize something grave had taken place. She looked at the article Mrs. Fillmore pointed to in the local news section.

Schenectady Gazette
March 8, 1927

Another Body Found in Cucumber Alley

The body of a young man was found last evening in Cucumber Alley. The victim had been stabbed multiple times. Police arrived and questioned numerous people, including the women who discovered the body. The police do not know if this murder is related to the two previous homicides in the same area. The victim's name is being withheld pending notification of next of kin. Anyone with information is asked to contact Schenectady City Police.

"Another victim!" she gasped. "No one is safe!"

Mrs. Fillmore agreed. "Perhaps they'll increase the patrols."

"A lot of good they've done," Alice said, rather bitterly. "The patrols didn't stop the murderer." She paused. "I wonder if my husband and son know about this."

Simon told her he planned to work at home today, finishing his journal article and then going to the post office. Rodney worked the late morning shift at the hotel and wasn't downstairs before she left. She thought of calling her husband but then changed her mind. She realized Mrs. Fillmore was speaking to her.

"…something's going on around here," she said nervously. "That makes three victims, Mrs. Longworth. Schenectady's always been such a safe, respectable place. The campus is lovely, especially in the spring. But now, things are different."

"Would you excuse me, Mrs. Fillmore? I want to see my sister. Do you mind if I take the paper to show her?"

Mrs. Fillmore told her she didn't mind at all. Alice grabbed her coat and cloche hat from the back room, and taking the newspaper, left the Nott Memorial Library on her way to the main academic building, in a harsh and gusty wind. She glanced at her watch. She saw it was only nine-thirty, but she wasn't sure if Agnes was teaching. Upon entering the building and brushing past numerous undergraduates, she climbed the stairs to the second floor and looked in each classroom, searching for her sister. She found her in the last classroom on the right, just before the far staircase, finishing a Latin class. Students were leaving and Alice stood aside, allowing them to walk past her. Agnes noticed her sister near the doorway and beckoned her to enter, although from the expression on her face, she could tell something wasn't right. Alice waited for the last student to leave, then approached her as she stood behind the teacher's desk.

"Agnes, I'm afraid I have terrible news," Alice said gravely. She opened the paper, folded back the page containing the article on the recent murder and held it out for her sister to read.

Agnes swayed slightly, then collapsed onto the chair in front of the desk. Another senseless murder took place in Cucumber Alley, with so many patrols and police guarding the area. She wiped away a few tears and then looked up at her sister.

Alice had walked over to the large windows overlooking the front of the campus. Always an admirable view, but at the moment she wasn't concentrating on the beautiful lawns or the Nott Memorial. She turned to her sister and expressed her shock and outrage.

"Do you suppose it's someone we know? Maybe Steven Banks?"

"Oh, my goodness, Alice, do you really think so? Mr. Banks and Wilma will be beside themselves if it turns out to be Steven. But why would he be in Cucumber Alley at night?"

"I had the same question for my foolish son," Alice said. "Rodney was lucky, he wasn't stabbed. But this young man, whoever he was, wasn't so fortunate."

"I should call Jerome and see if he's read about it," Agnes said worriedly. "Neither of us had time to read this morning's paper as we usually do. We were late getting ready for work and didn't bother with the paper."

"Same with Simon and I," Alice said. "Rodney works the late morning shift, but usually he doesn't read the morning paper, anyway." She paused, realizing the shock and horror of another murder victim in Cucumber Alley. "What should we do, Agnes?"

Agnes had regained her composure, after drying her eyes and clearing her throat. She had read the article several times but folded the paper and found it too painful to read again. She told her sister she had another class coming in soon but would call her later in the day.

At that moment, a few students entered the classroom and Agnes realized her next Latin group would soon start. She bid goodbye to her sister and then, putting on a brave face, began with the instructions and writing in Latin on the blackboard.

Descending the stairs, Alice was deep in thought. Three murders in Cucumber Alley, in less than a month. Approaching the exit on her way back to the Nott Memorial Library, she wondered if these gruesome deaths were somehow related.

Sloane got off the trolley at the corner of State and Lafayette Streets in downtown Schenectady and proceeded to walk to police headquarters on Liberty Street. It was not yet ten o'clock. He had left Albany early and took the trolley to Central Avenue until it arrived in the heart of Schenectady. He had moved his appointments scheduled for today to Friday, giving him a day to spend with Inspector James and to pay a visit to the Longworth family, by the afternoon. He also wanted to stop by the Hotel Van Curler to see Rodney at his place of work.

It was still blustery and chilly as he walked the two blocks to headquarters. Arriving amidst a snow shower, he opened the front door and was greeted by a policeman at the front desk. Almost immediately, Inspector James came from a back office and approached Sloane. They shook hands and the inspector invited him to his office.

Having spent much time at the Albany Police Department, Sloane was used to the daily routine and the unexpected catastrophes that occur with law enforcement. Policemen were busy writing reports, questioning witnesses, and answering phones. Entering the inspector's office, he took off his hat and coat, placed them on an empty chair, and then sat in a chair near the window. Before niceties could be exchanged, the inspector came straight to the point. Not what Sloane had expected to hear, but then in his line of work, he was rarely surprised. The inspector sat behind his desk, and looking at him gravely, cleared his throat and started to speak.

"We've had another, Mr. Sheppard. Another murder in Cucumber Alley."

Sloane lighted a cigarette, depositing the match in an ashtray on the desk. From long practice, he knew a murderer usually didn't stop with one or two victims if he felt threatened by someone or something. He waited for the inspector to continue.

"Two women who live nearby discovered the body last evening, around seven. Their names are Mrs. Edna Grey and Mrs. Marion Norris. They called the police and have already been questioned by the responding officers. As far as the victim, it's a young man, although we haven't released his identity yet. I can tell you his name is John Tucker, nineteen years old. He lived with his mother in a squalid apartment, not far from Cucumber Alley. We don't know why he was in Cucumber Alley. There was no evidence at the scene, so we have little to go on. As far as we know, there were no witnesses. We've spoken to people in the neighborhood."

Sloane drew heavily on his cigarette. "So much for the conclusion, the murderer was preying on just women. Looks like men are just as vulnerable."

Inspector James nodded. "We have his address from his wallet in his back pocket. Mr. Longworth's attack is another question, however."

"Perhaps Rodney Longworth was in the wrong place at the wrong time," Sloane said.

Inspector James agreed. "When he told us he saw something in the alley, he could've stumbled upon the murderer. He was attacked from behind and left for dead."

"But he wasn't killed," Sloane said thoughtfully. "I wonder if the murderer was in the alley at that time to meet someone as a payoff."

"Extortion is the better word," the inspector remarked dryly.

"Is there a connection between the two women and this Mr. Tucker?"

"None that we can see unless we uncover something." He paused. "Mr. Sheppard, what do you hope to gain by investigating this case?"

"Frankly, I had the same question," Sloane said honestly. "Rodney Longworth pleaded with me to look into his Miss Hayes's murder. I've handled many murder cases, in conjunction with the local police, of course."

Sergeant Eberhart entered at that moment. Seeing Sloane, he started to withdraw but the inspector told him to remain. He introduced himself to Sloane and asked if he heard about the recent murder.

"The inspector just told him. I'm working for Rodney Longworth to find who killed his companion. There's a possibility the person who killed Miss Hayes also killed the other two."

"And attacked Mr. Longworth in the alley," the Sergeant added. He then looked at the inspector. "Did you want to go to see the victim's mother?"

Inspector James looked at Sloane. "You're welcome to join us, Mr. Sheppard. Perhaps you can learn something about Mr. Tucker that would throw light on the murder of Miss Hayes."

Sloane rather doubted it, but he didn't voice his opinion. He butted his cigarette in the ashtray and joined the policemen in the lobby, where they put on their coats and hats. Once outside the police station, they made their way to a squad car and headed toward the stockade district.

The address on John Tucker's license was Green Street, not far from Washington Avenue. As they drove through the city streets, across

Liberty to Green Street, Sloane admired the brownstone houses, so well preserved. Inspector James found the building and parked the police car a block away. Arriving at the apartment house, not nearly as handsome as the other buildings, the inspector rang the bell of Mrs. Tucker's apartment. Without even asking who was calling, a buzzer sounded, allowing the men to enter. Inside the front hallway, it was dark and dreary, with a definite chill in the air and little heat from the radiator against the wall. They climbed rickety old wooden stairs until they came to the second floor. Inspector James led them along a hallway, to apartment 2B. Without even knocking, the door was opened suddenly. A woman appeared in the doorway, obviously distraught and her eyes blotched with tears.

"The police were here last night," she said, nervously. "Inspector James and Sergeant Eberhart? They told me you'd be coming today. Please come in." She had a cigarette between her fingers and was puffing nervously as she spoke. "I'm Mrs. Tucker, John's mother." She motioned for them to sit down, giving Sloane the chance to look around.

Squalid indeed, he thought, sparsely furnished, cold and damp as though this woman hadn't paid the heating bill. He was surprised she had electricity. In such slum-like conditions, obviously meant for low-income residents, he was also surprised her son had a driver's license. Living in such grimy disarray, could he have afforded a car? He rather doubted it.

The woman before them was about forty, dressed simply in a black dress as though in mourning for her son, her lips painted a bright red, her bobbed hair rather unruly. She was pacing back and forth in an agitated state and appeared ragged, but then given the manner of her son's death, how could she not be? He thought that was her permanent look, as though she had undergone many instances of turmoil and weathered them badly. She finished one cigarette and immediately lit another, smoking furiously, looking at the men before her, wondering if they could discover what happened to her son.

"Mrs. Tucker, my sincerest apologies for the loss of your son," Inspector James said. "This is Mr. Sloane Shepard, a private investigator from Albany. He's looking into the murder of Miss Theresa Hayes. I asked him to join us today."

"There may be a link with the three deaths," Sloane offered.

Mrs. Tucker continued smoking and pacing. "Johnny was a good boy; he just couldn't hold down a job. He was always in trouble of some sort and trying to find ways to make money."

"Do you know why he was in Cucumber Alley?" the Sergeant asked.

She shook her head and then collapsed into an armchair. She continued smoking, making little eye contact with the men. She started to cry but then regained herself in front of strangers.

"I didn't even know he had gone there," she said tearfully. "He liked those speakeasies, where he could drink. Maybe he just wandered there and saw something."

Sloane cleared his throat. "You mentioned your son was trying to find ways to make money. Did he work? What sort of jobs had he held?"

Mrs. Tucker looked at Sloane, as though just realizing he was there. She smiled briefly, finding comfort in his pleasing voice and appearance. She spoke weakly, almost forcing the words.

"He worked on a farm for a while. Then he worked shoveling sidewalks. Nothing steady."

"I just wonder if blackmail was something he was involved with," Sloane said.

Inspector James and Sergeant Eberhart turned his way. Mrs. Tucker also looked intently at him, surprised at hearing the word blackmail, not quite sure what it even meant.

"We have no proof of that, of course," the Inspector said, casting a rather dismissive glance at Sloane. "But we will continue to investigate until we find who is responsible, Mrs. Tucker."

Finding solace in the policeman's words, Mrs. Tucker tearfully thanked him. She wished she could tell them more about her son, but there was extraordinarily little. He dropped out of school at sixteen and drifted around the city, getting into trouble for shoplifting, vagrancy, and even bootlegging. Her husband had died in the war, and it had been difficult raising her son alone. They had lived in the apartment as it was the only place they could afford. Her job as a telephone operator paid the bills, as she called it, but it wasn't enough for them to find a better place to live.

"Do you know if your son had any enemies, Mrs. Tucker?" the inspector asked.

"No, I don't know. Johnny was reckless and irresponsible, so for all I know he may have had a ton of them. But who killed him in Cucumber Alley and why is beyond me."

Sergeant Eberhart had been writing in his notebook. He thanked her for her time, then the men got up, Mrs. Tucker joining them at the door. She implored them to find who was responsible for killing her son. He was basically a good kid, she told them, he didn't deserve this sort of end.

The policemen and Sloane thanked her, then left the apartment building. Once outside, they got in the car, where the snow had already blanketed the windshield. Turning on the wipers, the inspector commented they'd drive past Cucumber Alley and pointed it out to Sloane. He slowed down, allowing Sloane the opportunity to see for himself the desolate and rather forlorn alley although during the daytime it didn't seem too bad to him.

"We need to return to headquarters, Mr. Sheppard," Inspector James told him. "I can drop you off at the Hotel Van Curler, where you can speak with Mr. Longworth. And from there, you can walk to the Longworth house."

"You can catch the trolley back down to Albany on State Street," Sergeant Eberhart said.

They arrived at the intersection of Washington Avenue and State Street and the Hotel Van Curler. The inspector pulled up to the entrance and then turned and thanked Sloane for coming to Schenectady today. He shook hands with the policemen from in the car, then got out and climbed the steps of the hotel.

Sloane had never been in the Hotel Van Curler. He looked around the grandiose lobby, the ornate furnishings, and the crystal chandelier. He was favorably impressed with the décor as well as the clientele. Nearly everyone was dressed to the nines, and he didn't see a woman enter without a fur coat. A waiter walked past him and mentioned Governor Smith was in the building. Certainly, a high-class establishment. Sloane looked up and saw Rodney at the reception desk, just finishing checking in a party of four. He made his way over to him and greeted him pleasantly.

Rodney was surprised to see him. "Mr. Sheppard, I didn't know you'd be coming here. Welcome to the Hotel Van Curler." He paused. "This is Olive Mae, one of our guest clerks."

Sloane shook hands with the pretty brunette behind the counter. Rodney mentioned Mr. Sheppard was the private investigator he hired to look into Theresa's death. She cast a dubious look at both men, then proceeded to the farthest end of the counter, to assist a man checking in.

"I came to see the police," Sloane explained, meeting Rodney as he came from behind the counter. "I met with Inspector James and Sergeant Eberhart. We visited the woman whose son was found murdered in the alley last night."

"What?" Rodney gasped, loudly. A few people looked his way, apparently curious about his outburst in the otherwise refined lobby.

"Is there someplace we can talk, Rodney?"

He led Sloane to his back office, where it was quiet if not particularly comfortable. He lit a cigarette, didn't ask Sloane if he wanted one, and drawing heavily on the smoke, looked at the man across his desk in confusion and indignation. Sloane waited a few seconds so Rodney could compose himself, but he spoke before Sloane had the chance.

"Another murder? In Cucumber Alley? When did this happen?"

"Have you read this morning's paper? I'm sure it's been reported on the radio."

Rodney admitted he hadn't read the paper yet today or had the chance to listen to the radio. Puffing away on his cigarette, as though he hadn't smoked in months, he asked Sloane to tell him exactly what happened.

"A young man was found in Cucumber Alley last evening by a Mrs. Grey and a Mrs. Norris, who were out for a walk."

"I know Mrs. Grey and Mrs. Norris," Rodney said. "They're having lunch in the restaurant here. I saw them a little while ago."

"Where were you last evening, Rodney?"

Rodney drew on his cigarette. He looked at Sloane anxiously. "I worked the late shift and got home about eleven-thirty. I didn't see or hear anything unusual."

Rodney asked him if he planned to speak to his parents and his aunt and uncle.

"I plan to go there later today," Sloane said, lighting his own cigarette. "I want to get as much information as possible while I'm here in Schenectady."

"Why don't I introduce you to Mrs. Grey and Mrs. Norris," Rodney suggested. "I'll call Dad to make sure my parents are home later today when you arrive."

Finishing his cigarette, Rodney stood and led Sloane to the restaurant. It was practically full, as many dignitaries, including Governor Smith as well as the usual General Electric employees, were there. Rodney noticed one of the small dining rooms, just off the restaurant, was being used, so he assumed that was where the governor was lunching. From the waiters bustling in and out, he was sure that was the case. He located Mrs. Grey and Mrs. Norris seated at a corner table, on the other side of the restaurant, having coffee. Mrs. Grey smiled, albeit tiredly, when she saw Rodney approach their table.

"Hello, Rodney dear. So nice to see you. You know my friend, Mrs. Norris."

Rodney nodded at Mrs. Norris then introduced Sloane, a private investigator he hired to look into Theresa's death. They looked at him in surprise. Rodney told them Mr. Sheppard wanted to speak to them about their recent discovery. He told Sloane he needed to return to his office and left him with the elderly ladies. Sitting at their table, Sloane introduced himself again and proceeded to ask Mrs. Grey and Mrs. Norris about the body of the man they found last evening.

"It was dreadful, Mr. Sheppard," Mrs. Grey said, sipping her coffee. "Mrs. Norris and I decided to take a walk down Cucumber Alley."

"And then by the river, we saw the body," Mrs. Norris finished for her.

"Did you know who it was?" Sloane asked. He didn't want to reveal the identity yet, as it had not been released by the police. Looking carefully at the elderly women before him, he felt as though he were speaking to two Victorian maiden aunts, neither of whom were akin to trouble. Prim and proper, he could tell they shunned the loose morals of the younger generation and frowned upon the corruption brought about by Prohibition, although he hardly imagined they were against it.

"We went straight back to my house and called the operator," Mrs. Grey continued.

"Do you work, Mrs. Grey?"

"I'm a retired nurse. I teach at the college."

"And you, Mrs. Norris?"

"I retired several years ago. I'm active in our church and the community center."

"Did you know Miss Theresa Hayes?"

He caught a slight hesitation, as though they were afraid to admit the truth.

"We did know her," Mrs. Grey admitted reluctantly. "She worked at the college library. A most difficult young woman. I don't think she had many friends."

"Is there anything you can tell me about Miss Hayes and Mrs. Bradshaw?"

Mrs. Norris said she hardly knew either Mrs. Bradshaw or Miss Hayes and although she saw them around the village, she personally didn't know them. Mrs. Grey mentioned she knew Mrs. Bradshaw in passing but was not friends with her. She had little to add about Miss Hayes.

"I may be in touch with you again soon," he told them. He thanked them for their time, stood, and pushed the chair under the table. He left the restaurant on his way to the lobby.

From behind the registration desk, Rodney asked what he learned from Mrs. Grey and Mrs. Norris. He expected to hear a flood of information. Sloane related what they told him, and he could see the disappointment in his young face.

"I called my father," Rodney told him. "I told him you wanted to speak to him and my mother. My aunt and uncle plan to stop over later, so you'll be able to see them, too." He jotted down the address and then handed the slip of paper to Sloane. "I'll be home about five."

Rodney watched as Sloane left the hotel. He turned his attention to a guest needing his assistance. He glanced at his watch quickly. It was just past three o'clock.

Simon and Alice were in the living room, listening to the news and drinking coffee, although neither was relaxed. Simon had mailed his article to *Scientific American* and Alice had returned from the library an hour ago. Simon told his wife Rodney had called, telling him that Mr. Sloane Sheppard was at the hotel and would be there to see them shortly. Alice voice her displeasure. From his tone of voice, Alice could tell her husband was not pleased, either. From the radio, they heard the announcement of the discovery of another body in Cucumber Alley, that of a Mr. John Tucker, aged nineteen of Schenectady. The announcer gave few details and concluded that the investigation was continuing. Alice mentioned she read about it in the morning paper as did Simon. They assumed Rodney heard about it, too, if he hadn't seen the article in the paper. Perhaps someone at the hotel told him. It was now news all over the city.

"Who is this Mr. Tucker?" Alice wondered. "We don't know anyone here in the village with that name. Do you think Mr. Sheppard will speak to us about his death, dear?"

Simon was too preoccupied to speak. He finished his cigarette and quickly lit another. He exhaled a fine cloud of smoke, and took his time in replying, thoughtfully and carefully.

"I think Rodney is wasting his time and money with a private investigator."

Alice knew when her husband was deeply annoyed, as he usually lapsed into a long bout of silence. The radio was playing the latest popular tunes, but the calming music did nothing to alleviate the tension in the room. Within a half-hour, the doorbell rang. Alice entered the hallway and opened the door to see Sloane Sheppard standing before her. He greeted her, showed her his business card, mentioned he had just come from the hotel and saw Rodney, and asked if could come in. Alice stood aside allowing Sloane to enter. She offered to take his hat and coat and then proceeded to bring him down the hallway, to the living room, where Simon still sat, listening to the radio, and reading the newspaper. He folded the paper, put it on the coffee table, and rose to greet Sloane. He beckoned him to an armchair near the fireplace and then he and Alice almost together asked what they could do for him.

Sloane cleared his throat and asked them what they knew about the murders in Cucumber Alley, including the most recent death of Mr. Tucker. Both Alice and Simon shook their heads.

"I hardly knew Mrs. Bradshaw," Alice said. "Miss Hayes worked at the library, but she was a most disagreeable young woman. We didn't know Mr. Tucker. Are you also investigating who attacked Rodney?"

"There's a possibility the same person is responsible for the three murders and the attack on your son," Sloane said. "So far, the police have little to go on. There was no physical evidence left in Cucumber Alley."

"Isn't commuting from Albany to come here difficult, Mr. Sheppard?" Simon asked.

Sloane thought that a rather strange, unnecessary question. "I've handled cases everywhere, Mr. Longworth. Distant is not an issue where my investigations are concerned. Crime can happen anyway, including murder."

Alice got up from the sofa, clearly flustered. "We've never had a murder here in the village, Mr. Sheppard. I had my hours moved from evenings to days at the library so that I don't have to travel back here at night. My sister teaches at the college, but only one night a week." She turned to look at Sloane. "It isn't safe anymore to walk around."

"Rodney mentioned you're both retired," Sloane commented.

Simon told him he retired from General Electric while Alice was a retired French and English teacher. He spent his days writing journal articles for *Scientific American* and Alice volunteered at the Nott Memorial Library. Neither knew why the two women and Mr. Tucker were killed, or who could've attacked Rodney.

From long experience, Sloane knew that was most likely the truth, although there were bound to be secrets that they didn't wish to reveal. He was about to ask them more about Miss Hayes when the doorbell rang. Alice rather quickly went to the hallway again and opened the front door, admitting her sister and brother-in-law. Upon entering the living room, she introduced them to Mr. Sloane Sheppard, private investigator, from Albany.

"Terrible murders," Agnes said, maintaining her composure better than her older sister. She sat in an armchair across from the sofa. "Who'd kill these people and attack poor Rodney? The police must have some idea who's responsible."

Sloane shook his head. "Rodney hired me to look into the death of Miss Hayes. There may be a link between the three murders."

"You believe the same person killed the three of them?" Jerome asked. He lit a cigarette, offering one to his wife, who took it but didn't light it. She was continuing staring at Sloane in shock and disbelief.

Sloane asked them about their relationship with Mrs. Bradshaw and Miss Hayes, as well as Mr. Tucker. Neither acknowledged any involvement with the victims, although they reluctantly admitted an acquaintance with Miss Hayes. Agnes spoke before her husband had the chance.

"Miss Hayes was a most difficult young woman," she said firmly, mirroring the comments made earlier by her sister. "I don't know why they kept her on."

Sloane asked them about their work. Agnes mentioned she taught Latin at Union College and Jerome proudly spoke of his work at General Electric. They lived on Union Street, in the Realty Plot, which, Agnes added, was one of the best areas of the city.

From their demeanor as well as their haughty manner, Sloane could tell the Brennans, as well as the Longworths, had no financial worries, no perplexing issues clawing at their minds, no disruptions to their stability, and placid way of life. Even the attack on Rodney didn't seem to shake the Longworths and the Brennans too badly, although Mrs. Longworth seemed genuinely protective of her son.

On the other hand, they seemed congenial enough, if rather pompous and brusque in manner, but would one of them be capable of murder? Further questioning of the Brennans provided nothing helpful. Plenty of people had little regard for Miss Hayes but not to the extreme of killing her. Yet someone did and so far, he was baffled as to who and why.

Agnes asked Sloane about his work, his prior cases, and what he hoped to achieve by taking on this case. Her tone implied it was foolish and that Rodney should've known better than to hire a private investigator. Sloane mentioned his work in the criminal justice system in both Albany and Schenectady and his previous experiences in numerous kidnapping, divorce, and fraud cases. Agnes merely looked at him with raised eyebrows.

"Do you think you'll find who killed Theresa, Mr. Sheppard?" she asked him.

"That's what Rodney hired me to do," Sloane said, looking at the four people seated near him. An odd bunch if he ever saw one. He knew it'd be difficult to get more information from them and most likely they knew more than they were willing to reveal.

The doorbell rang once again. Sloane wondered if Mr. and Mrs. Longworth were used to people dropping over. From their expressions, he gathered they weren't. He watched as Simon, finding an excuse to leave, got up before his wife and went to the front door. A murmur of voices was heard from in the hallway before he returned momentarily with Mrs. Hayes and Mr. Banks. He took their coats and introduced them to Sloane.

"It's nice to meet you, Mr. Sheppard," Flora said, sitting on the sofa. She smiled and was polite. "My daughter was Theresa, Rodney's companion. I hope you'll find who killed her. It'd be a great weight off my mind." She paused, as though needing to clarify her appearance. "Russell and I wanted to stop by to see Rodney, but Simon mentioned he's working and won't be home till closer to five."

"You work in Albany, Mr. Sheppard?" Russell asked him. "I know Albany well. I'm a banker and stockbroker. I have several clients from Albany."

Sloane listened as Mrs. Hayes told him of her work in an insurance office while Mr. Banks elaborated on the opportune status of the stock market, adding that if he wished to invest, he'd be happy to help him.

While they were talking, Sloane looked carefully at Mrs. Hayes. An attractive woman, her blue dress highlighting her slender figure, her dark eyes alluring. She didn't appear to be in mourning for her daughter. He wondered if she had even bothered to mourn, her nonchalant attitude didn't give him the impression she was the type. Mr. Russell Banks seemed larger than life, rather stocky in his business suit, a stockbroker for sure. He also wondered if she and her companion made a habit of visiting the Longworth residence often. From the friction in the room, he sensed Mrs. Hayes wasn't too fond of Mrs.

Longworth, as she practically ignored her after realizing Rodney wasn't home, although she seemed pleased to see Mr. Longworth and the Brennans.

"Something must be done, Mr. Sheppard," Russell said, as though giving Sloane an ultimatum. "There's a maniac loose in this city."

Alice agreed. "My sister and I aren't comfortable walking around anymore."

"There are the patrols, dear," Simon said, patiently.

"They haven't done any good," Alice retorted. "This Mr. Tucker was murdered, and Rodney was attacked. The patrols obviously are not effective."

"You have a point," Russell said. "It's really up to the police to step up the security."

"Mr. Sheppard, do you plan to come to Schenectady often?" Jerome asked.

Sloane had the impression that Jerome wished he wouldn't. A rather quiet, observant man, there was something about Jerome Brennan that Sloane found disturbing. Perhaps his ambivalence toward law enforcement or his involvement with the case. Perhaps he had something to conceal which he feared Sloane would eventually find out.

"Until the case is resolved, I plan to come here often," Sloane said, looking at everyone. He then asked Flora and Russell, "Did you know Mr. John Tucker, who was murdered recently?"

They didn't know Mr. John Tucker, nor had they heard the name. Flora explained that the village was a tight-knit community, and most people knew one another. There were new people from time to time, of course, but most residents had been in the stockade for many years.

"What brought these people to Cucumber Alley in the first place?" Russell asked as though speaking to the entire room. "There must've been a reason because no one just goes there."

"I believe this case rests on Miss Hayes," Sloane said, glancing at Flora.

"But what about this Mr. Tucker who was murdered?" Alice asked innocently.

"He may have stumbled onto something," Sloane said.

Before he could elaborate any further, they heard the front door open. Knowing it was Rodney, Alice went to greet her son. Rodney was pleased to see his aunt and uncle, as well as Sloane. He smiled and sat in an armchair next to his father.

"We've been discussing the recent murders, Rodney," his father said.

"You *do* know there was another murder in Cucumber Alley, Rodney?" Flora asked him.

He nodded. "Yes, Mr. Sheppard told me earlier. I read it in the paper afterward. I don't know anyone named Mr. Tucker."

"Are you feeling better, Rodney?" Flora asked, rather awkwardly. "Be careful, dear, walking around the city, especially in the evenings."

Rodney mentioned he was much better and thanked Mrs. Hayes for her concern. A strange silence pervaded the room until Sloane spoke once again.

He asked more questions about each person's whereabouts the evening Miss Hayes was murdered. He cast a quick glance at Mrs. Hayes, who continued sitting near him, placidly, as though the rehashing of her daughter's murder didn't seem to faze her. Perhaps that was a cover-up for a deeper and hidden persona that few were aware of, except maybe Mr. Banks. Sloane then asked Mr. Banks if he could speak to his son and daughter-in-law in the future.

"Of course, Mr. Sheppard. Steven works with Mr. Brennan at General Electric and my daughter-in-law works at the United Cigar Store on Jay Street."

Sloane thanked them and with Rodney, walked to the front door, where Rodney handed him his hat and coat. Sloane mentioned he'd be in touch soon, then stepped out onto the snowy sidewalk. Walking up Washington Avenue, he was rather tormented by an unease that this case was far from over. The genteel stockade neighborhood was not used to murder. It was far from the serenity that held this upscale neighborhood intact.

He could not rid his mind of the disturbing thought that the killer was someone he had recently encountered. A false face, hiding beneath a veneer of respectability. Someone must be lying, and that person had the most to hide, but he didn't yet know who or why.

CHAPTER ELEVEN

At the United Cigar Store the next day, Wilma Banks heaved a sigh of relief as the customer she was recently attending, a pleasant but rather exacting businessman made a purchase and left the store. Sometimes they never want to leave, she thought, glad that the store was empty for the moment. She walked to the back of the counter and picked up the morning paper.

Thursday, March 11, 1927, almost a month, she thought wryly looking at the front page, and no one brought to justice for the murders in Cucumber Alley. She scanned the headlines, the world news, and the local stories. Finding nothing of interest, she gazed out the front windows across Jay Street, to the other shops and restaurants. It was noontime and Steven would soon arrive from General Electric as he promised to take her to lunch today.

While she waited, she lit a cigarette and continued looking out the store windows. Light snow was falling, and the wind was gusty, but Wilma learned to brave the weather, rather than complain about it. She looked in the counter mirror, smoothed down her bobbed hair and, taking her pocketbook from underneath, she opened it and found her lipstick. She was about to apply it to her lips when the front door opened, the chimes on the inside clanging noisily, much to Wilma's annoyance, and instead of seeing Steven, it was Rodney who entered. He smiled upon seeing her.

"Hi, Wilma," he said, walking up to the counter. "How's it going?"

"Fine, Rodney," she said, returning the smile although she didn't think he came to the store to chit chat. She waited to see what he wanted. She glanced at the back door, to make sure her boss was in there. It was closed, a good sign, meaning she had the store to herself. She asked Rodney how she could help him today.

"Two packs of Lucky Strikes, please," he said. Wilma reached in the back for the cigarettes and rang them up at the register, depositing the thirty cents Rodney handed her. He was about to leave when Wilma decided to ask him a few questions.

"On your lunch hour, are you?"

Rodney nodded, and nervously pulled his cap lower on his head. A bad habit, but with the tumultuous events recently, he was inclined to anxious gestures.

"Yes, and I'm out of cigarettes. Thought I'd come here to get them."

"How's the hotel these days?"

"Busy. Governor Smith visited recently. Steven stopped in a few days ago. Why don't you and Steven stop by for lunch when I'm working? We can talk more then."

"Steven's coming here today to take me to lunch. We might try that new café that opened up further along Jay Street."

Rodney felt uncomfortable, although he wasn't sure why. Steven and Wilma were his friends, weren't they? He never quite knew how to take Wilma. Certainly, pretty in her own style, but far from beautiful, she was the ultimate flapper, just not a flamboyant one.

"The private investigator I hired was here yesterday," he told her. "He spoke with Mrs. Hayes and your father-in-law at our house last evening. He plans to find out the truth."

"Yes, Russell mentioned he spoke with a private detective at your house last night." She hesitated. "What do *you* think is the truth, Rodney?"

He paused, rather irritably. "I don't really know, Wilma. Someone had a vendetta against Theresa and even Mrs. Bradshaw. I was attacked in Cucumber Alley. I could've been killed."

"That Mr. Tucker was murdered, too. Did you know him?"

Rodney shook his head. "The name doesn't sound familiar. Mr. Sheppard will find the underlying cause of this mess, even before the police do."

"Are you doing the right thing, Rodney, hiring a private detective to look into this?"

"The police in this city drag their feet. It could take months before they finally get to solving it. By that time, the killer will have got off scot-free."

Before Wilma could say anything more, the door opened again and this time it was Steven who bustled in, shaking snow from his coat. Looking fresh and robust, with his cheeks red from the chilly air, he greeted his wife and was surprised to see Rodney.

"Rodney, old boy, what brings you to the United Cigar Store?"

He looked at him questioningly and Rodney felt even more uncomfortable, unsure if his friend was implying something that wasn't happening.

"I came for cigarettes," he said, holding the packs up as though he needed to prove it to Steven. "It's my lunch hour, so I thought I'd come here, it's the closest to the hotel."

"Don't they sell cigarettes at the hotel gift shop?" he asked him.

"Of course, but I wanted to take a walk," Rodney said, again not sure why he needed to explain his actions to Steven Banks. At times like this he wondered if he really was a friend.

"I came to take Wilma to lunch," Steven said, smiling at his wife. Handsome to a degree but not close to Rodney's debonair appearance, he exuded charm and manners, along with a certain arrogance, and most people were convinced of his appeal.

They made small talk for a few more minutes and then Rodney decided to return to the hotel. He was about to turn for the door when Steven suddenly stopped him.

"Rodney, this evening there's a lecture and demonstration by Dr. Alexanderson on the future of broadcasting. It starts at six o'clock. Why don't you stop over?"

Rodney hesitated. "I heard on the radio recently that he planned to lecture at General Electric. Isn't Dr. Alexanderson the scientist who talks about television?"

"He is indeed," Wilma said, before her husband could speak. "Soon they predict we'll be watching shows on a box and hearing them, too."

Even Steven was impressed. "Before long, there'll be talking pictures, too."

"I read *the Jazz Singer* will be the first talking film," Rodney said, sharing the enthusiasm. "But that won't be till later this year."

"In the meantime," Steven said, as he helped Wilma on with her fur coat, "why don't you come over to General Electric later and listen to Dr. Alexanderson? Your uncle will be there, and he's probably told your father about it, too."

Steven and Wilma then joined Rodney outside, talking about the lecture at General Electric that evening. In the crowded pedestrian thoroughfare of Jay Street, busy with the lunchtime crowd, Steven and Wilma said goodbye to Rodney as they found the new café and entered. He then turned and entered bustling State Street, crowded with shoppers and General Electric employees on lunch. He unwrapped the cellophane on a pack of Lucky Strikes and lighting a cigarette, decided he would go to the lecture at General Electric this evening. Why not, he thought, it'd be better than brooding at home over the Cucumber Alley murders. Maybe he'd ask Olive Mae to join him. He'd call his parents to see if they planned to attend. He was sure Mr. Banks would attend as well as Mrs. Hayes.

Satisfied with his plans Rodney crossed at the light and entered the Hotel Van Curler to return to work, unaware of the unforeseen circumstances that would occur that evening.

The lecture and demonstration by eminent electrical engineer Dr. Ernst Alexanderson at the General Electric facility was regarded as topical and paramount to those interested in the future of electronics. Family members and friends of employees were welcome to attend and by the time six o'clock came, the auditorium had few vacant seats. Dr. Alexanderson was held in high esteem as a valuable employee of General Electric, a premier researcher in the new medium of broadcasting and his lecture was highly anticipated by those in attendance. WGY and the *Schenectady Gazette* sent reporters to cover the event.

Rodney had called his parents, telling them he planned to have dinner with Olive Mae at the hotel before heading over to General Electric. He told them about the lecture and to his surprise, his father already knew about it. Jerome called to tell him that he and Agnes planned to attend. Simon told his son that he and Alice would also attend and that they'd see him there.

Rodney and Olive Mae left the hotel and waited on Washington Avenue for the trolley to General Electric. Upon arriving at the main building, and after confirming they were guests of Steven Banks, they were instructed by a guard to proceed to the auditorium on the lower floor, where a crowd had already gathered.

Rodney spotted his parents, along with the Brennans, closer to the front. In back of them were Steven and Wilma. He waved to his father, who beckoned him and Olive Mae to join them.

"This should be quite an event," Steven said, loud enough for the entire row to hear.

"I'm glad you made it, Rodney," Wilma said, her red paisley scarf around her neck.

"Rodney, dear, so lovely to see you," Agnes said turning in her seat. "You're looking handsome as always. And Olive Mae, you certainly are a pretty girl."

He then did a double take. He noticed his Aunt Agnes's red paisley scarf draped around her neck, like Wilma's. Why would he see those infuriating red scarves again? He didn't notice the red marks on his aunt's scarf, so she must have washed it. He looked to his right and spotted Mr. Banks and Mrs. Hayes approaching. Mrs. Hayes wore a red cloche hat, like the one Mrs. Grey usually wore. Didn't he see red in the alley just before he lost consciousness? Something just wasn't right with this picture, he thought irritably.

The auditorium was filling up and the sound of chatting was a steady hum. Wilma motioned to two empty seats next to her. Mr. Banks and Mrs. Hayes nodded hello to everyone and then sat down, eagerly awaiting the lecture and demonstration.

Rodney sat in back of his parents, with Olive Mae next to him, but oddly felt uncomfortable, the red scarves bothering him. The murmur of voices was strangely annoying, as though it took away the thoughts he wanted so much to clarify and understand. He brushed it off and listened to Olive Mae rattle on and on about the latest Clara Bow film and how much she enjoyed reading *Vanity Fair* and *Harper's Bazaar* magazines.

"Rodney, I must come to the hotel for lunch," Jerome said, turning in his seat to address his nephew. "I haven't had the chance. I've been so busy."

"You're always welcome, Uncle Jerome," Rodney said and smiled.

He then looked to his right and noticed Mrs. Hayes and Wilma talking intimately, engaged in what seemed a serious conversation. He wondered what they were talking about. His eyes then traveled further along the rows. He noticed several prominent politicians, with their wives and even Mr. Lennox and his wife. He saw Mrs. Grey and her friend Mrs. Norris making their way down the aisle. She made eye contact with him, smiled, and nodded. Rodney nodded in return, although he didn't understand why Mrs. Grey and Mrs. Norris would want to listen to a lecture on electronics and broadcasting. Mrs. Norris must have relatives working here, he thought. He noticed Mrs. Grey's red cloche hat and red paisley scarf, prominent against her white dress. He then looked at his parents, chatting amicably with the Brennans. Mr. Banks was talking with his son, and Wilma and Mrs. Hayes were still conversing. As six o'clock approached, an announcer from General Electric walked onto the stage, the house lights dimmed, and a hush fell over the audience. He greeted the crowd pleasantly and then proudly introduced General Electric's own Dr. Ernst Alexanderson.

Rodney watched as a distinguished gentleman took center stage, thanked his colleague, and then stood behind a podium. He was tall with a thick mustache and thinning brown hair. As he spoke, he held the audience spellbound, as everyone was curious to know more about the development of television.

"Good evening, ladies, and gentlemen. My name is Dr. Ernst Alexanderson, and I am an employee of General Electric. It is my intention to discuss the future of broadcasting, with its beginnings here in Schenectady."

A murmur of astonishment rippled through the crowd. Rodney was extremely impressed with the technology developed in his hometown. Like the rest of the audience, he listened, fascinated to what Dr. Alexanderson was telling them.

"In January, I lectured in New York City, and I predict that every home will have a television set within ten years." He explained further the mechanical television he created, using an extremely sensitive neon light. He then pointed to a large upright console, similar to a radio set, which was the mechanical television he had labored for so long. He demonstrated this by holding a motor control in his hand. He used it to synchronize the picture which utilized mechanical scan technology.

"Here at General Electric, the future of electronics will continue to grow, and television broadcasting is at the forefront of that innovation."

Rodney listened and watched in awe, wondering if his parents would eventually purchase a television set. He couldn't fathom watching shows on a screen, but Dr. Alexanderson enthusiastically continued his demonstration, enthralling the audience.

"With the developments in broadcasting I have researched, and as an experiment, I will successfully send the first television images from my home here in Schenectady to a few homes in the area. I will transmit voices over radio to accompany the image. I propose the first public demonstration of television at Proctors Theater using a projector by sometime next year."

A round of applause and even a few whistles erupted from the exuberant crowd, obviously pleased, and perhaps a little overwhelmed by the brilliance and the technological foresight of Dr. Alexanderson. His lecture on television broadcasting continued for another half hour and concluded just before seven-thirty. Thunderous applause reigned in the auditorium and Dr. Alexanderson again thanked everyone kindly and bowed slightly, before walking offstage.

The house lights remained dim at first, then became brighter as people started to rise, and conversations began in earnest. Nearly everyone was fascinated by Dr. Alexanderson's lecture and television demonstration and talk was regulated to what the future held not only for Schenectady but the whole country, maybe even the world.

Rodney heard Olive Mae speaking to him, but he wasn't really listening. He saw Mrs. Grey and Mrs. Norris make their way over and begin to chat with his mother and his aunt. Wilma and Steven were chatting with his father and uncle, while Steven started to talk with a few people who were seated behind them, although he didn't know who they were.

He squinted in the bright house lights in stark contrast to the dimness during the lecture. He saw several workmen remove the podium and then others carried the large console off the stage. Other workmen began cleaning and getting it all in order. People were filing out of the auditorium, talking animatedly about the lecture and demonstration.

Rodney turned to Olive Mae and was about to suggest they leave when suddenly a man from the stage shouted something in a language he wasn't familiar with. It was a loud, obnoxious flood of nearly excitable speech that took those still in the auditorium by surprise. At first Rodney didn't know what was happening and neither did anyone else. The man, speaking in a crescendo of incomprehensible outrage, was pointing to the small group near the stage. He continued speaking excitedly and was breathing torturously, his face red, veins bulging on his forehead. He was subdued by other General Electric employees, who ushered him backstage. People were looking at each other in stark confusion, not understanding what they just saw and heard.

"What was that all about?" Olive Mae asked, turning to Rodney.

"That guy must've been crazy," Steven said, coming up to them. "He was pointing at something and screaming in some language at the top of his lungs!"

"It was Russian," Agnes said, ever the authority on languages. She put on her fur coat and her red paisley scarf as she, Jerome, Alice, and Simon joined Rodney and Olive Mae. "I studied Russian while an undergraduate."

"Who was he?" Wilma said, behind her husband, wrapping her red paisley scarf around her neck. She shivered more from nerves than cold.

Rodney thought she looked intimidated, even scared. And that infuriating red scarf again. He then noticed Mrs. Grey with her red paisley scarf, Mrs. Norris and Mrs. Hayes who equally looked scared, as though any loud, obnoxious behavior was foreign to their serene way of life.

"We don't need to concern ourselves with it," Mr. Banks said sensibly.

"He certainly seemed angry," Mrs. Norris said, almost shivering.

"Indeed, he did," Mrs. Grey said firmly. "Perhaps he's envious of Dr. Alexanderson's contributions. Some foreigners are anarchists, you know. And very resentful, too."

Even Mrs. Hayes agreed. "I read in the paper about anarchists, even here in Schenectady. A Russian may have a vendetta that only he knows about."

"Russians in Schenectady?" Alice said, bundling her coat around her.

"Oh yes, dear," Mrs. Grey said. "Many anarchists proliferate, even in Schenectady."

"Especially after the war," Simon said, putting on his hat and coat. "We've had our fair share of refugees and immigrants."

Rodney listened to the conversation and wondered if that was the case. The man was obviously disturbed by something and perhaps it did deal with Dr. Alexanderson. What else could it have been? Steven and Jerome reiterated that they didn't know the man and had never seen him before. Their tones implied they were on the upper echelon of General Electric and had no contact with a laborer. Rodney wanted to say that of course, they wouldn't know him, would they ever encounter a laborer in the labs in which they worked? Even his uncle and Steven displayed a haughty air at times.

Simon, Alice, Jerome, and Agnes mentioned they were ready to leave. Simon told his son they'd see him at home soon. Mrs. Grey and Mrs. Norris had already proceeded to the exit, while Steven and Wilma were putting on their coats and hats, then joining the rest of the audience to the exit. Mr. Banks and Mrs. Hayes said goodnight and started walking up the aisle behind Steven and Wilma. Rodney watched as they retreated through the exit doors, leaving him and Olive Mae practically alone in the auditorium. They too proceeded up the aisle, but Rodney stopped, turning back to the now empty stage, meditatively. He was silent for a moment before Olive Mae asked him what was wrong.

"Oh, it's nothing," he said, turning back to her. "Let's get going."

He put any thoughts of the screaming man and those disquieting red paisley scarves behind him as he and Olive Mae left the auditorium on their way to the exit.

It was close to eleven-thirty. Rodney and his parents arrived home several hours ago at almost the same time. After walking Olive Mae home, Rodney continued up North Ferry Street, to Front Street, passing Cucumber Alley before arriving at Washington Avenue and his parent's house.

They stayed up rather late, chatting in the living room and listening to the radio. Alice made coffee and Simon had rekindled the fire. It was still chilly out and the warmth from the fire was comforting. Conversation ensued about Dr. Alexanderson's lecture and the future of broadcasting, but Rodney's mind was too far away to concentrate on what his parents were saying. Putting her coffee cup on the end table, Alice noticed her son seemed rather disturbed.

"You've been so quiet since you got home, Rodney. Is everything all right with Olive Mae? You didn't stop at Cucumber Alley before coming here, did you?"

Rodney puffed on his cigarette. "Olive Mae's fine, Mother. I didn't stop at Cucumber Alley." He added nothing more and even Simon sensed his son's disconcertment.

"We've had a long evening," he said to his son, folding the evening paper and leaving it on the coffee table. "Everything was going well until that lunatic started his rampage."

"It's best not to discuss it," Alice said. "Especially so late at night. It's too disturbing."

Rodney butted his cigarette in an ashtray and announced he was retiring for the evening.

"I'm on the three o'clock shift tomorrow," he told his parents, getting up and heading for the hallway. "Hopefully, I'll sleep late. I need the extra rest."

But as he lay in bed, tossing and turning, sleep was far away for Rodney. He heard his parents ascend the stairs fifteen minutes ago, and the house took on its usual nighttime quiet. He listened while the grandfathers' clock in the downstairs hallway chimed the midnight hour and then the half-hour, still without falling asleep. He sat up irritably, pushed aside the bedsheet and blanket, switched on his bedside lamp, and fumbled for his pack of cigarettes. He stretched out on the bed, lit a cigarette, exhaled a large cloud of smoke and tried to sort out the chaotic thoughts circling in his mind.

Something strange happened this evening. That Russian man or whatever he was, speaking so excitedly, and pointing at them as they stood near the stage while they were putting on coats and getting ready to leave. But who was he pointing at and why? He spoke little to no English, but he must've had a gripe with someone or something. It seemed odd that he would venture to address a particular person or persons in such a brutally opprobrious manner.

Dr. Alexanderson's lecture and demonstration were timely and informative. But that man didn't start shouting until it was over, and most of the audience had left, except us, he thought. What made him speak so excitedly? He could see the convulsed face as he pointed at the crowd.

Rodney sat up, rather wearily, but still feeling wide awake. He extinguished his cigarette in the ashtray on the bedside table. Mrs. Bradshaw, Theresa, Mr. Tucker…three unsolved murders. And his attack, nearly left for dead until the policeman discovered him. Would there be other victims? There must be a madman loose somewhere, luring his victims to Cucumber Alley. But so far the patrols and the police hadn't uncovered anything. And this Mr. Tucker, what was he doing in Cucumber Alley so late at night? Did he stumble upon something he shouldn't have and had to be silenced?

Now an unknown foreign man, screaming vituperation at someone or something. Maybe he saw someone he recognized. But would he let out a stream of invective? No one understood him, but by his tone of voice and his expression, he seemed angry but at who or what? Maybe it was nothing. And maybe he was just wasting hours dwelling on it.

For some time, Rodney sat motionless, his mind deep in troublesome thoughts. He didn't know how long it was before sleep overcame him. In the early morning, as daylight slowly filled the room, he awoke, lying curled in a cramped fetal position on the edge of the bed.

CHAPTER TWELVE

S loane Sheppard arrived at his office in downtown Albany later than usual the next morning, as he met with a client at the Albany County Courthouse. By ten o'clock, he was at his desk, looking at his March 1927 calendar for the week of the fourteenth. He had briefly reviewed his notes on the Cucumber Alley murders and intended to give his full attention to the case when the candlestick phone on his desk rang sharply. Upon answering it, he heard a rather excitable young man's voice. He knew it was Rodney before he identified himself. Before he could ask the purpose of his call, Sloane heard about the bizarre behavior he witnessed during a lecture at General Electric last night.

"Start at the beginning, Rodney," Sloane said, loosening his tie as he figured it'd be a long discourse, whether valuable to the case remained to be heard.

Rodney was holding the candlestick phone somewhat impatiently, standing in the hallway in his robe and slippers. He had stayed in bed later than usual given his sleep pattern last night. He took a deep breath and told him about the lecture and demonstration by Dr. Alexanderson at General Electric and of the high-strung man who, at the conclusion of the lecture, spoke belligerently and pointed wildly at the group of people near the stage, of which he was one, as though he had a vendetta against somebody or something.

Sloane waited for him to say more. When he didn't, he asked how he thought it related to the murders of Miss Hayes, Mrs. Bradshaw and Mr. Tucker.

"I really don't know," Rodney said hesitatingly. "It may not have anything to do with the case. But he was pointing at someone or something."

Sloane agreed that it was indeed strange but failed to see how it would be important to the case. Unless the man recognized someone or something and reacted as he did. He still did not see the relevance but kept it to himself. He told Rodney he had yet to review his notes but planned to do so today. Before ending the call, he asked him about Theresa's employment at the college.

"She worked as a clerk at the Nott Memorial Library," Rodney told him, feeling as though he had already supplied that information.

Sloane heard a slight annoyance in his voice. "It might be beneficial to speak to people at the college who knew Miss Hayes I'll see if I can get an appointment to speak to the library dean later today." He paused. "Rodney, how often did Miss Hayes speak to Mrs. Bradshaw?"

Rodney frowned. "I remember I was busy checking in guests, and I saw them talking, but what they discussed, I don't know. I assumed Theresa was just chatting with Mrs. Bradshaw, passing the time of day."

"It may have been more than that," Sloane said gravely.

"What do you mean, Mr. Sheppard?" Rodney asked him.

Sloane asked when he saw them talking. Rodney patiently mentioned it was recently, but he couldn't remember the exact date. He started to ask more questions, but Sloane told him he'd be in touch soon, after speaking to the dean of the library. After a few more words of encouragement on Sloane's end, the call ended. He reached for his cigarette pack and taking one out, thoughtfully tapped it against the desk blotter. Putting it to his lips and lighting it, he decided to call the Nott Memorial Library. First, he consulted a Schenectady city directory, which he kept on a bookcase against the far wall. Finding the number, he returned to his desk, grabbed the candlestick phone, and waited for the operator. As usual, the circuits were busy in the morning but within a few moments, he heard a female voice asking for a number please, and after giving her the Schenectady exchange, he was soon connected to the library at Union College.

"Good afternoon, may I speak to the dean of the library?" he asked the woman who answered. He could hear talking in the background. So much for a quiet library, he thought.

"The library dean isn't available at the moment," a crisp female voice spoke. "May I help you with something, sir? We're quite busy today with freshmen orientation."

Sloane explained who he was and his purpose in calling. The woman identified herself as Mrs. Fillmore, the chief librarian. She again asked if she could help, hoping to terminate the inquiry as soon as possible but Sloane was not to be put off.

"Is the dean available this afternoon?" he asked her.

"Well, I'd have to check his calendar, Mr. Sheppard," Mrs. Fillmore said, stalling for time.

"I can meet with him this afternoon. This is a criminal investigation, and it's imperative I speak with people associated with Miss Hayes."

Mrs. Fillmore caught her breath. She paused, glancing at the calendar on the check-out desk. "The dean is here later this afternoon, at four. His name is Dr. Bennett, although honestly, Mr. Sheppard, I don't know what he could tell you about Miss Hayes. He hardly saw her."

Sloane thanked her and mentioned he'd be there at four o'clock today. He hung up and sat brooding, wondering if speaking to the dean of the library would be beneficial. He took up the candlestick phone, asking the operator to call Union College again. The college switchboard connected him to the president's office, but his secretary mentioned he was out till Monday. He asked for an appointment, after explaining the purpose of his call and was given a later afternoon time on Monday, the fourteenth. Sloane replaced the handset and looked at his calendar. Monday morning was booked solid with appointments, but he was fortunate to have only one, a divorce case, for the early afternoon, leaving him plenty of time to get to Schenectady.

He then grabbed his jacket from the back of his chair, his coat from the rack behind the door, and after locking up, headed for the elevator. A middle-aged woman got off as he got on and once the gates were closed, the elevator clanged downward, toward the lobby.

Once outside, it was still chilly as March days go in Albany, so Sloane buttoned his coat to the neck. He first stopped at a diner and had a roast beef sandwich and coffee. Paying at the cashier, he left the diner and waited on North Pearl Street for a Schenectady bound trolley. Glancing at his watch, he realized he had plenty of time to get there. Within a few moments, one approached, and Sloane stepped on, depositing a nickel in the slot near the conductor.

He was pleased it wasn't as crowded during the mid-afternoon as it would undoubtedly be within a few hours, with workers erupting from office buildings. Taking off his Fedora hat, Sloane sat next to a young woman, who was engrossed in the latest issue of *True Confessions* magazine. He noticed a businessman reading the morning paper while to his left another young woman was immersed in Mary Roberts Rinehart's current novel *Lost Ecstasy*. There were several passengers who got off and many more who got on along the way. It seemed like a long ride but before he knew it, the trolley was on State Street in downtown Schenectady. He got off at the corner of State and Lafayette Streets and once on the sidewalk decided it was too cold to walk and flagged down a cab to take him to Union College. Arriving at the driveway of the imposing campus, he paid the driver and proceeded to the Nott Memorial Library.

Approaching the stone-masonry masterpiece, Sloane couldn't help but marvel at the Nott Memorial Library. He didn't think he had ever seen anything like it, even in Albany. Passing several students as he entered the opulent building, he saw a woman behind the circulation desk, checking out books and assisting students. She looked up and asked Sloane if he needed assistance.

"My name is Sloane Sheppard. I have an appointment to speak to the dean. I'm investigating the death of Miss Theresa Hayes."

"Oh yes, Mr. Sheppard. I'm Mrs. Fillmore, the chief librarian." She hesitated as a student needed her attention. Briefly, she turned away before returning to where Sloane stood in front of the circulation desk. "Is there anything I can help you with, Mr. Sheppard?"

"Did you work with Miss Hayes?" he asked her.

Mrs. Fillmore nodded. "Yes, Miss Hayes and I shared several shifts. I was her immediate supervisor. Although her work was satisfactory, I admit she was a most disagreeable young woman." She spoke with finality as though that was all he'd get from her.

Sloane smiled, hoping to encourage her to speak further. "Where were you the evening she was killed?"

Mrs. Fillmore explained she was working the evening shift, along with Miss Hayes, during a snowstorm. Mrs. Longworth was a volunteer, shelving books and periodicals. She mentioned how Mrs. Longworth went to see her sister in the main academic building where she was teaching a Latin class. Only after her shift ended, she added.

Sloane nodded. "And Miss Hayes? Do you remember her actions that evening?"

"I was busy at the reference desk and here as well, checking out books for students and a few faculty members. I remember Dr. Longworth stopped by and asked for a periodical. Mrs. Grey also was here and requested a nursing journal." She paused. "But Theresa, I don't know where she went. It was as though she disappeared."

"Disappeared? Did you look for her?"

Mrs. Fillmore nodded. "Her shift hadn't ended yet, but she must've left, because Mrs. Longworth and I searched the entire library, and she was nowhere to be found."

At that moment, a tall, rather heavy-set middle-aged man approached the circulation desk. He introduced himself as Dr. Arthur Bennett, the dean of the library. Sloane shook hands with him and mentioned he had an appointment to see him.

"Mr. Sheppard, nice meeting you. The meeting I attended ended earlier than expected so I am free if you wish to speak to me now."

Sloane thanked Mrs. Filmore and then followed Dr. Bennett up several stairs to a back room, small yet well-furnished with a desk, two file cabinets and two chairs. Dr. Bennett returned to his desk while Sloane sat at the chair in front of him, allowing him a careful look at the man before him. Certainly, well educated, his doctorate degree from Harvard hung on the wall behind him. He had thinning brown hair, speckled with gray, and brown eyes which were curious yet friendly. He asked Sloane how he could help him.

"I'm investigating the murder of Miss Theresa Hayes. What can you tell me about her, her work here, and her overall disposition?"

Dr. Bennett paused, lit a cigarette without offering one to Sloane, leaned forward on his chair, and threw the match in an ashtray. He moved the candlestick phone from one side of the desk to another and shuffled a few papers as though stalling for time before looking up at Sloane. His tone was grave and unpretentious.

"Well, Mr. Sheppard, I didn't have much contact with Miss Hayes. Mrs. Fillmore recommended to terminate her, but she commented her work was adequate and she did not have sufficient cause to do so."

"Was she involved with anything inappropriate that you know of?"

"Inappropriate? I'm afraid I don't understand, Mr. Sheppard."

Sloane chose his words carefully. "Mrs. Fillmore mentioned she vanished that evening. She and Mrs. Longworth looked but didn't find her. Could she have had a meeting or a tryst with someone you didn't know about?"

"If Miss Hayes was involved with something illegal, that was no concern of mine. Frankly, I tried to avoid contact with her. Although, I found she could be pleasant at times. When I needed her assistance, as did the president's office, she was a good worker."

Sloane had been writing in his notebook. "I'll be speaking to the president on Monday. Rodney Longworth, Miss Hayes's companion, told me she could be secretive, as though she were hiding something. Did you have that impression of Miss Hayes?"

Dr. Bennett exhaled a long stream of smoke before answering. "I can't say. I remember her talking to Mrs. Longworth, Mrs. Brennan, Mrs. Grey, and Dr. Longworth numerous times. I don't believe they had high regard for her. In fact, I don't think anyone did. Perhaps she was a threat in some way."

"What makes you say that about her, Dr. Bennett?"

He crushed his cigarette in the ashtray. "Mrs. Fillmore and I noticed that she changed, became even worse if that were possible after she finished working at the president's office. She was moody with us, the students, and the faculty, as though she knew something she wasn't privy to. I asked the president's office what she worked on while there. They told me she filed papers, old records, insurance and business matters."

Sloane nodded. "But she may have had access to other records, too."

Dr. Bennett cleared his throat. "I wish I could help, Mr. Sheppard. We're looking to replace Miss Hayes, so we've been busy in that endeavor."

"How long did she work in the president's office?"

"About three weeks. The president's office handles hiring, along with personnel. They may have more information about Miss Hayes."

"She was hired for the library, is that correct?"

Dr. Bennett nodded. "But earlier this year, she was needed at the president's office for a few weeks. She divided her time between there and the library. We've been short-staffed recently, so her services were needed in the administration office as well as here."

Sloane continued scribbling in his notebook. He asked him a few more questions about Theresa Hayes, but his answers were evasive, as he reiterated, he rarely saw her. He realized he could learn nothing more of value from Dr. Bennett. Sloane stood, shook hands with him, and gave him his business card, asking if he remembered anything that could help in the investigation, to please call him. Dr. Bennett opened the door and thanked Sloane for stopping by. He showed him how to get to the main floor which Sloane discovered was rather like a maze in the atrium-style library, but after climbing down several flights of stairs, he arrived at the main floor. He nodded to Mrs. Fillmore who was still at the circulation desk as he made his way to the exit.

Once outside, he glanced at his watch and saw it was just three o'clock. As he had finished with Dr. Bennett earlier than expected, he decided to stop by to see Mr. and Mrs. Longworth. On Union Street, he caught the trolley to the corner of Washington Avenue. He arrived at their house in no time and rang the doorbell. He could hear a flurry of activity before muffled steps sounded as the front door was partially opened. Sloane looked into the face of Mrs. Alice Longworth.

"Hello, Mrs. Longworth. I'm Mr. Sheppard. I'd like to speak to you and your husband if this is a convenient time."

Sloane thought she looked depressed and rather agitated, as though the emotional turmoil of the murders and the attack on her son had finally caught up with her. Mr. Longworth entered, holding the evening paper, wondering who his wife was talking to. He was not too pleased upon seeing Sloane again.

"Hello, Dr. Longworth," Sloane said, shaking hands with Simon. "I was at the Nott Memorial Library and wanted to speak to you and your wife again."

"Haven't we already told you what we know, Mr. Sheppard?" Simon said, rather irritably.

Alice agreed. "We've already spoken to you, Mr. Sheppard. There isn't anything more we can help you with," she said. "But please come in, Mr. Sheppard. Would you like coffee or tea?"

Sloane declined either and followed them to the spacious and comfortable living room, where the fireplace was already lit and the radio was on, tuned to WGY. Soft music filled the air, creating a placid and inviting atmosphere. Alice motioned for him to sit in an armchair and then she and Simon sat before him on the sofa.

Sloane cleared his throat before speaking. "There've been three murders here in the stockade village in addition to the attack on your son. The police have no leads so far."

"Do you have leads, Mr. Sheppard?" Simon asked, almost sarcastically.

"Yes, I do," Sloane said, surprising even himself. He could tell the animosity from Simon and a more latent but apparent animosity from

Alice. "The third victim, Mr. Turner, may have been blackmailing someone. And that person killed him, to keep him quiet."

"Blackmailing?" Alice said. "We know most of the neighbors. Murders don't happen in the village. I've always felt entirely safe in this area."

Simon agreed with his wife. "There's no crime here in this part of Schenectady. And as my wife mentioned, murders don't happen here."

"Your son was involved with Miss Hayes and contemplated marriage, is that correct?" Sloane asked, sensing the uncomfortableness in the room.

Alice grimaced. "Fortunately, that didn't happen."

Simon looked at his wife with such apparent anger that Sloane thought he'd slap her, as though he preferred that she'd kept her opinions to herself. Sloane wondered if this well-mannered couple in their opulent brownstone house was just a front for a different and distinct home life, beneath the quiet façade. He blinked as he realized Alice was speaking again.

"...Rodney knew how we felt about Miss Hayes. But people make their own mistakes, Mr. Sheppard. I don't know of anyone, other than our son, who genuinely liked Miss Hayes. Most of the neighbors didn't care for her, either."

"Would that include your sister and brother-in-law? As well as the Banks and Mrs. Grey?"

Alice nodded. "Yes, that's correct. The people you just mentioned have all been bullied by Miss Hayes. Even her own mother wasn't very fond of her."

"Where did you graduate college, Dr. Longworth?"

Simon looked at Sloane, taken off guard by the question. "At NYU for my graduate degrees. My undergraduate degree was at Union." He went on to explain before Sloane asked that he and his brother-in-law, Jerome, both worked at General Electric.

"Schenectady is still a wonderful city," Alice put in. "General Electric is growing, too."

Sloane asked about the lecture by Dr. Alexanderson and the ensuing chaos afterward. He mentioned Rodney had called him this morning to tell him about it.

"Do you think it has a bearing on the case, Mr. Sheppard?" Alice asked.

"Frankly, I don't know. According to Rodney, this man pointed at someone or something in the crowd. Do you remember what you saw?"

"That's what happened," Simon said. "We didn't know the man. He didn't speak English."

"My sister said it sounded like Russian," Alice said.

Sloane nodded. As he thought when speaking to Mr. and Mrs. Longworth previously, they were an odd pair but courteous. He didn't think he'd get anything more from them. It was possible they knew or suspected something but declined to say more. He then asked about Rodney. Alice told him he was working the late shift today and wasn't expected home till after eleven o'clock.

Sloane stood and thanked them for their time. Simon and Alice saw him to the door and then abruptly closed it practically on his heels. He stood on the sidewalk in front of their house, and then proceeded down Washington Avenue, to see if Mrs. Hayes was home. He had written her address, along with the addresses of Mrs. Grey and the Banks, in his notebook. If Mrs. Hayes wasn't home, he'd try Mrs. Grey. He noticed it was now almost five o'clock, so perhaps she was home from work. It'd be either Mrs. Hayes or Mrs. Grey, Sloane decided, as it was getting dark, and he wanted to return to Albany before it got too late. He came upon Flora's house and was reassured when he saw someone move past the front windows. He'd try to see Mrs. Grey at another time. He climbed the snowy steps and rang the bell.

As he waited, he looked to his left and noticed in the distance the Longworth house and further down on Washington Avenue to his right was Mrs. Grey's brownstone house. Strange how they lived so close by, and nobody knew anything about what happened in Cucumber Alley. He cast his eyes even further and could see where Washington Avenue and Front Street met, at the beginning of Cucumber Alley. With the encroaching darkness, he noticed Washington Avenue was certainly well-lit but glancing up the avenue he noticed the area around Cucumber Alley was covered in darkness. Just then the door was abruptly opened, and Mrs. Flora Hayes stood before him, looking disheveled, as though she had just woken up from a deep sleep.

"Mrs. Hayes, I'm Mr. Sheppard. I'm investigating the murders in Cucumber Alley."

"Yes, I know who you are," Flora snapped. There was a distinct pause. "I'm afraid you've come at a bad time. I can't see you right now."

"Another time, perhaps? I'll be back in Schenectady on Monday."

Flora pursed her lips. "I'm not sure at the moment."

Sloane looked at her carefully as she stood in the doorway. She didn't look nearly as attractive as when he had met her previously. Maybe she had just returned from work. She appeared tired and forlorn, and apparently miserable. Even the gray dress she wore matched her mood. He didn't think whatever was troubling her was her daughter's murder. He caught a certain condescension and haughtiness in her manner.

"What time on Monday?" Sloane asked, giving her a taste of her own medicine.

"I work all day and am quite busy in the evenings."

Sloane nodded. "Then another time. Thank you, Mrs. Hayes."

As Flora closed the door, Sloane turned to descend the steps when he thought he heard a man's voice in the background. He looked back at the door, wonderingly, then proceeded on his way up Washington Avenue.

As he came to the corner of Washington Avenue and State Street, Sloane decided to visit Rodney at the Hotel Van Curler. He noted where he'd catch the trolley back to Albany and then upon crossing at the light and entering the renowned hotel, he saw him behind the registration desk, assisting several guests checking in. He waited for him to be free before approaching him.

"Mr. Sheppard," Rodney said in surprise. "How did it go with the library director?"

Sloane smiled at Rodney, standing behind the desk. An intelligent young man and a persistent one. He told Rodney he had indeed spoken to Dr. Bennett, the dean of the library. Before he could ask for the details, Sloane briefed him on what he learned from Dr. Bennett and Mrs. Fillmore. He concluded they were not able to add anything new to the investigation.

"What about the foreign man at Dr. Alexanderson's lecture?" Rodney asked, as though Sloane had resolved it all. "Maybe Dr. Bennett and Mrs. Fillmore know about him."

"I didn't mention it to them," Sloane said. "I did mention it to your parents, who I just finished speaking with. They didn't know the man and had never seen him before."

Rodney frowned, his brown hair falling slightly over his forehead. He looked puzzled and worried. He asked Sloane what he thought of the foreign man at the lecture.

Sloane cleared his throat. "I don't know yet, Rodney. As I told your parents, he could've recognized someone or something." He paused. "I mentioned the possibility that Mrs. Bradshaw, Miss Hayes and Mr. Tucker may have seen or heard something they shouldn't have and decided to blackmail the killer."

"You really think that's the issue here?" Rodney asked.

Sloane nodded. "I don't see any relation between the three victims. When someone is threatened, the person may resort to murder."

"But who'd blackmail someone in the village?" Rodney stammered. He came from around the desk. It was quiet in the grandiose lobby and there were few people about. He looked imploringly at Sloane. "Whoever killed Theresa also killed Mrs. Bradshaw and that Mr. Tucker."

"And attacked you in Cucumber Alley," Sloane added.

"Do you think that foreign man is responsible? He did act really strange, screaming at the top of his lungs and pointing as we were leaving."

"The police may know more about it," Sloane told him. "In the meantime, I don't recommend you walk around by yourself at night, Rodney." His tone was grave, and Rodney looked at him with wide eyes. "The killer may be someone you know," he added.

Rodney was soon needed at the front desk. Sloane assured him he'd be in touch soon and left the hotel, to get the trolley back to Albany. As he walked on State Street, his mind was reeling. While waiting with a sizeable crowd, he wondered if the solution of this case, or at least part of it, centered around the machinations of Miss Theresa Hayes.

That evening, Steven and Wilma Banks paid a visit to Mrs. Edna Grey at her home on Washington Avenue. Edna had called Wilma at the United Cigar Store earlier in the day and invited her for coffee and dessert. Wilma, surprised by the invitation, asked if her husband could come along to which Mrs. Grey pleasantly told her Mr. Banks was welcomed, too.

Before leaving the house, Steven asked his wife why they were going to Mrs. Grey's house and on a Friday evening no less, when they could be at a speakeasy, even at one of the local dance marathons. Wilma eyed her husband as they walked up Washington Avenue.

"After standing up all day at the store, do you think I'd want to get involved in a dance marathon?" she told him. "Sometimes, Steven, I don't think you have a brain."

Rather rebuffed, Steven joked and told Wilma he'd go dancing with her anyway. "Besides, you dance a mean Charleston."

It was close to seven o'clock when they rang the doorbell at Mrs. Grey's handsome brownstone. They had passed the Longworth's house and were not too far away from the beginning of Cucumber Alley. Wilma wondered how they could all live so close and not have seen or heard anything happening in Cucumber Alley. She also wondered why Mrs. Grey invited them for coffee unless she was becoming sentimental in her elderly age.

The front door was opened and Mrs. Grey, looking matronly and overbearing as usual, stood before the Banks, smiling, and ushering them inside her pristine and spotlessly clean home. She took Wilma's fur coat and red paisley scarf, commenting it was just like the one she owed, and Steven's coat and cap, and then directed them to the living room, where a fire was blazing, and the radio was tuned to a station playing popular tunes. Mrs. Grey told her guests to make themselves comfortable, while she went to the kitchen and returned shortly with a tray, bearing cups, sugar, cream, and plates containing applesauce cake she had baked during the afternoon.

"Applesauce cake was my husband's favorite," she said, smiling, handing them the plates and the coffee cups. "On a blustery day, it's nice to have warm cake and coffee!"

She sat in an armchair while Steven and Wilma were on the sofa. An awkward silence ensued until Wilma, putting down her coffee cup, asked Mrs. Grey if she mind if she smoked.

"Well, I don't smoke myself, dear." She rose to retrieve an ashtray from on top of the mantel, then brought it over to Wilma. "Please feel free to smoke. My late husband was a smoker."

Steven also lit a cigarette, more from nerves than an actual desire to smoke, still wondering why this old matron invited them to her house in the first place. He puffed quite heavily on his cigarette as did Wilma, neither saying anything of much interest. Mrs. Grey commented how well they looked and then the terribly cold weather for mid-March, wasn't it just awful? When would spring arrive, she lamented? She mentioned the church rummage sale and the community center activities, her science classes at the college, and how much she enjoyed teaching.

Wilma listened and smiled but really could have cared less about the weather, the rummage sale, the community center or her science classes. A quick glance at Steven told her he felt the same, although neither showed it.

"…and there'll be a summer rummage sale at the church, too," Mrs. Grey was saying, rambling on and on about the church activities so much that Wilma thought she'd burst from the strain of not telling her to stop talking.

"I suppose you're wondering why I invited you here," Mrs. Grey said at last, as though clearing away the preliminaries and getting down to her real intentions.

"Well, it was rather unusual, Mrs. Grey," Wilma said, sipping her coffee. She picked up the cigarette she left in the ashtray and continued smoking, waiting to hear what Mrs. Grey had to tell them. She couldn't imagine it'd be anything of much importance. She'd realize within a few minutes she was totally wrong.

Mrs. Grey cleared her throat as though preparing for a narration that would take all her reserve. Steven looked at her and wondered what was happening and was thinking of excuses to leave when she started to speak.

"I hope what I have to say isn't too disturbing, dears, so please forgive my impertinence if I appear meddling."

That's all she does is meddle, Wilma thought, what else does an old Victorian matron have to do. She looks strong, so it couldn't be something with her health. So, what in the world did she want to tell them?

"As you know, I worked at the hospital for many years. I saw many patients and worked in different wards." She paused and then spoke abruptly. "Steven, I believe your father is the father of Theresa Hayes."

Silence. A silence so strong with undercurrent that, at a glance at her husband, Wilma realized Steven was totally shocked and speechless. The only sounds were the ticking of the grandfathers' clock in the hallway and the soft music from the radio. A bombshell so totally unexpected that it left both Steven and Wilma dumbstruck. Wilma put down her cigarette and looked at her husband who was still in complete shock. She then looked at Mrs. Grey, furious that this interfering old busybody would call them here to tell them this news. She reached out to her husband, but Steven irritably shook her hand off and addressed Mrs. Grey. His tone was firm and indignant.

"How dare you make such an accusation!" he said angrily before Wilma had the chance to speak. His voice rose, clearly an indication of his wrath. "What proof do you have? Dad never mentioned it to me. He would've told me."

"Not necessarily, dear," Mrs. Grey said soothingly. "I believe that's why Mrs. Hayes's husband divorced her because he found out she was pregnant by another man. And the same for your mother. She divorced your father after finding out about his affair with Mrs. Hayes."

"You're telling me Theresa Hayes was my half-sister?" Steven said, clearly livid. "How do you know that? And why would you decide to spring this on us after all this time?"

"Please, don't be upset, dear," Mrs. Grey said, sipping her coffee. She put the cup and saucer on the coffee table. "I worked at the hospital."

"That doesn't mean anything," Steven retorted, smoking incessantly.

Mrs. Grey shrugged. "I believe it does, Steven."

She gave the impression she knew much more than she told. But by now Steven and even Wilma had heard enough. He stood up and towered over Mrs. Grey, who remained seated in the armchair, looking up at him, unfazed by his wrath. He continued looking at her, gesticulating with his cigarette as though making a point while speaking.

"I don't believe this, Mrs. Grey. Dad would've told me, years ago."

"It is strange that you didn't mention it sooner, Mrs. Grey," Wilma said, coming to her husband's defense. "Personally, I don't see what business it is of yours, anyway."

"She used her mother's last name and by all accounts, she was the daughter of Mrs. Hayes's husband." Mrs. Grey paused, addressing Steven. "I believe she was your father's daughter, your half-sister. Ask him yourself."

Steven stood in front of Mrs. Grey, with the cigarette between his lips. Wilma thought he'd slap her so evident was his anger. She was about to stand between them when Steven unleashed his venom on the woman in the armchair.

"So, you worked at the hospital? Hundreds of people work at the hospital. You're nothing but a quack! What proof do you have of this nonsense? You're a phony!"

Steven and Mrs. Grey locked eyes and Wilma thought her husband would lash out at her. Instead, he butted his cigarette in the ashtray and strode to the hallway, collecting his coat and hat and calling for his wife to do the same. Wilma looked at Mrs. Grey as she calmly sipped her coffee, oblivious to the disruption she had caused.

"You'll regret this, Mrs. Grey," she told her firmly. She joined her husband in the hallway and within a moment the front door opened and closed with a bang.

Mrs. Grey sighed, put down her coffee cup, and walked to the front door. She looked out the side window and saw Steven and Wilma walking up Washington Avenue toward their house. She then locked the door, returned to the living room, and sat back down on the armchair, as though nothing out of the ordinary had occurred. She picked up *True Story* magazine and contentedly began to read. But then she thought back to what Wilma Banks told her. Was she threatening her? She did say something about regretting this, didn't she? Those were her last thoughts as her eyelids became heavier and heavier, the words on the page were fuzzy and she fell into a deep sleep.

It was not until several hours later, close to midnight when Mrs. Grey awoke. She realized she was still in the living room and had fallen asleep in the armchair. The lamp on the end table was on, but the magazine was on the floor, an indication she had dozed. She was about to turn off the lamp when a distinct sound from outside caught her attention. She paused, listening. She crept to the hallway and stood motionless. Was someone trying to break in? She crept to the side windows and looked out. It was pitch dark with lampposts providing only dim light. She saw the upper part of Cucumber Alley. She then squinted and thought she recognized someone on the sidewalk just outside her house.

Without waiting a moment longer, Mrs. Grey scurried toward the candlestick phone on the hallway table and upon picking up the handset, asked the operator to call the police.

CHAPTER THIRTEEN

S chenectady Police Headquarters was strangely quiet early on Saturday mornings. Chilly air with light snow and an even colder police station greeted Inspector James upon his arrival. He took off his hat and coat and leaving them on a chair, settled at his desk. He picked up the report left for him by the policemen on duty last night and gave it a quick overview. He saw it was a busy Friday night in the city; a disorderly conduct arrest, two arrests for drunk driving, a shoplifting arrest at Woolworth's, a stolen purse at Proctor's Theater, and a possible break-in at a home in the village.

Inspector James read the particulars of the arrests and the incidents carefully. Certainly, nothing too unusual for a Friday night. His attention was then drawn to the last item. A possible break-in at a home in the village, belonging to Mrs. Edna Grey of Washington Avenue. He noted the details.

Saturday, March 12, 1927, 1:14 a.m.

Mrs. Edna Grey reported a burglar outside her home. Responding officers arrived at the scene and reported

Mrs. Grey was visibly upset, although no evidence of a break-in was evident. Officers combed the area around the lower block of Washington Avenue, including Cucumber Alley, but found nothing. An imprint of a size twelve shoe in the snow near Mrs. Grey's house was observed. Mrs. Grey commented she had not been out all evening and insisted a man was standing outside her house after midnight.

Inspector James put the report aside. He and Sergeant Eberhart had questioned Mrs. Grey at the college about the Cucumber Alley murders over a week ago. He wondered if Mrs. Grey was a target, that the killer was planning on making her his next victim. Then why stand near her house after midnight? Was he hoping to lure her outside and to Cucumber Alley? He had the impression Mrs. Grey was a strong and formidable woman, not given to hallucinations. He doubted that she'd open her front door upon seeing a stranger. He'd go to her house later today to see what more he could find out. At that moment, Sergeant Eberhart entered, carrying the morning paper.

"We need more clues to find the man responsible for the Cucumber Alley murders," he said gravely, tossing the paper on the desk. He sat across from the inspector, looking preoccupied.

"Mrs. Grey contacted the police early this morning. She claims someone tried to break into her house." Inspector James showed the nightly report to his colleague.

"Tough luck she and her friend found Mr. Tucker," the sergeant said. "Mrs. Norris told me Mrs. Grey suggested they walk down Cucumber Alley that evening. Of course, they didn't know what they'd find there."

Inspector James agreed. "That makes three murders and no leads. Unless we're dealing with a madman, killing his victims in Cucumber Alley for no apparent reason."

"The foreign man at General Electric who caused a commotion on Thursday evening has been spoken to," the sergeant said. "He wouldn't say why he yelled and pointed at someone or something in the crowd. He works as a foreman at the facility. Maybe he recognized someone?"

"It may not tie in with the murders," Inspector James concluded. "But whoever was outside Mrs. Grey's house earlier this morning may be the killer."

"Mrs. Grey could be a target," Sergeant Eberhart said to which Inspector James agreed.

"We have to act fast before another victim is found in Cucumber Alley."

Saturday mornings were usually quiet and peaceful for Rodney. It was the perfect opportunity to sleep late. He'd get up at his leisure, and have an unhurried breakfast, with plenty of coffee and cigarettes, without having to dress for work.

He stretched his long legs in bed and glanced at the alarm clock on his nightstand. It was only eight o'clock, which wasn't too bad, given he worked till eleven last night and didn't get home until past eleven-thirty. He sighed, contentedly, feeling comfortable in his warm blankets, reluctant to get up to start the day, when suddenly he heard a loud cry from downstairs. He raised his head from the pillow and listened. There it was again. It sounded like his mother.

He threw back the covers and jumped out of bed. Forgetting his robe and slippers, he hurried down the stairs. Upon arriving in the hallway and expecting to hear about another murder in Cucumber Alley, he saw his mother talking on the phone, clearly alarmed by her expression. His father had also heard the commotion and entered, looking at Rodney at the bottom of the stairs and his wife, perplexed and overwrought, as she stood in the hallway, holding the handset and the candlestick phone.

Rodney looked at his father and then again at his mother. Simon wondered what was happening, looking at Alice, as though for answers. She continued mumbling into the handset and then concluded the call, replacing the candlestick phone on the table and silently brushing past her husband and son, as though in a trance. Rodney looked at his father uncomprehendingly, and then followed him into the kitchen, where Alice was busy at the stove, pouring coffee and making breakfast. She turned when she heard them enter. She forced a wry smile.

"Oh, Rodney dear, you're up early on Saturday. It looks like the sun's trying to come out for a change. Here's your coffee."

She deposited two cups on the table, but Rodney knew something was troubling her. He lit his first-morning cigarette, eagerly awaiting her answer.

Alice sat across from her son and husband, stirring her coffee with a forlorn expression. She appeared nervous, not wanting to talk, looking down at her coffee cup absently.

"There must be something bothering you, dear," Simon said, sipping his coffee. "What was the phone call all about? It must've disturbed you."

"Please tell us, Mother," Rodney implored, drawing heavily on his cigarette, and forgetting the coffee in front of him.

Alice cleared her throat. "That was Steven calling for you, dear."

Rodney blew smoke and through the haze looked at his mother. "Steven? For me? Why didn't you tell me?"

"You were still in bed, dear. I didn't want to disturb you since you hadn't gotten up yet."

Rodney and Simon looked at her questioningly, waiting for her to continue. Alice meekly sipped her coffee. She cleared her throat and then spoke bluntly, getting right to the point.

"Steven mentioned he and his wife visited Mrs. Grey last night. She told them she believes Mr. Banks is Theresa's real father."

"What!" Rodney practically shouted, almost knocking over the coffee cup in front of him, his cigarette dangling from his mouth. He was in such shock he was rendered speechless.

"I've never heard that before," Simon said, trying to make sense of it. "What proof does she have? Of course, at the turn of the century, records weren't kept like they are today."

Alice agreed. "Even at the school where I taught, many children didn't have birth certificates. It was worse during the war and the pandemic."

"Mrs. Grey was wrong to tell him," Rodney said. "It'd cause friction between Steven and his father, and I imagine, Wilma too."

"And Mrs. Hayes," Alice put in, although she personally couldn't stand Flora Hayes.

"I should go to see Steven," Rodney said. "How did he sound, Mother?"

"He was understandably upset," Alice told him. "I don't blame him. Now he knows he had a sister. I hope it doesn't cause a rife between Steven and his father."

"I imagine it would indeed," Simon said logically.

"Do you think this ties in with the murders?" Rodney asked his parents.

Alice and Simon looked at their son, wondering why he'd make such a superfluous remark.

"I don't see how it could, Rodney," his father said, patiently. He continued sipping coffee.

"Mrs. Grey can be obstinate," Alice said thoughtfully. "Maybe she shouldn't have told them. But she's involved with our church and highly regarded in the community."

"That foreign man who acted belligerently at the lecture Thursday evening," Rodney added. "That could have something to do with the murders, too!"

"Rodney, dear, please," his mother said, sweetly. "You hired Mr. Sheppard, didn't you? Why don't you let him find out the truth, since you're paying him to do it?" Her tone hinged on sarcasm which wasn't lost on Rodney.

But by then he was too disturbed to continue sitting at the breakfast table. He crushed his cigarette in the ashtray and stood, announcing he'd visit the Banks this morning.

"You should shave, dear," Alice said disapprovingly as though her son should look his best first thing in the morning. "And those brown slacks came back from the dry cleaners yesterday. I hung them up in your closet."

Rodney felt the stubble on his face feeling self-conscious as though on inspection by his mother, who despite the early hour always looked pristine and fresh. He was about to leave when Alice noticed he was barefoot.

"I was going to buy you a new pair of Oxford shoes, too, dear," she told him.

Simon noted there was a sale at Barney's and Alice added she planned to go there today.

"Thanks, Mother," Rodney said, gratefully. "Remember, I wear size twelve."

He then turned and headed for the stairs and his bedroom to get ready for the day.

The atmosphere in the living room of the Banks' brownstone house was tense. Russell was still in his robe, pajamas, and slippers, a cold cup of coffee next to him on the end table. He had said all he could say to his son and daughter-in-law, but he realized it wasn't enough to satisfy them. Wilma was seated on the sofa, coffee, and cigarettes on the coffee table, but she was still in shock to actually speak, drink coffee, or smoke. On the other hand, Steven continued his rampage, this time directed at his father. He also was in his pajamas and robe but clearly disheveled, having slept little, his hair tousled, his face a mixture of anger and remorse. He smoked one cigarette after another, speaking quite forcefully to his father. He paused only to stub out one cigarette before lighting another, all the while pacing back and forth in front of the fireplace, as though to emphasize his torrent of speech.

"Dad, why didn't you tell me about Theresa? That's why Mother divorced you, isn't it?" He paused. "We wanted to wake you last night when we got back from Mrs. Grey's, but I decided to wait until this morning. How could you keep this from me?"

Russell continued looking at his son, speechless, unable to articulate words.

"If it comes out in the open, we'll be the laughingstocks of the village," Steven said, finally collapsing next to his wife on the sofa. He smoked incessantly, obviously upset and confused. He looked up at his father. "Did Theresa know?"

Russell looked at his son as though he didn't know he was there. "No, Steven, she didn't know. Your mother filed for divorce after she learned Theresa was my child. I believe she was an acquaintance of Mrs. Grey at the time."

"That's how she found out," Steven said. "That old battle-ax ruined your marriage, Dad!"

"I called Mrs. Hayes earlier," Wilma said, sipping her coffee which also was cold. "I think I got her out of bed."

At that moment, the doorbell rang, and Wilma went to answer it. She returned shortly with Flora Hayes. She left her fur coat and cloche hat on a hallway chair, and upon entering the living room, greeted Russell and Steven cordially but by the electric air in the room, she could tell something was wrong. She glanced at Russell and then Steven and finally at Wilma, who invited her to sit near the fireplace and offered her coffee, which she refused.

"I came as soon as I could," Flora said, smiling and settling in an armchair, slightly out of breath. "I'm going shopping this morning and plan to visit a few friends later." She wondered what was happening. Looking at Steven as he sat on the sofa next to Wilma, his expression alone was enough to convince her that the dreaded day had come. Russell confirmed it.

"They know, Flora," he said, quietly.

She looked at them, not knowing what to say. Usually not at a loss for words, she turned to Wilma who appeared the only one who maintained a semblance of stability.

Wilma related to Flora the circumstances behind their finding out the truth of Theresa's parentage. She told her about their visit to Mrs. Grey last night, of how she remembered when Theresa was born in the hospital.

Flora was livid. "How did she even know about it?" She hesitated. "What business did that miserable woman have in telling you? I figured she knew something, she's always been so nosy. I could kill her with my bare hands!"

"Please, try to relax, Mrs. Hayes," Wilma said, soothingly.

"I'm so sorry, Steven," Flora continued. "I can tell this has been a tremendous shock, understandably." She fumbled for words. "It just happened, Steven, and I'm sorry again for your distress. Your father and I loved each other, but we were both married at the time."

"How did your husband learn the truth?" Wilma asked, curiously.

"Well, I'm not sure," Flora admitted. "It may have been Mrs. Grey."

Russell agreed. "My ex-wife was an acquaintance of Mrs. Grey."

Flora spoke with righteous anger. "Insufferable woman, always sticking her nose into other people's business."

Steven spoke weakly as though all strength was taken from him. "Dad, it would've been better if you had told me years ago."

"I would've had to tell Theresa, too," Flora said thoughtfully. "I never wanted her to know. She was bitter after the divorce and this news would've destroyed her."

"Forgive me, Steven," Russell said, compassionately, understanding his son's inner turmoil. "My life was different then. Your mother and I didn't have a good marriage and Flora was there when I needed her." He cast a wry smile at her.

"The same for me," Flora said fighting back tears. "My husband was incensed when he learned I was expecting a child by another man."

An awkward silence followed broken by the abrupt ringing of the doorbell. This time Steven went to the front door. Upon seeing Rodney, he welcomed him in, took his coat and cap, and brought him to the living room. Rodney greeted everyone, feeling a little embarrassed as Russell, Wilma and Flora looked at him, clearly distressed. Sensing their discomfort, he spoke rather nervously.

"Sorry if I'm interrupting anything. My mother told me the message you left, Steven. I was still in bed when you called." He sat next to him. "This must be a great shock."

"Thanks, Rod, for stopping by," Steven said, casting a faint smile at him. "The shock isn't over yet. I think it'll take some time."

"Why did Mrs. Grey tell you about it in the first place?" Rodney asked. "With these terrible murders happening, we don't need anything else to upset us."

"Maybe she's senile," Wilma offered. "Or just a busybody."

"I should go see her," Flora said, with a determined look on her face. "I'll get even with her for causing so much turmoil for us."

There reigned a deep silence, as though Rodney, Steven, Wilma, and Russell agreed with her as though they wanted to get even with her themselves, in their own way. Wilma offered to make fresh coffee and prepare breakfast.

"Let me help you, Wilma," Flora offered. "I think a good breakfast will be the best for all of us. Will you have breakfast, Rodney?"

"Yes, I'd be glad to stay," he told them, not wanting to mention he had already eaten. He expressed his apprehension to Steven, who looked at him and thanked him for his concern.

"I need to get ready for the day," Steven said, stubbing out another cigarette. "And maybe a hearty breakfast is the best thing, after all. It'll help alleviate this shocking news."

Flora noticed the morning paper unopened on the coffee table. Impulsively she reached for it, while Rodney joined Steven upstairs. Wilma went to the kitchen to make more coffee and start on the pancakes, while Russell remained immobile in his chair, looking at Flora. Neither spoke until Flora, scanning the local news, came upon the police section of the previous day.

"There's a notice here that Mrs. Grey reported an intruder last night," Flora said, in surprise. "Police were at her house. I don't remember hearing sirens earlier this morning."

"Neither did I," Russell said. "What else does it say?"

Rodney and Steven came downstairs and entered the living room. Steven was dressed in shirt, tie, and pleated slacks, but wearing only socks as he couldn't find his shoes.

"In the paper it says there was an intruder at Mrs. Grey's house," Flora told them. "There was a man on the sidewalk, but it doesn't say there was a break-in."

"Perhaps she was just imagining it," Russell said.

"It says there was a size twelve shoe imprint in the snow," Flora said, meditatively while reading the notice again. She folded the paper and put it back down on the coffee table angrily. "Frankly, I could care less about Mrs. Grey. She's nothing but a busybody."

At that moment, Wilma appeared in the doorway and urged them to come to the kitchen. Russell and Flora followed her, but Steven hesitated, telling them he'd join them momentarily. He sank onto the sofa, looking more presentable but still drained. He reached for his cigarettes in his shirt pocket, lit one, and offered one to Rodney. They sat smoking in silence for a few moments.

"Why don't we go out later," Rodney suggested. "The best thing for you right now."

Steven agreed an evening out was a good idea, then asked Rodney if he'd see if his shoes were in the hallway. Rodney went to the hall and returned with a pair of patent black leather shoes.

"Those are Dad's," Steven told him. "They're size ten. Mine are twelve."

Rodney disappeared to the hallway again and soon returned, handing a pair of brown dress shoes to Steven. He put them on and then they joined the others in the kitchen, where the aroma of fresh coffee and pancakes was awaiting them.

Several hours later, the Longworths and the Brennans arrived at the restaurant in the Hotel Van Curler. As usual for a Friday evening, most tables were full. A steady murmur of conversation and the clatter of dishware greeted them as the head waiter showed them to their reserved table. Upon handing them the menus, another waiter mentioned that Tom Mix and his wife were having dinner and in a separate dining room Buster Keaton and his family were hosting a private dinner party. It was quite a festive evening at the Hotel Van Curler.

They settled comfortably at their table, reviewing the sumptuous dining choices. After dinner, the Longworths and the Brennans planned to attend Proctor's Theater to see Noel Coward's hit play *Fallen Angel*. Agnes loved the theater and especially admired playwright Noel Coward's work. Jerome wasn't as literary as his wife but showed an interest more to please her than an actual interest in the theater.

"Did you read about Mrs. Grey in this morning's paper?" Alice asked her sister, as well as her brother-in-law. She knocked ash from her cigarette into an ashtray.

Agnes nodded. "Just terrible, poor Mrs. Grey. I thought there were patrols around the village overnight?"

"The police have stepped up patrols," Simon said. "But the men of the village can only do so much. Frankly, I wouldn't want to patrol late at night, especially in this cold weather."

The waiter approached and wrote down their dinner choices. Within a short time, their orders arrived, and they enjoyed a hearty meal. Afterward, they relaxed with coffee and dessert.

Jerome finished a dish of ice cream and a second cup of coffee. "Do the police have any leads who killed the people in Cucumber Alley? And attacked Rodney, too?"

"Unfortunately, no," Alice said. "That's why Rodney hired Mr. Sheppard from Albany to look into the matter. So far, he hasn't resolved anything." Her tone implied it was a waste of Rodney's time and money.

"Let's not talk about those horrible murders tonight," Agnes said, changing the subject. "We've had a wonderful evening so far, this beautiful hotel and the delicious food. And now we're off to the theater!"

"Proctor's opened in December, and it's been a big hit," Simon commented.

"The theater is beautiful inside," Agnes said, dreamily. "We should get going soon."

"Agnes, what do you think happened to Rodney?" this from Alice, putting down her coffee cup and looking at her sister, her brother-in-law and then her husband.

It was an odd question and an awkward moment. Agnes looked at her older sister with surprise, that she'd insist on mentioning such unpleasantness on their evening out. She finished her coffee and addressed her sister, rather curtly.

"I really do prefer not to discuss the recent events, Alice, if you don't mind. Poor Rodney was extremely fortunate to survive his attack. I'm sure the police will find the underlying cause of it. Or that Mr. Sheppard."

Alice mentioned Steven's call from this morning and the revelation of Theresa's real father. Both the Brennans were taken by surprise, if not totally taken aback by the news.

"Well, that opens a new can of worms," Jerome said dryly, with raised eyebrows.

"Indeed, it does," Agnes said thoughtfully. "I hope Steven is taking it well."

"Rodney spent time with him earlier," Alice said. "They're going out tonight."

"Does Flora know that Steven and Wilma were told about it by Mrs. Grey?" Agnes asked her sister. "Personally, I don't see why Mrs. Grey would mention it at all."

"It wasn't any of her business," Jerome agreed with his wife.

"I assume Flora Hayes was told Steven and his wife know the truth," Alice said, rather uncaringly. "But I really don't know."

Another strange silence pervaded the table in the opulent dining room. A band soon started, and many people were on the dance floor, enjoying the fox trot and the Charleston. It was a lively evening and before leaving for the theater, the Longworths and the Brennans decided to enjoy a twirl around the dance floor.

They then gathered their coats and belongings from the cloakroom attendant in the magnificent lobby. Agnes wished she could ask Tom Mix for his autograph. She wanted to speak to Buster Keaton too, but the head waiter advised her that it was a private party and not open to uninvited guests.

Alice, Simon and Jerome put on their coats and hats and were at the front doors. As Agnes joined them, they descended the stairs to Washington Avenue on the way to Proctor's Theater, and once on the sidewalk, the red paisley scarf around her neck began to flap gently and noticeably in the chilly evening air.

At the Longworth's house, Rodney ate the casserole his mother prepared and afterward washed and cleaned up the kitchen. He turned off the kitchen light and proceeded to the living room, where he strode moodily around, irritable, and restless. He was home alone, waiting for later in the evening when he'd meet Steven and Wilma at the coffee house on State Street, where a local jazz band was performing. He joined his parents and aunt and uncle to the door as they left for the hotel restaurant and then to the theater. He had called Olive Mae, but she was going to Utica to visit relatives and wouldn't be back until Monday.

It was early evening, but the days were slowly growing longer and there was more daylight than in the previous weeks. Rodney put on his coat and cap and decided to walk to a small store on Union Street, before it closed. He handed the clerk thirty cents for two packs of Lucky Strikes and once outside, undid the cellophane wrapper and flicked his lighter to ignite a cigarette.

Drawing on the smoke and feeling satisfied, he headed north on Union Street and back to Washington Avenue, where he intended to proceed south toward Cucumber Alley and Front Street. He walked aimlessly, watching several trollies go by, the cigarette helping to calm his nerves. His mind was too cluttered to sort out the facts of the last few weeks.

Just who was that foreign sounding man at the lecture on Thursday evening and why did he become so belligerent? Aunt Agnes thought it was Russian. Maybe he was a spy or even an anarchist, like Mrs. Grey suggested. After all, General Electric, where the man worked, was a major scientific environment. Maybe he was trying to infiltrate our research projects? He'd call Mr. Sheppard again and relate his thoughts to him.

Upon reaching the lower part of Washington Avenue, right at the entrance to Cucumber Alley, he noticed a small crowd gathered around two children, who were crying and upset. He approached and saw Mrs. Grey and her friend Mrs. Norris standing amidst other neighborhood women, trying to console the little boy and girl, both of whom were wailing endlessly.

"There, there, child," a woman said softly, trying her best to comfort the little girl.

The little girl merely shrugged her off while the little boy wailed even louder. A few of the women tried to take control but to no avail. Mrs. Norris thought she recognized the children as belonging to a refugee family who lived in an apartment on Green Street. Then why were they near Cucumber Alley? They must have wandered off by themselves. She'd return them to their parents, of course. Maybe they had gotten lost and didn't know their way back? The poor parents must be sick with worry. One of the women commented the little girl had a fever.

Mrs. Grey looked at the crying girl. She felt her forehead and looked closely at her eyes but straightened up and reported that the girl did not appear feverish. She'd have other symptoms, she commented. She needed a good night's sleep, poor child.

Mrs. Norris offered to walk the children home, commenting that the little girl felt feverish just by holding her hand. The crowd dispersed, with the women returning to their houses and Mrs. Norris leading the children down Green Street. Mrs. Grey looked up and spotted Rodney. She smiled and went over to him.

"Hello, Rodney, dear," she bundled her red paisley scarf closer around her neck. "I don't think winter will ever end, do you? Care to join me for coffee? I baked an apple pie this afternoon."

Rodney momentarily was struck by the red paisley scarf and kept pushing distorted thoughts from his chaotic mind. He realized Mrs. Grey was speaking to him again, so he apologized and smiled wanly.

"A lot on your mind, dear? Me too. Someone was standing right outside my house on the sidewalk during the night. The police came to see me earlier today. Nice gentlemen. It was in this morning's paper. The evening edition, too. Did you see it?"

Rodney commented that he had seen it in the paper, which wasn't entirely the truth. Mrs. Hayes told him while he was at the Banks' earlier, but he wouldn't mention that to Mrs. Grey. He also wouldn't mention the torment she caused by revealing the true parentage of Theresa Hayes to Steven and Wilma.

"I'm afraid it isn't safe anymore around the village, Rodney. You should be careful, too. You were attacked and left for dead in the alley."

Rodney continued puffing on his cigarette and shivered slightly in the chilly air. He thought that was rather a shallow remark. He didn't need to be reminded of his recent brush with death. But then, he knew Mrs. Grey was given to bouts of candidness and forthrightness.

"Thanks, Mrs. Grey. I'm just out for a walk." He paused. "Good night."

Mrs. Grey smiled. "Good night, Rodney dear. Feel free to stop over any time."

Rodney watched as she unlocked her front door and went inside, turning on the lights, and illuminating the windows. Realizing it was getting darker and that he'd be meeting Steven and Wilma soon, he turned and walked back up Washington, toward his house.

The red paisley scarf, almost like a ghostly apparition, remained locked in his subconscious. It was in his mind still when he went out with Steven and Wilma, listening to the jazz band at the coffee house, when he arrived home, greeted his parents in the living room, who had recently gotten home themselves from the theater and when he went upstairs to bed.

Lying in bed, finding it difficult to sleep again, he knew a pattern was forming in his mind, and it rested on that infuriating red paisley scarf.

CHAPTER FOURTEEN

O n Monday morning, the fourteenth, Sloane Sheppard was at the
kitchen table in his apartment, finishing breakfast. Still in his
robe and pajamas, it was rather early for Sloane. Glancing at the clock
on the wall, rather sleepily, he saw it was only seven-fifteen which was
not his accustomed rising time. He was unshaven and barefoot, his
black hair tousled from sleep. He had arisen early, to get a head start
on his investigation of the murder of Theresa Hayes. He had canceled
appointments today and tomorrow, moving them to later in the week,
giving him plenty of time to investigate in Schenectady. Going to the
stove, he filled his cup with more coffee and then entered the living
room to use the phone.

Yawning slightly, he sat in an armchair and picked up the candlestick phone on the end table. He didn't know if Inspector James
would be in at this early hour, but he tried it. He asked the operator
to connect him with the Schenectady Police Department. Once the
operator determined it wasn't an emergency, she mentioned circuits
were busy, and as usual for a Monday morning, he had to wait for a
free line. The operator called him back within a few moments and soon
Sloane was speaking to Inspector James.

"Good morning, Inspector. This is Sloane Sheppard in Albany. I'll be coming to Schenectady today. Any leads on the Theresa Hayes murder investigation?"

Inspector James coughed. "Well, Mr. Sheppard, we have no new leads. We were made aware of a disturbance at a lecture at the General Electric facility recently, although I don't see that it relates to the murder of Miss Hayes."

"Yes, Rodney Longworth told me about it."

"A foreign man went berserk for apparently no reason. His name is Mr. Boris Ivanov and his sister's name is Mrs. Ludmilla Kalamanov. We've spoken to him through his sister, she speaks better English, but we didn't learn anything. He says he didn't know what he was doing and that it was nothing important. If you speak to him, I don't know what more you can get out of him."

"You believed him?" Sloane asked.

"Honestly, no, he may be hiding something or protecting someone. We don't have sufficient cause to arrest him, Mr. Sheppard."

"Or possibly he recognized someone from the crowd and in his limited English, tried to make the people there aware of it."

Sloane then mentioned he had an appointment to speak to the president of Union College this afternoon. He also mentioned he wanted to speak to others who knew Miss Hayes.

"Dr. McIntyre is well-respected at Union College," the inspector told him. "He may be able to shed some light on Miss Hayes's character." He paused. "Mr. Sheppard, you should know that Mrs. Edna Grey reported an intruder outside her house early Saturday morning. We sent patrolmen there, but all they found was an imprint of a size twelve shoe in the snow. They took her statement, of course, and we're increasing patrols in that area."

"I'd like to speak to Mrs. Grey, this morning before visiting Dr. McIntyre."

"We've spoken to her as well," Inspector James said. "We didn't learn anything new."

Sloane mentioned he wanted to speak to Mr. Boris Ivanov at General Electric and would call there to arrange an appointment. He added if time permitted, he'd stop by police headquarters, then thanked the inspector and ended the call. He then looked in his notebook that he always kept near his phone and asked the operator to call Mrs. Edna Grey in Schenectady. After giving her the number, he waited a few moments, until he heard the ringing on the other end. It lasted for at least six rings and Sloane was about to replace the handset when Mrs. Grey answered, rather breathlessly.

"Mrs. Grey, this is Sloane Sheppard. I'm investigating the murder of Miss Theresa Hayes. I'd like to speak to you today if that's convenient." His tone implied that it needed to be, as that was his appointed time in Schenectady. He waited for her answer.

Mrs. Grey sighed. "Oh, hello, Mr. Sheppard. I do remember you from the hotel when Rodney introduced us." Her tone became grave. "Mr. Sheppard, there was someone outside my house. I was too afraid to approach the front door, but there was a man standing on the sidewalk!"

"Yes, the police told me. That would've been early Saturday morning, Mrs. Grey?"

"That's correct, Mr. Sheppard. I called the police but didn't find anything, except an imprint of a size twelve shoe in the snow. I told them I don't wear that size and hadn't been out during the evening."

Sloane looked down at his bare feet, knowing his own shoe size was twelve. Certainly, a common size for a man. That helped narrow down the stranger outside her house. Although he thought, it could equally have been a woman. He wondered who wore a size twelve shoe that was acquainted with Mrs. Grey unless it was a total stranger, which he thought rather unlikely.

"Will you be home this morning, Mrs. Grey?"

Mrs. Grey paused. "Yes, but why do you wish to speak with me again, Mr. Sheppard? We spoke at the hotel restaurant last week, with my friend Mrs. Norris. I hardly knew Miss Hayes and saw her only occasionally in the library."

"I've spoken to Mrs. Hayes, the Longworths and the Brennans." He paused. "What time is best for you?" he added persuasively.

"Well, I need to stop by the church to prepare for the rummage sale, but I should be back by eleven. I have an afternoon class and must prepare for it, of course."

Sloane thanked her and ended the call. In his notebook, he had scratched off the Longworths, the Brennans, Mrs. Hayes, Mr. Banks and now Mrs. Grey. He wanted to speak to Mr. Steven Banks and his wife, Mrs. Wilma Banks. He made a note to see them while in Schenectady today. He entered the bathroom, showered, and afterwards filled the sink with water to shave. As usual for Sloane, his wardrobe was of the utmost importance. His suit, vest, dress shirt, pleated slacks and tie were impeccable as always.

He soon left his apartment on Madison Avenue and instead of catching the trolley downtown to his office, he crossed Madison and hopped on the northbound trolley until it came to the corner of Western and Colvin Avenues. He got off and walked to Central Avenue. Crossing at the light of the busy intersection, he waited for another trolley to take him to Schenectady. In no time, a northbound trolley appeared and as it was still the morning rush hour, it was full of people heading for work. Sitting rather uncomfortably between a heavy-set middle-aged woman and a businessman reading the morning paper, he anxiously waited for the trolley to arrive in downtown Schenectady. It made many stops along the way, but sooner than he realized, it came to the corner of State Street and Washington Avenue.

A brisk wind and partial sunshine greeted Sloane as he stepped off the trolley. He proceeded to walk on Washington Avenue, past the brownstones belonging to Mr. and Mrs. Longworth and Mrs. Hayes. He walked until he almost reached Cucumber Alley before arriving at the handsome and well-kept brownstone house of Mrs. Edna Grey. A distinguished and striking historic home, dating at least from the 1700s, Sloane was equally impressed with the ornate lighting near the front door, reminiscent of an old gas lamp. Obviously, the house was well attended to. Upon climbing the steps to ring the doorbell, he was surprised Mrs. Grey allowed snow to pile up, even underneath the windows. He glanced to his right and assumed that was where the shoe imprint must have been spotted. Soon enough the front door was opened, and Mrs. Grey appeared, smiling and delighted to see him as though he was her close friend.

"Coffee, Mr. Sheppard? I baked an apple pie. Come along to the kitchen, so we can talk."

Sloane felt like a schoolboy being led by a strict teacher. She took his hat and coat, leaving them on a hallway chair. Following her to the kitchen, he settled at the large, circular table and as he expected, it was a neat and orderly room, rather large as city kitchens go, with the most modern furnishings including a shiny gas stove and a new toaster. Mrs. Grey had gone to the counter and then turned bearing a tray, containing cups, cream, sugar, and two plates of apple pie. She returned to the stove, grabbed the coffee pot and filled the cups, handing one to Sloane before sitting down across from him. She placed the pot near her on the table and then began to eat the apple pie as though she was ravenous and hadn't eaten in days, stopping to sip her coffee, without waiting for Sloane to speak. He watched her for a moment before proceeding.

"Thank you, Mrs. Grey, for having me here this morning. I wanted to speak to you further about Miss Hayes, Mrs. Bradshaw and Mr. Tucker."

Mrs. Grey looked up from her slice of apple pie. "I don't know what more I can tell you, Mr. Sheppard. I hardly knew Mrs. Bradshaw and I was not acquainted with Mr. Tucker." She put her head back down to continue eating, as though that was the end of the discussion.

Sloane decided to steer the topic in a different direction. "Did you enjoy nursing, Mrs. Grey? How long were you in the profession?"

"Yes, very much. Almost thirty years," she told him, wiping her mouth on a napkin.

"Which hospital?"

"Ellis Hospital, here in Schenectady."

"When did you start working there?'

Mrs. Grey frowned. "Let me think. Around 1870." She found the question rather odd.

"What departments did you work in?"

"It varied. I worked in pediatrics and also maternity. That's how I remember when Miss Hayes was born." She regretted it and then added more before Sloane could ask to elaborate. "Miss Hayes was the child of Mr. Banks. That may be why his wife divorced him and I'm sure why Mrs. Hayes's husband divorced her. They discovered Mrs. Hayes's daughter belonged to Mr. Banks."

Sloane had hardly sipped his coffee and had taken only a few bites of the pie. "Are you sure of this information?"

Mrs. Grey nodded. "Quite sure. I told it to Steven Banks and his wife last Friday evening. And then afterward, I saw that strange man outside my door, underneath the living room window."

"You're saying it was Steven Banks?"

Mrs. Grey shrugged. "He was livid when I told him the truth about Theresa. He seemed to blame me for it. He and his wife threatened me. Told me I'd pay for it."

Sloane stopped sipping the coffee. "Was there anyone else who heard her say that?"

"No, I invited them for coffee and the only people here were the Banks and myself."

"Perhaps his father should have been the one to tell him."

Mrs. Grey shrugged. "I knew Mr. Banks's ex-wife. I may have mentioned it to her."

Sloane figured that was most likely the case. How else would the woman have learned the truth? He could understand if Steven Banks and his wife were upset, perhaps even devastated.

"After Theresa's death, I felt Steven should know. Russell Banks is one of those stockbrokers." She made it seem like stockbrokers were gangsters or worse. "The Banks know more than they are willing to tell, Mr. Sheppard. Steven Banks has a temper, and his wife is a flapper of the most lurid sort." She shook her head and continued drinking the coffee. "She and her husband frequent speakeasies. They like to drink and smoke, too."

"Would Steven commit murder knowing he had a half-sister? Or attacked Rodney?"

"If he did kill Theresa, he wouldn't have known she was his half-sister. But he could've killed her for other reasons, the same for Mrs. Bradshaw and Mr. Tucker. And attacked poor Rodney, too."

"Which college did you attend, Mrs. Grey?"

Her face seemed to brighten. "The State Normal School. I started my career at Albany Hospital and then came here to Schenectady at Ellis Hospital."

"What do you teach at Union College?"

"Mostly science and pre-nursing classes."

"Do you have any idea who would kill three people in Cucumber Alley, Mrs. Grey?"

She shook her head while finishing her coffee. "I'm sorry, Mr. Sheppard, I can't be of help to you." She hesitated, then her face turned grave and rather dark. "I think you should speak to the Banks. I don't trust them." She smiled tiredly. "I suppose I shouldn't speak in such derogatory tones about my neighbors. The police have been here to speak to me. They were most kind and understanding. They suggested I stay a few nights at the home of my friend, Mrs. Norris, not far away, but I just couldn't leave here." She looked around at the immaculately clean kitchen. "I do enjoy my house. My husband also loved it. He died several years ago. I keep busy with part-time teaching, my church and the community center."

Sloane finished the coffee and thanked Mrs. Grey for her time. He followed her to the hallway where he put on his hat and coat and realized he learned nothing of value from speaking to this rather intimidating woman. He didn't think anyone could pull the wool over her eyes. She certainly was no fool. But there was something else about this shrewd elderly matron standing before him, showing him to the door, thanking him for stopping by and waving goodbye as he stepped out onto the sidewalk, but what was it?

Another strange character, obviously concealing something but just what he didn't know. Just like Alice and Simon Longworth and Agnes and Jerome Brennan. And Theresa Hayes was the daughter of Mr. Russell Banks. Well, that's an exposed secret, Sloane thought, dodging two unruly children and their mother in the crosswalk at the light. He arrived at the other side of State Street and walked down the sidewalk, pensively. He didn't see how that information was connected to the murders or the attack on Rodney. Did Mrs. Grey imply that Steven Banks was a ruthless killer? Or possibly his father or his wife? And the Brennans and the Longworths, were they too good-natured in public that there were a few skeletons rattling that they kept hidden?

He decided to eat lunch at a diner he spotted as the trolley came into State Street. He entered a small, homey restaurant with a long counter and a medium-sized dining room. He removed his hat and coat, sat at the counter and ordered a turkey sandwich and coffee. Settling in his seat, he had no sooner taken out his pack of cigarettes, when Rodney entered. He was surprised to see Sloane and stammered when he spoke.

"Mr. Sheppard, what a surprise seeing you here!"

Sloane nodded. "Hello, Rodney." He knew he had to ask him to join him, it'd be odd if he didn't. He was surprised Rodney would come to a diner when the hotel had that fabulous restaurant. As though reading his mind, Rodney grinned and seemed to relax.

"I like to get out of the hotel sometimes," he told Sloane. He took off his cap and jacket and asked Sloane if he could join him, saving him the trouble of having to ask him himself. He sat at an empty swivel seat next to him and picked up the menu he had just looked at.

"I thought of stopping by the hotel to see you this afternoon, Rodney," Sloane told him truthfully. "I have an appointment to speak to Dr. McIntyre at the college first."

Rodney nodded, thanking Sloane for his work in the investigation. A waitress approached from behind the counter. He ordered a ham sandwich, French fries and coffee. After she departed, he lit a cigarette and looked at Sloane. He too puffed at his cigarette, knocking ash into an ashtray. Neither spoke until Rodney asked him what he thought of the stockade village. Sloane thought that an odd question, as though it masked another more important comment.

"It's quite historic. Homes in the village date back to the 1600s. Do you like living there?"

Rodney nodded. "It's convenient to the hotel. I walk unless it's snowing or raining. Then I take the trolley. It goes straight up Washington Avenue."

Just then their orders arrived, and Rodney dug into his sandwich and French fries. Sloane ate his turkey sandwich and drank his coffee, finishing before Rodney. He asked the waitress for more coffee while Rodney was still eating.

"Anything more you've learned, Mr. Sheppard?" he asked with a mouthful of French fries.

"I spoke to Mrs. Grey this morning," Sloane told him. "She couldn't tell me anything helpful. As I mentioned, I have an appointment to speak to the college president this afternoon."

"I've never met him, but I hear he's a decent man," Rodney said, washing down the French fries with coffee. "I remember Theresa told me she worked at the president's office for a while."

"What did she tell you, Rodney?"

Rodney thought back a few months, wiping his mouth with a napkin. "Well, I remember she mentioned she found out information on people. She wasn't specific even when I asked her." He paused. "Theresa was kind of nosy, anyway. She liked to butt into other people's business."

"Perhaps she found out something she shouldn't have?"

Rodney shrugged. "She didn't say anything more about it."

"She may have said something to Mrs. Bradshaw," Sloane said.

"You think that's why she was killed?" Rodney asked, his eyes wide open.

"Can you think of anyone else who had a grudge against Miss Hayes?"

"A lot of people had a grudge against her. Even her mother didn't find her too appealing."

"Mrs. Grey told me Mr. Banks is Theresa's real father."

Rodney smoked angrily. "That interfering battleax told you that? She had a nerve! It's bad enough our finding it out, now she's spreading it all over!"

"It's bound to come out, Rodney," Sloane said calmly. "And I don't intend to mention it to just anyone. Your parents know, I assume?"

He nodded. "They mentioned it to Uncle Jerome and Aunt Agnes." He made it sound as though it was a top military secret, something extremely clandestine, that only certain people should be privy to. He then changed the subject altogether.

"Mr. Sheppard, what do you know about paisley scarves?"

Sloane looked at him strangely. "Paisley scarves? I don't know anything about them. I see women in downtown Albany wearing them."

Rodney nodded. "Wilma Banks, Aunt Agnes and Mrs. Grey have a red paisley scarf."

Sloane expected him to add more as he didn't see the significance of his comment. He asked him what he meant about the scarves.

"Aunt Agnes had red stains on her scarf, but she washed them out. Wilma Banks always wears hers and so does Mrs. Grey. My mother, Aunt Agnes and Mrs. Grey meet for lunch often at the hotel. Aunt Agnes and Mrs. Grey have the same red paisley scarf. That's when we noticed the stains."

"Was this before or after Miss Hayes and Mrs. Bradshaw were murdered?"

Rodney thought. "It was after, I think."

"Mrs. Grey mentioned an intruder outside her house early Saturday morning. Police found an imprint of a size twelve shoe in the snow."

"I wear size twelve," Rodney said, impulsively. He finished his coffee. "I think Steven wears twelve, too."

Sloane asked the waitress for the check, and he picked up the tab for Rodney as well. He smiled and thanked Sloane for his generosity as they walked out of the diner. He noticed it was not yet one o'clock.

"I still have time before my lunch hour is over," Rodney said, shivering in the gusty wind. "Do you want to meet Wilma Banks? She works at the United Cigar Store. It's right over there, on Jay Street."

Sloane glanced at his watch and saw it was early, so he decided to follow Rodney across State Street, to the pedestrian thoroughfare that was Jay Street. Certainly, a busy and commercial area, with plenty of stores on both sides, cafes and restaurants. Rodney walked over to the United Cigar Store, opened the door for Sloane and together they entered and found Wilma talking to her husband in front of the counter, near the cash register. His back was to them, but Wilma's face registered surprise upon seeing Rodney.

"Hi, Wilma," Rodney said, jovially as was his custom. "This is Mr. Sloane Sheppard. He's investigating Theresa's murder."

At that point, Steven turned and saw Rodney and Sloane. He smiled briefly at Rodney and gave Sloane a quick once over, wondering what he was doing here. He explained he was visiting his wife during his lunch hour. Sloane found it odd that he felt he needed to justify his presence. Several customers walked past them, and Wilma eagerly went to assist, ringing up a few sales and gift wrapping an ashtray. Sloane noticed how she placed it in a box and handed it to the customer, and then joined her husband to hear what he and Rodney were discussing with Steven.

"I understand you've spoken to my father," Steven said to Sloane, rather suspiciously. "And to Mrs. Hayes, too." He paused. "I don't know what my wife and I can tell you. Neither of us had a favorable impression of Theresa. She tried to break up our marriage."

Sloane found that information interesting. "Did you go out with her, Mr. Banks?"

Steven relented, as though he didn't want to admit it. "Only briefly. We've been married three years, but Theresa had ways to ruin people's lives."

Wilma agreed. "She'd think nothing of wreaking havoc for someone. She was jealous of me and my marriage. We've told this to the police when they questioned us."

"I understand Mrs. Grey imparted some devastating news to you last Friday," Sloane said, choosing his words carefully.

"You spoke with her?" Steven asked, obviously perturbed.

"Last week at the hotel when she was having lunch with Rodney's mother and aunt. And earlier this morning, too. She told me about your father being the real father of Theresa Hayes."

"You think it's related to the recent murders?" Wilma asked him.

"I'm continuing my investigation," Sloane said, looking at Rodney. "I can't say much more until I'm satisfied when I've arrived at the truth. The police are also looking into these murders, of course. I've been in contact with them."

"And do you think the end is in sight, Mr. Sheppard?" Steven asked, almost maliciously.

"Yes, Mr. Banks, I do," Sloane told him, causing Steven to look at him with surprise. "I do believe the end is in sight. The more I find out, the more confident I am that I will arrive at a satisfactory conclusion."

"Did Rodney mention the man who went berserk at the lecture last Thursday?" Wilma asked. "It was just terrible. He pointed at something in the audience and keep shouting."

Rodney agreed. "We don't know what it was about."

"I work at General Electric," Steven said with an air of superiority. "I never saw the man before." He explained his work in the laboratories with Mr. Brennan, Rodney's uncle. His work involved scientific research; therefore, he would not have had contact with a laborer.

"Is there anything more you require, Mr. Sheppard?" Wilma asked as the store was getting busy with several customers asking for assistance.

"No, thank you, Mrs. Banks," Sloane said. He left his business card and mentioned if she thought of something that could help, to let him know and Wilma told him she would do just that.

Sloane, Rodney and Steven walked out of the store into a rather heavy snow shower and a gusty wind. Rodney thanked Sloane for coming to Schenectady today.

"I was glad to bump into you," he said, shivering while puffing away at a fresh cigarette. "Good luck with Dr. McIntyre. And you'll let me know what else you found out?"

"You're seeing the college president, Mr. Sheppard?" Steven asked in surprise.

Sloane nodded. "He might be able to tell me more about Theresa's work at the college."

They arrived at the trolley stop. Rodney shook hands with Sloane and Steven, crossing at the light to get to the Hotel Van Curler. Steven also crossed to the other side, hopping on the next trolley headed to General Electric.

With snow showers stinging his face, Sloane walked down Washington Avenue to Union Street, to catch a southbound trolley. His mind returned to the conversation he had with Rodney in the diner. He said something rather curious. He wore size twelve shoe and so did Steven Banks. The snow imprint of the intruder's shoe outside Mrs. Grey's house was size twelve. A common men's size, but still… And Steven and Wilma Banks, another odd pair, he thought grimly.

At that moment, a trolley approached, and Sloane eagerly jumped on, paid the nickel in the slot near the conductor, and settled in a seat for the ride down Union Street to Union College.

Arriving at the Union College campus, Sloane walked through the main entranceway and proceeded to the administration building, not far from the Nott Memorial Library. Upon entering, he approached the receptionist who verified his appointment and directed him to the fifth floor, the location of the president's office.

The lobby, flanked on both sides by an ornate staircase, gave Sloane the opportunity to observe as much as possible. He noted several academic departments on each floor, students brushing past him, going up and down the staircase. Finally, arriving at the fifth floor, he found the office of the president, Dr. Walter McIntyre, in a rather isolated corner on the left, overlooking the back lawn of the campus. He entered and spoke to the secretary, a pleasant middle-aged woman with brown hair and expressive blue eyes, who greeted him with a professional smile. She welcomed him to a chair and then disappeared into an inner office, to verify that Dr. McIntyre could meet with him. She soon appeared at the doorway, telling Sloane to enter.

Sloane was immediately impressed by the man seated behind the desk. He got up and shook hands with Sloane, motioning to a chair in front of him. Certainly, a distinguished professor of long merit, Sloane looked at his degrees on the wall, including those earned at Harvard and Yale. He was a middle-aged man, with brown hair turning to gray and a rather serious disposition. He moved the candlestick phone and a pad from one end of the desk to the other, and as though not wasting time, came right to the point and asked Sloane what he could do for him.

Sloane reiterated the purpose of his visit. "I'm investigating the murder of Miss Theresa Hayes, a former employee here. Can you tell me anything about Miss Hayes?"

Dr. McIntyre cleared his throat. "She didn't have a good relationship with many on staff. It was recommended she be terminated, but her work was adequate here and in the library."

"What did her work here involve here?" Sloane asked.

"In January, we were cleaning up old files and papers in this office, many dating back to the 1870s and 1880s. She stored them in other file cabinets, in a back room, to clear up space for newer files and related papers."

"Is that all she did with the files?"

"No, she made reports on current and past employees, so we could have a quick reference on file. Occasionally, we receive letters asking for references on former employees."

"So, she actually spent time going through the files as well as moving them from this office to another room for storage?"

"Yes, that is correct."

"Are you familiar with Mrs. Jerome Brennan?"

"Of course, Mr. Sheppard. A highly regarded professor here. Latin is her specialty."

Sloane nodded. "And Mrs. Edna Grey?"

"Yes, she's a part-time lecturer. Her background is in nursing and the sciences."

"How long has Mrs. Brennan worked here?"

"Many years. She was here before I arrived."

"And Mrs. Grey?"

"She also was here before I arrived. I wasn't involved in their appointments. I believe the committee members who hired them years ago are now retired, some are deceased."

"I spoke with Dr. Bennett already," Sloane mentioned. "He told me he recommended Miss Hayes's dismissal to Mrs. Fillmore, but as you mentioned, her work was satisfactory. He also didn't speak highly of her."

"I'm afraid Miss Hayes did not have a good reputation here at the college."

Sloane mentioned Rodney Longworth and Dr. McIntyre smiled in recognition.

"I didn't know Rodney personally, but Mrs. Brennan speaks well of him. After all, he is her nephew. He graduated in 1921."

"This is a beautiful campus, Dr. McIntyre," Sloane commented, looking out the large window over his shoulder at the back lawn which showed the magnificent homes of the General Electric Realty Plot in the distance. "I'm impressed with the Nott Memorial Library."

Dr. McIntyre smiled. "Thank you, Mr. Sheppard. The library is the centerpiece of the campus. Union College is growing rapidly." He then elaborated on the college's increased enrollments, and the need for Friday evening classes, thanks in part to Mrs. Brennan. He commented this was his fourth year as president, having come from a college in western New York State. He then concluded his narrative by giving Sloane the chance to speak.

"May I review the files Miss Hayes worked with, Dr. McIntyre?"

He showed surprise. "Those files contain personal information, Mr. Sheppard. They are not open to the public."

"This is a murder investigation," he reminded him. "I'd appreciate the opportunity." Dr. McIntyre hesitated, then reluctantly stood and asked Sloane to follow him. In the outer office, he told his secretary he'd return shortly and then led Sloane down a long and dimly lit hallway. Arriving at the last door on the right, he took out a key ring from his pocket and finding the one to open the door, inserted it and turned on the ceiling light. Sloane followed him inside to a small windowless room obviously used for storage, several file cabinets were against the far wall and two long tables were in the middle, both holding several boxes of files. Dr. McIntyre smiled wryly.

"These boxes contain files pertaining to recent staff hires," he said, glancing at the boxes on the tables. "Over here are the file cabinets where Miss Hayes worked." He led Sloane to the back of the room. "Is there anything in particular you wish to look at, Mr. Sheppard?"

"No, not really," Sloane said, hoping he'd leave so he could rummage around himself. "May I open this file cabinet here?"

"Yes, by all means," Dr. McIntyre told him, then sat down at one of the tables, while watching to see what Sloane would look at.

At a cursory inspection, Sloane saw files for the years 1850 to 1880 but didn't recognize any names. There was a mustiness to the files and Sloane wanted to hold his nose from the unpleasant smell. He felt uncomfortable as he knew Dr. McIntyre's eyes were on him, watching his every move. By a stroke of good luck, he heard high heel shoes coming down the hallway hurriedly, as though something urgent had occurred. His secretary stood at the doorway, requesting his assistance.

"Excuse me, Dr. McIntyre, but Mr. Jennings, the chemistry teacher, is here to see you and he says it's particularly important. He's adamant about seeing you this minute."

Reluctantly, Dr. McIntyre got up with a tired sigh, as though he knew the whims of professors. "When you're finished, Mr. Sheppard, just turn off the light and close the door. I'll lock it up later. And please stop back before you leave."

Sloane thanked him and watched as he and his secretary left the storage room, chatting on their way to his office. Feeling more confident now that he was alone, he turned his attention to the other file cabinets Theresa Hayes worked with, next to the one he was looking through. Randomly opening the top drawer, he saw it was stuffed with files, dating from the late 1800s to the early 1920s. Thumbing through them, he didn't see any names he knew, but upon further inspection, he noticed a file on Mrs. Agnes Brennan, Professor of Latin. Taking it out, and opening it, he saw college transcripts, her curriculum vitae, teaching observations, a letter offering a full-time professorship dated June 1897, newspaper clippings on numerous academic awards, induction into the National Latin and Greek Society, letters from professors recommending tenure, receipts from a cruise line class trip to Rome in 1920. Other miscellaneous papers about her earnings, tax papers, sick leave, committee meetings, and guest lecturers. Looking further, he saw memorandums on the Friday evening classes. He took a small notebook and a pen out of his jacket pocket to write down information. He looked at the memorandums carefully.

The first was from Agnes herself, declaring a sustained interest in Latin studies and the need for Friday late afternoon and evening classes to accommodate students. Another was a petition from various professors, dated 1926, just last year, protesting the Friday evening classes and a request to Dr. McIntyre to stop it at once. Sloane then noted a letter from a Dr. Harold Peters to the then-president recommending that Mrs. Jerome Brennan be terminated for unethical practices. Sloane found that interesting, jotting it down in his notebook. He read it again, but it didn't say what Mrs. Brennan may have done that was unethical. He noticed it was dated May 10, 1921. He found nothing else of interest in the file.

He returned it and realized the files were not in alphabetical order. He saw in the back a file on Mrs. Edna Grey. He had to yank it out as it was full of papers, too many for him to go through quickly.

Would her part-time teaching warrant such a full folder, Sloane thought, thumbing through the papers. Teaching observations, tax forms, sick leave memos, a letter from the then-president offering her a part-time position dated May 1915, and permission slips on class visits to Ellis Hospital. He saw a document, supposedly a transcript, dated 1870, but it wasn't from the State Normal School. Didn't she mention she graduated from college in Albany? He didn't recognize the school, and it didn't look like an authentic transcript. Looking further, he saw a memo from the personnel office to the then-president, stating they were unable to procure an official transcript from Mrs. Grey or the college she listed. Another document, dated 1914, from a Mrs. Carol Osborne, a health and science professor, to the then-president questioned Mrs. Grey's preparation in nursing, which, according to an attached memo, prompted a thorough but inconclusive investigation by the administration. A letter from a Dr. Leonard Seymour, another professor of health and science, to the president, stated that from his part-time work at the hospital, he believed Mrs. Edna Grey was responsible for a patient's death at Ellis Hospital in 1913, by her mishandling the diagnosis and not properly responding to the patient's acute symptoms, further explaining he was of the opinion Mrs. Grey was not qualified or capable of teaching pre-nursing or science classes. He wrote he would also make these claims known to hospital administration. Sloane noted it also was dated 1914.

Except for the Friday evening classes issue, most likely Dr. McIntyre was unaware of the other matters with Mrs. Brennan and was probably totally ignorant of the concerns over Mrs. Grey, as these personnel issues occurred before his arrival on campus. Since the issues noted were dated years ago, it was also likely they were no longer being investigated.

He was about to look further when he heard footsteps coming down the hallway. He stuffed the folder on Mrs. Grey back into the file cabinet and noticed a folder on Mr. Russell Banks. Quickly, he took it out and upon opening it, saw a memorandum that blatantly stated under no uncertain terms would Mr. Russell Banks be rehired at Union College. He didn't know Mr. Banks was once employed at the college. Was he a professor? He had just returned the folder when at that moment, Dr. McIntyre returned.

"Find anything to interest you, Mr. Sheppard?" he asked, joining him at the file cabinet. His tone was pleasant but firm, as though he'd prefer Sloane finish his snooping.

Sloane closed the file cabinet and thanked Dr. McIntyre for letting him look through the files. He commented he didn't find anything to help with his investigation, but it was worth the look. He tried to make light of it and fortunately, Dr. McIntyre seemed to accept it.

He mentioned that if he could be of further assistance, to contact him. He led Sloane down the hall to the main stairway, where they shook hands and Sloane thanked him for his time.

He walked down the staircase and out of the administration building, past the Nott Memorial Library, on his way to catch the trolley. Upon returning to his office, he'd call General Electric, to see if he could make an appointment to speak to Mr. Boris Ivanov as soon as possible.

"Boni officium, discipuli. studere in altera septimana experiri. Salvete, discipuli mei," Agnes said to her Latin class. A good group of students, and so dedicated to the wonderful study of Latin. She reminded them to prepare for next week's test and watched as they collected their belongings and walked out of the classroom. She turned to erase the blackboard when she saw her husband enter, taking her by surprise.

"Darling, how nice seeing you here! Is it five o'clock already?"

She knew it wasn't, as her class ended at four, but she gave Jerome the benefit of the doubt. While erasing the board, she waited to hear why he decided to come to the college, she assumed there was a reason. For research, she knew he used the library at General Electric and hardly ever visited the Nott Memorial Library. She finished erasing and looked curiously at her husband.

"I decided to take the afternoon off," Jerome said simply, approaching his wife and kissing her on the cheek. "I've been too engrossed in work for so long, I needed a break." He paused, sensing incomprehension in his wife's face. "We can eat out tonight or go to Proctor's to see another play. Or shopping at Barney's or Carl's."

"I think I'd rather cook at home tonight, dear." She paused. "It's been too much, Jerome. The three murders, Rodney's attack, and that Russian man at the lecture. Who was he, anyway?"

"Nobody knew him," Jerome said.

"Maybe he screamed at one of us," Agnes said, sensibly.

"One of us?" Jerome said, practically in shock. "Why do you say that?"

Agnes shrugged and fiddled with papers on the desk. "The murderer must be someone we know. Personally, I'm rather suspicious of the Banks. They were at the lecture that evening."

"You think Russell would kill his own daughter? And why would he kill Mrs. Bradshaw and that Mr. Tucker? Unless they were a threat in some way."

Agnes nodded. "Maybe they knew something about Russell that he didn't want to come out in the open. On the other hand, I wouldn't put anything past Steven or Wilma."

"What reason would Steven or Wilma have for killing Theresa?"

"She threatened them, didn't she? I know she tried to break up their marriage."

"That's not a legitimate reason for murder, dear."

Agnes shrugged. "Perhaps not."

"I wonder if Flora and Russell will get married."

Agnes showed surprise. She put the homework papers in a folder. "Why should you care what they do, dear? As much as I like Flora Hayes, she bore an illegitimate child, which is not to my liking. Now we know why her husband divorced her."

"And why Russell's wife divorced him."

Agnes agreed, then reached for her fur coat. "I'm finished for today, dear. I want to tidy things up here. I can grade these papers when we get home."

Jerome approached the large windows overlooking the front grounds of the campus. Always an admirable view, even in the winter. He looked at the Nott Memorial Library in the distance, with students and professors going in and out.

"What's *he* doing here?" Jerome suddenly exclaimed, still looking out the window.

Agnes had collected her textbook and the folder. "What, dear?"

Jerome stayed planted in front of the large window. Agnes joined him, looking down at the front lawn. She didn't see anything special, until her husband pointed to Sloane Sheppard walking across the campus, passing the Nott Memorial Library. They watched as he left the school grounds, heading toward State Street.

"What *is* he doing here?" Agnes said irritably, shrugging into her fur coat, wrapping her red paisley scarf around her neck and putting her pretty cloche hat delicately on her head. "He's snooping around. I don't like that."

Jerome looked at his wife. "I don't like it, either Agnes."

"The past should stay buried," Agnes said slowly. "Buried and forgotten."

Simon and Alice decided to have dinner at the Hotel Van Curler, as Alice had little food in the icebox and admitted she did not feel much like cooking. Simon suggested stopping in to see Jerome and Agnes, but Alice knew her sister finished teaching around four, and most likely wouldn't welcome company while she had just gotten home.

Walking in the crisp evening air, they arrived at the hotel, finding it busy even for a Monday evening, with new guests checking in and waiters rushing in and out of the kitchen, carrying trays full of sumptuous food.

They walked over to the registration desk, surprising Rodney, as he was not expecting to see his parents until he arrived home. He glanced at his watch and noticed it was a little after five o'clock. His shift ended at six, so he looked at his parents uncertainly, wondering why they were there. He handed the room keys to a middle-aged businessman who had just checked in and then turned his full attention to his parents.

Simon smiled at his son. "We decided to have dinner here tonight. Why don't you join us after your shift ends?"

"We'll have a nice relaxing meal, Rodney," Alice said. "I think we need it, after all we've been through the last month or so."

Rodney thought that was an excellent idea. "And no talk about the murders."

Simon and Alice agreed. They decided to wait in the lobby, in the luxurious chairs near the ornate fireplace, for Rodney to finish his shift. They had no sooner sat down when Russell and Flora entered, making their way through the lobby to the restaurant. They stopped when they saw Simon and Alice.

"Hello, Simon, hello Alice," Russell said, rather uneasily. He knew Steven had called Saturday morning to speak to Rodney about Theresa, but this was the first that he saw the Longworths since the revelation about Theresa was made known.

Flora smiled at Alice, even though she personally could not tolerate her, finding Alice Longworth arrogant to the extreme and condescending in nature. She mentioned she and Russell were having dinner at the hotel this evening, as Monday evenings were usually not as busy as other nights. She wore a simple evening dress, with her fur coat and cloche hat, very feminine and chic. She thought she caught a glimmer of envy in Alice's eyes, which surprised her, as she knew Alice Longworth could certainly afford better clothes than what she was wearing. Flora thought she looked well, a black dress highlighted by white pearls and too much make-up as was usually the case with Alice.

"We're staying for dinner, too," Simon said. "Rodney's joining us after his shift ends at six." He stopped speaking as the obvious question hung in the air between them.

Russell and Flora hesitated, unsure if they should ask them to join them. Flora thought Simon and Alice could have asked if they'd want to join *them*. As neither took place, Russell and Flora wished them a pleasant meal and entered the grand restaurant, where they were greeted by the head waiter. A piano player was playing soft tunes in the background creating a most luxurious dining experience.

Simon and Alice chatted among themselves while waiting for Rodney, who entered the lobby sooner than six o'clock, as the evening desk clerk had already arrived, giving him the chance to leave a bit earlier. Entering the restaurant, they were seated at a corner table and the waiter, an acquaintance of Rodney, was pleased to offer them the best service possible.

"My sister's birthday is coming up," Alice said after the waiter wrote down their orders and scurried off to the kitchen. "Perhaps this is the time for a celebration. Help take our minds off the recent events." She paused. "Maybe another play at Proctor's. We saw the new Noel Coward play on Saturday. Agnes especially enjoyed it."

"It'll play there for a while, dear," Simon said. "Why don't you look in the paper for other shows? Maybe there's something else we can see this week."

Alice motioned for the waiter. "Can you see if you have this evening's paper?"

The waiter, eager to please, went to the lobby in search of the evening paper. He soon returned with the *Schenectady Gazette* and handed it to Alice decorously. She thanked him graciously and started to look through the pages until she came to the theater section. She scanned the current plays and movie showings but didn't see a new production at Proctors. Obviously, the Noel Coward play was doing quite well.

"Oh, how sad," she exclaimed suddenly. "How terribly sad."

The waiter returned, to refill their coffee cups. Rodney sipped his coffee and looked at his mother curiously.

"This poor little girl died yesterday," Alice lamented. She read the brief article to her son and husband. "*Sally Bowen of the village, aged five, died of rheumatic fever yesterday, Sunday, March thirteenth, at Ellis Hospital.*" She paused. "There's a picture of her here. Poor child."

She folded back the paper and handed it to Rodney and he and Simon looked at it together. The article gave details of Sally Bowen of Schenectady and her sudden death from rheumatic fever. It mentioned next of kin and pending funeral arrangements. The picture was of a little girl, in pigtails and a plain dress, smiling at the camera.

"I don't know the Bowens," Alice said, finishing her coffee. "Of course, there are several new families in the village. No one with that name belongs to the church."

"Maybe they live in the apartments on Green Street," Simon said.

"Well, that's none of our concern, dear," Alice added, as though the residents of the apartments on Green Street were of a lower class than the inhabitants of the magnificent brownstone houses on affluent Washington Avenue.

Rodney almost gagged on the coffee. That little girl was the same one he saw Saturday evening on Washington Avenue! He stared at the picture as though memorizing it and read the notice again. He then handed the paper back to his mother, who caught the waiter's attention to return it to him. He lapsed into an unsettling silence, as his parents were chatting about preparations for Agnes's birthday party.

But Rodney's mind was far off, thinking, too cluttered and too disturbed to pay attention to what they were saying.

CHAPTER FIFTEEN

Russell sat at his desk in his office at the Schenectady Trust Company, where he was finishing notes on an investment transaction he secured for a man and his wife. A wonderful time to invest, he advised his clients as the stock market was seeing record increases. The wife was hesitant but Russell, ever the stockbroker, advised her the market was stable and a proliferation of stocks was forecast for the future. He smiled in satisfaction, knowing his business was growing exponentially.

It was Tuesday, a bright sunny morning, still cold but a hint of spring was in the air. He had enjoyed dinner with Flora at the hotel last evening and upon arriving home, spent time with his son and daughter-in-law, both still reeling from the revelation of Theresa's parentage. He had just put the top on his pen when he looked up and saw Sloane Sheppard in the doorway.

"Good morning, Mr. Banks. I'd like to speak to you."

Russell silently cursed his secretary for allowing him in but then realized she was on vacation for the week, and he never found a replacement. He put aside his ledger book and reluctantly welcomed Sloane in and invited him to sit at the chair in front of his desk.

Rather a rugged sort of person, Russell noted of the young man seated in front of him, handsome, too, with jet black hair, worn back from a prominent forehead, a formidable presence. He cleared his throat and asked Sloane how he could help him.

"I'm wrapping up my work on the murder of Miss Hayes," Sloane said, choosing his words carefully. He took off his trench coat and hat. "I understand Miss Hayes was your daughter."

Russell cringed and did not meet Sloane's eyes. "Yes, Mr. Sheppard, that's correct. It was a long time ago. Flora and I fell in love, but we were both married at the time. My wife divorced me, and Flora's husband divorced her. She let Theresa use her married name so that there wouldn't be any questions while she attended school or even as she got older." He paused. "What else can I say, Mr. Sheppard?"

"It must have been difficult for both of you," Sloane said.

Russell nodded. "That's behind us, Mr. Sheppard. Flora and I have gotten closer in recent months. We may marry someday but we haven't decided yet." He looked at Sloane closely. "You say you're wrapping up your investigation. Have you discovered the identity of the killer?"

Sloane avoided his question. "I understand you once worked at Union College. Next to General Electric, the college is a major employer. What did you do at the college?"

"How did you know I was employed there?" Russell asked, resenting an intrusion into his private life. "I don't remember mentioning it to you."

"I'm a private investigator, Mr. Banks. I investigate people who are under suspicion of a crime. That includes you."

"That also was a long time ago. I was hired by the finance department. I was accused of forging records and embezzling funds, none of which was true. I resigned as they continued their investigation. Later I learned they found their mistakes, but I had already left."

"You were not to be rehired under any circumstances," Sloane commented.

Russell shrugged. "I'm not surprised. I'm sure I made an enemy or two while there."

"Was your son on good terms with Theresa?"

Russell hesitated. "They didn't get along, but then Theresa didn't have a good relationship with a lot of people, including my daughter-in-law. She tried to break up their marriage. She was a very vindictive young woman."

"Do you know why Theresa would go to Cucumber Alley that night?"

Russell shook his head. "The police asked us the same question. Neither myself, my son, my daughter-in-law or Mrs. Hayes knew why Theresa went to Cucumber Alley that night."

"At the lecture last week, Rodney told me a man went berserk, causing quite a sense. Did you know the man? Had you seen him before?"

Russell shook his head. "No, never. He spoke another language, and no one understood what he was saying."

"Did your daughter know things about certain individuals that was private?"

Russell frowned. "No, not that I'm aware of. Theresa didn't know I was her father. Her mother and I decided not to tell her."

"But Mrs. Grey knew."

Russell sighed, rather impatiently. "I'm afraid Mrs. Grey is the village busybody."

At that moment a young man, a clerk, knocked on the door and asked to speak to Mr. Russell, as an important banking issue had come up. Several clients were requesting his assistance.

Sloane realized he wouldn't learn much more from Russell Banks. He stood, shook hands with him, and thanked him for seeing him.

Russell joined him at his office door, watching as he walked through the lobby and out the front doors.

Sloane glanced at his watch and saw it was only ten o'clock. He shivered as a gust of chilly air swept up the sidewalk. He pulled his Fedora hat lower on his head. He had a full day planned while in Schenectady, including meeting Mr. Ivanov. His next visit was to Mrs. Hayes.

At the corner of State and Clinton Streets, Sloane came to the insurance office where Flora worked. It was a small building, sandwiched between a coffee shop and a dry-cleaning store. Upon entering, the receptionist greeted him and asked how she could assist. Sloane told her he wanted to speak to Mrs. Hayes. The receptionist said Mrs. Hayes saw customers by appointment. Sloane mentioned he was not a customer and showed her his business card.

"Oh, a private investigator," the young woman said in surprise. "Let me see if Mrs. Hayes is available. One moment, please."

She disappeared into another room and returned momentarily, saying Sloane could go in. He thanked her and met Flora at the doorway, where she asked him bluntly why he was here and what she could possibly do for him.

"I've answered enough questions, Mr. Sheppard," she said firmly.

"You didn't have time to speak with me when I came to your house last week. I thought I'd come here instead. I'd like to speak to you."

Reluctantly, Flora stood back and allowed Sloane to enter her office, a small, rather cramped space with a desk, two chairs and a table containing folders, an adding machine and assorted loose papers. Once seated, Flora cleared her throat and told Sloane she was quite busy this morning.

"Thank you, Mrs. Hayes. I have a few questions to ask. What was your relationship with Mrs. Bradshaw? You must have known her as she lived in the village."

Flora nodded, mentioning again she had discussed this already with the police. "Only in passing. I didn't know her well."

"Did your daughter know her?"

"Again, only in passing. Theresa told me she spoke to her at the hotel when she'd visit Rodney after work, but other than that, I don't think they were friends."

"Did you get along with your daughter, Mrs. Hayes?"

Flora eyed Sloane carefully, not wanting to fall into any traps. "We had our differences, of course but she was my daughter. I cared for her well-being."

"She was Mr. Banks's daughter as well," Sloane commented.

"Yes, that's news for the whole world to know," Flora said indifferently. "That has no bearing on the murders."

"It doesn't, Mrs. Hayes?"

"What are you implying, Mr. Sheppard?"

"Do you think someone you know is capable of murder?"

"You're asking who I think killed Theresa?" Flora thought before replying. "Mrs. Longworth didn't like my daughter. I don't think Dr. Longworth cared for her, either." She paused. "Mrs. Brennan didn't get home till late that night. Her husband, too, since he often works late."

"I believe Mr. Brennan was with Dr. Longworth and Rodney that evening," Sloane said.

Flora pursed her lips. "Well, I wouldn't put anything past the Longworths."

"Do you get along with the Brennans and the Longworths?"

"Agnes and I get along. She's the opposite of her sister. Alice is more self-centered. I don't know Dr. Longworth well or Alice's husband, Jerome. Dr. Longworth and Mr. Brennan knew each other from General Electric."

Sloane had the impression she wanted to say more but decided against it. He then asked her about the lecture at General Electric last Thursday evening.

"Did you know the man who caused a scene at the lecture last week?"

Flora showed surprise. "No, I had never seen him before. I was taken aback, as we all were. Even Mrs. Grey and Mrs. Norris, her friend, were upset by his outbursts."

"Do you wear a red paisley scarf, Mrs. Hayes?"

Again, Flora showed surprise. She found the question superfluous. "No, I don't, but I know Mrs. Banks does. Mrs. Brennan and Mrs. Grey also wear paisley scarves. Personally, I don't care for that design."

"Were you aware of information your daughter may have had on someone in the village?"

"Information?" Flora asked. "I can't say, Mr. Sheppard. My daughter was certainly inquisitive but if she knew things about certain people I wasn't aware of it."

Sloane smiled. "Thank you, Mrs. Hayes. I won't take up any more of your time."

He rose to leave and shook hands with Flora as she came from around her desk, seeing him to the door. Before he entered the outer office, she asked him a question, rather hoarsely.

"Mr. Sheppard, is the same person responsible for the murders and the attack on Rodney?"

Sloane put on his trench coat and Fedora hat. He looked Flora squarely in the eyes.

"Yes, Mrs. Hayes, I believe the same person is responsible for the three murders and the attack on Rodney."

"Then you know who it is?"

Sloane looked at her carefully. "I have a very good idea."

CHAPTER SIXTEEN

ontinuing his investigation in Schenectady, Sloane arrived at the General Electric facility just after the lunch hour. He had already made an appointment to speak to Mr. Boris Ivanov. After clearing it with his immediate supervisor, who was skeptical of his employee being questioned as part of a murder investigation, it was then arranged that Sloane would meet Mr. Ivanov and his siter, Mrs. Ludmilla Kalamanov at one o'clock. Mr. Ivanov insisted his sister be present, as she spoke English fluently. Both were employed at the facility.

Stepping off the trolley, Sloane entered and was stopped by a security guard. He gave his name and told the man he had an appointment to speak to Mr. Boris Ivanov and Mrs. Ludmilla Kalamanov. The guard made a call and before long Sloane was allowed into the building, where he was directed to the basement and the facilities department.

He had no sooner approached the stairs when he saw Steven Banks and Jerome Brennan walking down the hallway, talking animatedly about a meeting they just attended, both carrying folders full of papers. They looked at Sloane in surprise.

"Mr. Sheppard, small world," Steven said, in an unfriendly tone. "What brings you to General Electric?" His tone implied he had no reason to be there and was not welcome.

Sloane looked at Steven Banks, a handsome but arrogant and rather crude young man, distinguished in his vest and tie, looking ever the research scientist. He gazed quickly at Jerome Brennan, who appeared aloof and gave a false appearance of simple frankness. He looked at Sloane questioningly, wondering why he was there.

"I'm interviewing people who knew Mrs. Bradshaw," Sloane lied. He didn't feel he needed to explain to Steven Banks, who he found flippant and rather irritating, his real reason for visiting General Electric.

"I didn't know she knew people here," Jerome said honestly. "But the village is small enough where we all seem to know each other."

"Any new leads on Theresa's death? Or should I say my half-sister," Steven said.

Sloane ignored the last comment. "Not yet, Mr. Banks, but I anticipate wrapping this case up before too long."

"We've never had murder in the village before, Mr. Sheppard," Jerome told him. "These deaths have had a terrible effect on us. My wife isn't used to anything so unpleasant."

Her unethical practices at the college would've been unpleasant, Sloane felt like saying. Mrs. Brennan must have done something years ago to prompt a professor to write a letter demanding her termination. Certainly, Mr. Brennan knew about it, or did he choose to ignore it?

"I plan to conclude my inquiry soon," Sloane told them.

"Perhaps Mrs. Bradshaw was worth a lot of money," Jerome suggested. "I don't think she had any inheritors. Even Theresa could've come into money somehow."

Steven agreed. "If someone's obsessed with money, murder wouldn't matter."

"I'll be in touch with everyone soon," Sloane said.

He started to walk down the stairs but was suddenly arrested by Steven. He looked at Sloane and his manner was disingenuous as well as cynical, adding mirth to his duplicitous tone.

"You don't need to suspect me, Mr. Sheppard," Steven told him, with a snicker. "I'd never kill anyone."

After reaching the lower floor of the building, Sloane looked around for the facilities department.

He passed the boiler room, the mailroom, the laundry facility, and the receiving area before finally reaching the facilities office. Upon knocking, he heard a deep male voice telling him to enter.

He saw a young man seated behind a desk full of papers and folders. Behind him was another door with a sign claiming FACILITIES in bold letters. Sloane introduced himself and explained the nature of his visit.

"My supervisor told me you'd be here," the young man said. He had a quick way of talking, rather nervously. His brown hair receded slightly, and Sloane didn't think he was older than thirty. "My name's Tim Nielsen. Please sit down. Mr. Ivanov knows of your visit. Did you wish to speak to his sister? I believe she's here, too. I'll call his area to let them know you've arrived."

Sloane thanked him and sat on a small sofa, with end tables on each side. Tim Nielsen dialed an extension and spoke to a foreman, letting him know Mr. Sheppard was here to see Mr. Ivanov. Within a few moments, a foreman, a large, gruffy middle-aged man appeared at the door behind the desk, unsmiling and rather abruptly told Sloane to follow him.

They walked down a well-lit hallway, with an unappealing, pungent smell of oil, gasoline, and cleansers permeating the walls. Arriving at the last room on the right, the foreman went in first, and then Sloane saw a young man, perhaps no older than twenty-one or two, seated in a metal chair, a woman was seated next to him.

"These are the people you wanna see," the foreman said and then turned and left.

It was a simple room, perhaps used for meetings, with a small table, and a few chairs. Sloane looked at the faces before him, before grabbing a metal chair, unfolding it, and sitting in front of them. The young man appeared timid, perhaps even scared as though he didn't know what to expect. He had thick black hair, almost matching Sloane's wavy black hair and brown eyes. He was dressed in a workman's uniform, blue slacks with a matching blue collared shirt, a name tag embroidered above the right pocket. The woman next to him, who Sloane assumed was the sister, was older, perhaps thirty, and rather pretty with curly brown hair, a soft face, and vivid green eyes. She cleared her throat and spoke first.

"Hello, Mr. Sheppard. My name is Mrs. Ludmilla Kalamanov. We were informed you wish to speak to my younger brother, Boris." She paused. "This is a private room where we won't be disturbed. My brother doesn't speak English too well. We came to this country from Russia a year ago. My brother arrived recently. He's concerned about his immigration status. He was afraid to speak to the police when they came here to see us. He's afraid of being deported. Does this have anything to do with immigration?"

Sloane shook his head. "No, this has nothing to do with immigration, so he doesn't have to be concerned in speaking to me."

She seemed relieved and expressed this to her brother, who nodded and smiled gratefully. Sloane nodded. "The red paisley scarf. Most likely she was waiting for Mr. Tucker to pay him hush money. She didn't want you to witness her meeting with him."

"The police have already spoken to us," Ludmilla said. "My brother apologized for his outburst. The police dismissed it." She wondered why Sloane wanted to speak to them.

He was surprised the police dismissed it so easily without realizing Boris may have information pertinent to the Cucumber Alley murders.

"What is your job here, Mrs. Kalamanov?" he asked her.

"I'm a supervisor in the laundry facility," she explained. "The foremen and electricians at General Electric wear uniforms. My unit is responsible for washing, ironing and sewing." She paused, looking at her younger brother, who seemed to dread this interrogation.

"What was your job the night of Dr. Alexanderson's lecture?" Sloane asked him.

Boris hesitated. "I set up a speaker and then I took it down, with the tables."

Sloane nodded. "Did you see something or someone that upset you?"

Boris turned to his sister for help. She interpreted in Russian and the effect on the young man was obvious. Sloane hoped he'd provide useful information, something the police overlooked or failed to uncover. Instead, he remained tip-lipped, and said nothing.

"I was told you shouted quite loudly, pointing at something or someone."

Boris still did not say anything. Sloane decided to use another approach.

"Do you like working here, Boris?"

"Yes, I like it," he said. "People are nice here."

"Where do you live?"

"I live with my sister and her husband on Green Street."

Sloane recognized the area, most likely the apartments where the Tuckers lived, not far from Cucumber Alley. He started to see a pattern, but it was crucial Boris Ivanov provide much-needed information. He patiently continued his questioning, speaking as gently as possible.

"Do you ever walk around the village, Boris?"

Boris nodded. "Yes, I like to walk."

"Do you walk around Cucumber Alley in the evening?"

He looked down at the floor, unwilling to add anything further.

"Cucumber Alley is where Miss Hayes was murdered," Sloane told them. He relayed information about the unsolved murders in Cucumber Alley and the attack on Rodney Longworth. Ludmilla interpreted for her brother, expecting him to reply, but still, he said nothing.

Sloane leaned forward and looked at Boris Ivanov intently. "Boris, if there's something you saw, you must tell me. Do you want to be killed, too?"

Ludmilla interpreted and this time Boris shivered slightly, obviously, Sloane's words had an effect. He moistened his lips, feeling awkward and rather uncomfortable.

"What do you mean, Mr. Sheppard?" Ludmilla asked, quite concerned.

"A young man, Mr. Tucker, was murdered in Cucumber Alley. He may have been killed because he saw something and was blackmailing someone. Are you blackmailing someone, Boris? Is that why you don't want to talk?"

Ludmilla wasn't sure what blackmail meant, although she was able to interpret in Russian what Sloane wanted to convey. Again, Boris shook his head in denial.

Sloane had the impression Boris Ivanov was an intelligent young man, simply seeking a new life in America, with his sister and brother-in-law, and Schenectady and General Electric were good places to start. Boris sat up straighter, looking at Sloane.

"Did you see something in Cucumber Alley or recognize someone at the lecture?" Sloane persisted. "If you did, you must tell me."

Boris appeared to understand. He looked at his sister as though for support and then took a deep breath and quite bravely, without hesitation, told Sloane what he needed to know.

CHAPTER SEVENTEEN

On Wednesday, Alice was up before eight o'clock. She sat at the kitchen table, drinking coffee and scribbling on a tablet. She was in her robe, nightgown, and slippers, enjoying the early morning solitude. She was planning a luncheon this Saturday, to celebrate her sister's birthday. She considered it an ideal time for a celebration, to block at least momentarily the memories of the murders and to return to at least some semblance of normalcy in their lives.

She'd call her sister and ask if she and Jerome would attend. No sense planning, preparing food, and inviting people if Agnes wasn't up to it. She continued adding names to the list: the Banks, Mrs. Hayes, Mrs. Grey, Dr. McIntyre, and his wife, and Mr. and Mrs. Lennox, Dr. Bennett and his wife. She finished writing and sighed in satisfaction. She was free today and tomorrow, so she'd have plenty of time to prepare. She had no sooner put the cap on her pen when she heard footsteps coming down the stairs and Rodney appeared in the doorway.

"Good morning, dear," she said, smiling. "I'll fix oatmeal for you."

Rodney stifled a yawn, still sleepy, not quite awake. He sat at the table, looking as though he hadn't slept. With the recent tumultuous events and the suspicions nagging at his brain, his sleep patterns had been far from normal. He squinted and ran his hand across his face.

"Have you spoken to Mr. Sheppard lately?"

"No, not yet." He lit a cigarette while sipping the coffee his mother had placed before him. He decided to tell her about the little girl he saw on Saturday evening when his parents and Aunt Agnes and Uncle Jerome went out for the evening. He mentioned how Mrs. Grey was there, along with Mrs. Norris and several other neighborhood women. It was the same little girl they read about in the evening paper while they had dinner at the hotel. Alice didn't see any relevance in what her son was telling her. She placed the coffee pot on the table, along with plates, and utensils.

"There's something fishy with that, Mother," Rodney said.

Alice returned to the stove and stirred the oatmeal in the large pot. "You certainly don't blame Mrs. Grey?"

"No, but she was there."

"Mrs. Grey is highly regarded in the community and at the college," Alice said. "If that little girl was ill, she'd have noticed it. Her death cannot be attributed to Mrs. Grey."

Rodney continued puffing on his cigarette, sipping coffee, his stomach in knots. He noticed the tablet with the lists. Alice told him about her plans for a luncheon on Saturday afternoon.

"To celebrate Aunt Agnes's birthday. You don't work on Saturday, do you?" She made it seem like even if he did, he'd need to rearrange his schedule. Fortunately, Rodney shook his head, smiling slightly.

"No, I have the weekend off, finally. I can help with the arrangements."

"Do you think Mr. and Mrs. Lennox would like to attend?"

"I really don't know. I'll ask Olive Mae to attend."

Alice smiled. "Yes, please ask Olive Mae. I'll call Dr. Bennett at the library and Dr. McIntyre's office later today. When you go to work, you can ask Mr. Lennox."

At that moment, Simon entered, greeting his wife and son sleepily. He sat across from Rodney, still not quite awake, and helped himself to coffee.

"Dad, we're having a house party Saturday afternoon for Aunt Agnes," Rodney told him.

"For her birthday, dear," Alice said sweetly.

Simon frowned. "You've made up your mind already? Who are the guests?"

Rodney handed over the list of names. Simon frowned again, glanced at the list of names, and then tossed it across the table, reaching for his cigarettes and lighting one without saying anything. Alice sensed his obstinacy.

"Don't worry, dear," she said, bestowing a steaming bowl of oatmeal in front of him. She did likewise with Rodney, sprinkled with just enough nutmeg. She placed a bottle of milk on the table and sat down to finish her coffee. "It'll be a grand time, Simon. I'll make your favorite, beef stroganoff. Besides, what could possibly go wrong?'

Early in the afternoon, as Rodney came downstairs dressed for work, the phone rang in the hallway. Since he was the only one present, he decided to answer. He picked up the candlestick phone and heard Sloane Sheppard, asking for him.

"Mr. Sheppard, I'm getting ready to leave for the hotel. I'm glad you caught me!"

"I've reached a conclusion on the murder of Miss Hayes," Sloane said, looking at his notes.

Rodney loosened his tie as though he couldn't breathe. "You know who's responsible for killing Theresa?"

Sloane didn't answer him directly. "I plan to speak to your parents, as well as your aunt and uncle, the Banks, Mrs. Hayes and Mrs. Grey."

An idea occurred to Rodney. "We're having a luncheon on Saturday afternoon. We're inviting the people you'd like to speak to."

Sloane hesitated. If it was a house party, he didn't know if it'd be the right setting for relaying his findings on the case. He asked Rodney if his parents would mind if he stopped by.

"I'm sure it'll be fine," Rodney told him, still elated that Sloane had figured out who was guilty of the murders. "It starts at one o'clock on Saturday."

Sloane expressed his gratitude and told him he'd be there later in the afternoon and then ended the call. Rodney replaced the handset on the candlestick phone slowly, thoughtfully, then put the phone back on the table. At that moment, Alice came downstairs, wearing a simple blue dress with pearls and just enough Chanel No. 5.

"Did I hear you speaking to someone just now, Rodney?" she asked curiously.

Rodney nodded. "Mr. Sheppard. He said he's reached a conclusion on the case. He wants to speak to all of us. I invited him here on Saturday."

Alice glared at her son. "Rodney, we're having a luncheon for family and friends. Mr. Sheppard is neither family nor friend."

"He's doing me a service," Rodney said, not willing to back down to his bossy mother.

"I think another time would be more appropriate," Alice said firmly.

"Well, I don't," Rodney said, equally firmly. "He wants to speak to us, Aunt Agnes, Uncle Jerome, the Banks, Mrs. Hayes and Mrs. Grey. Since they'll be here on Saturday, I don't see any harm in it."

The front door opened, and Simon entered. He had gone to a corner store for bread and milk. He stopped upon seeing his wife and son in the hallway. From their expressions he could sense something was wrong. He took off his coat and Fedora hat, left them on a hallway chair, and then looked from Rodney to Alice, wondering what was happening. Rodney told his father that Mr. Sheppard called, as he had reached a conclusion on the case. He invited him to the luncheon on Saturday, as he wanted to speak to everyone concerned. Suddenly realizing he'd be late to the hotel Rodney grabbed his coat and cap from the closet and hurried out the front door.

With her son gone, Alice added that it was not the right time as it was her sister's birthday. If she expected her husband's support, she was taken aback by his nonchalant manner.

Simon shrugged, almost uncaringly. "Let Mr. Sheppard come on Saturday."

Alice started to protest but Simon waved her off, walking down the hallway to the kitchen with the bread and milk.

"I wouldn't worry, dear," he told her. "Unless you have something to hide."

In his office in downtown Albany, Sloane replaced the handset on the candlestick phone after speaking with Rodney and looked again at his notes. He had arrived early, seeing two clients before calling

Rodney. And before calling Rodney, he had placed other calls of importance.

The first was to the State Normal School in Albany. Upon speaking to the registrar, he was informed that nursing, while not a major course of study, was offered as a component through science classes with an emphasis on health care. Inquiring further, he was told many students were prepared for positions in public schools.

A call to Dr. McIntyre's office at Union College verified that the science staff from 1900 to 1920 had either retired or passed away. Sloane asked if he could speak with Dr. McIntyre again but was told he was at a conference and would return tomorrow. He inquired about Dr. Leonard Seymour and was told he passed away in 1919. He also inquired about Mrs. Carol Osborne. She retired in 1920 and passed away, just last year. The secretary mentioned the science department contained newer, younger faculty, most hired within the last seven years. He then asked about the claims made against Mrs. Brennan regarding unethical practices by Dr. Harold Peters. The secretary mentioned Dr. Peters had retired in 1922 and was living somewhere out west. She wasn't familiar with the unethical practices he accused Mrs. Brennan of. She commented that some professors had such claims made against them, especially during the war, when enrollment was at an all-time low. She added most claims were dismissed by the administration.

Another call to Ellis Hospital in Schenectady. After several connections, and numerous dead ends, he was finally able to speak to a head nurse who remembered Mrs. Grey. Fondly she praised her work and her decorum in the hospital. He referenced the letters written by Dr. Leonard Seymour and Mrs. Carol Osborne of Union College claiming her lack of preparation in nursing and oversight of a patient's condition leading to the patient's death at the hospital, but the head nurse was not aware of such claims. He remembered Mrs. Grey telling him she began work at the hospital in 1870 and he mentioned that to the head nurse, inquiring into staff who knew Mrs. Grey from the beginning of her employment. The head nurse told Sloane staff from such a long time ago were either retired or deceased. She did not know of anyone currently employed at the hospital who began in the 1870s or 1880s and was still working there.

He then spoke to the head of personnel, a Mr. Collins, who although reluctant at first to give information over the telephone, upon learning it involved a murder investigation, gave a thorough check on records pertaining to Mrs. Edna Grey. He verified her dates of employment from 1870 until her retirement in 1914. Sloane asked if her last name was Grey when hired, and he confirmed she was Mrs. Walter Grey of Schenectady, her first name being Edna. He could add little else. He reported no such memos existed pertaining to those claims made by Dr. Seymour and Mrs. Osborne. He mentioned that many records of patients and employees during the late 1800s, the Great War and the flu pandemic were either lost or simply not kept, as the hospital saw an influx of patients, including refugees and homeless children, and record-keeping was often overlooked. He added the hospital was in a chaotic state during the Great War, being extremely short-staffed and doctors and nurses were overworked and overwhelmed, with the flu pandemic stretching their resources even further.

Replacing the handset, Sloane wasn't surprised. Glancing at his notes again, he had jotted down the dates 1914 when the memos were written about Mrs. Grey, and 1913 when the neglect and the patient's death occurred. He noted she retired a year after the patient died.

The memo on Mrs. Brennan was written in 1921, but that also led nowhere. Obviously, it wasn't followed up and must have been dismissed at some point. Even ten or fifteen years were like an eternity, as people moved on, changed jobs, and retired, leaving few if any individuals who could remember events from the past.

275

A lot had happened since that time, too, Sloane thought grudgingly, that would distort people's memory. Certainly, the Great War and the flu pandemic affected nearly everyone. There were other perplexing headlines; President Harding's Teapot Dome controversy, his unexpected death in 1923 and Vice President Coolidge assuming office, the murder of little Bobby Franks by Leopold and Loeb in 1924, the Scopes Trial in Tennessee two years ago, the execution planned this year for Sacco and Vanzetti from an alleged bank robbery in Massachusetts in 1920. Sloane heard on the radio that protests to stop the execution had even reached Albany, where a rally was being held tomorrow in front of the state capitol.

He picked up the handset again on the candlestick phone and asked the operator to place a call to the State Office of Licensure and Permits. It was a long shot, but he had to obtain as much information as possible to support his conclusion. The woman he spoke to was reluctant to give information over the phone, as Sloane assumed, despite his telling her the importance of the request, that it pertained to a murder investigation. She confirmed that insurance salesmen, stockbrokers, and medical personnel were required by law to hold the state license in their profession. Pertaining to medical staff, without the appropriate license, it'd lead to dismissal and even criminal charges, especially in cases of malpractice. He thanked her and ended the call.

He lighted a cigarette, exhaling a large cloud of smoke. He jotted down on his pad the names of everyone he interrogated. He tried to cross certain ones off but was not quite sure yet.

The red paisley scarf, that Rodney mentioned. What bearing, if any, did it have with the murders? And the size twelve shoe imprint outside Mrs. Grey's house. Unlikely a woman wore size twelve shoes. But Steven Banks wore twelve as did Rodney.

He sat thoughtfully at his desk, puffing at his cigarette incessantly as was his custom when finishing a case. Impulsively, he picked up the phone again and asked the operator to call General Electric in Schenectady. After a few moments, the call went through and was answered by the switchboard operator. He asked to be connected with the laundry facilities. He was pleased when Ludmilla Kalamanov answered herself.

"Hello, Mr. Sheppard, nice hearing from you again," she said pleasantly.

Sloane heard laundry machines in the background and voices in a language he didn't recognize, most likely Russian. He cleared his throat before speaking.

"Do you know the size shoe your brother wears, Mrs. Kalamanov?"

"Excuse me, Mr. Sheppard?" she asked, not sure she heard him correctly.

"His shoe size, if you know it," Sloane repeated, feeling hopeful.

Ludmilla hesitated. "My husband and I recently bought new shoes for Boris. He wears size twelve." She paused, finding the question rather odd. "Why do you want to know, Mr. Sheppard?"

He told her he'd be in touch soon, thanked her, and ended the call. That confirmed my suspicions, he thought, and repeatedly circled a name on his pad with a vengeance.

CHAPTER EIGHTEEN

I t was Saturday morning, and although the sun was trying to break through the thick clouds, it remained blustery, with intermittent snow showers and occasional gusty winds. Pedestrians scurried along the streets, the milkman and the mailman made deliveries. The Cucumber Alley murders hung over the city like a dead weight. But life went on as usual in the stockade village.

While his parents were already up, Rodney managed to sleep late, as it was his day off. Groggily getting out of bed, he paddled over to the bathroom, filled the sink with water to shave, then after finishing, he rinsed his face with cold water. He reached for a towel on the rack, dried his face, and splashed shaving lotion on his cheeks. He slicked back his hair and then returned to his bedroom, where he put on a dress shirt, his customary vest, and pleated slacks, along with his formal shoes. He stood in front of the mirror, getting rather agitated at tying his tie. With his nerves racked, and after several tries, he succeeded in a halfway decent knot. He sat on his bed and smoked a few cigarettes, wondering what Mr. Sheppard planned to tell them.

Crushing his cigarette into an ashtray, Rodney decided to go downstairs. He entered the kitchen and helped himself to coffee from the pot on the table and a corn muffin. He saw his mother busy at the stove while his father was collecting plates, cups, and silverware, and placing them on the counter. They were still in their robes and slippers. So absorbed in their chores they didn't hear him enter. Simon looked up and smiled.

"Good morning, Rodney. We're getting things ready for this afternoon."

"Anything I can do to help?" he offered, sipping his coffee.

Alice turned from the stove. "Good morning, dear. Would you turn on the radio? WGY usually plays popular songs on Saturdays. You can bring Aunt Agnes's gifts into the living room." She pointed to three wrapped boxes on the far counter.

Rodney collected the boxes and brought them into the living room, depositing them on the coffee table, then turned on the radio console to WGY. The soothing sounds of Duke Ellington, Josephine Baker, and Ruth Etting soon filled the room, creating a rather carefree atmosphere. The room was immaculately clean so there was little for him to do. Returning to the kitchen, Alice asked her son to mind the kitchen while she and Simon went upstairs to dress.

Checking the beef stroganoff, which smelled delicious, the salad in the icebox, the bottles of ginger ale, the coffee and the chocolate birthday cake on the kitchen table, Rodney was satisfied the luncheon would be a success. He even looked forward to it, after all, it was his aunt's birthday.

The grandfathers' clock in the hallway chimed the half-hour, already twelve-thirty. He had just simmered the casserole when the doorbell rang. The first of the guests had arrived.

Rodney went to the front door, expecting to see his aunt and uncle, as he assumed they'd arrive early. To his surprise, he saw Mrs. Grey, her face beaming, looking much younger than her years.

"Hello, Rodney dear," she smiled, as he stepped aside, allowing her to enter the hallway.

"So windy, but refreshing, nonetheless. I bought a nice gift for Mrs. Brennan."

She removed her long coat, red paisley scarf, and red cloche hat and handed them to Rodney, leaving him speechless. She noticed his bewilderment and asked if he was all right.

"Yes, I'm fine," he stammered. He looked at the red paisley scarf in consternation, leaving her belongings on a chair. "Please come in, Mrs. Grey. My parents will be down shortly."

Rodney looked at her quickly. She looked pleasant in a simple gray dress, a long string of pearls, her gray hair fixed neatly in the bob style, although Rodney didn't think she was a true flapper. Upon entering the living room, she smiled upon hearing Ruth Etting's latest hit song emanating from the radio console and then noticed the gifts for Agnes on the coffee table. She added her birthday present to the pile and addressed Rodney pleasantly.

"The radio is just wonderful, Rodney. Ruth Etting's one of my favorites!"

Rodney agreed. "Ruth Etting's the bee's knees, for sure. Can I get you something to drink, Mrs. Grey? We have ginger ale and coffee."

"Thank you, dear. Ginger ale's fine."

Mrs. Grey sat down in an armchair near the fireplace, seemingly engrossed in the jazz music. Rodney thought she appeared so lost in the upbeat tunes that upon returning from the kitchen he wondered if she even realized he had left the room. She thanked him as he handed her the sparkling beverage and sat down on the sofa across from her.

At that moment, Alice descended the stairs and appeared in the living room. She greeted Mrs. Grey warmly.

Alice was dressed to perfection as always, her pristine beige dress, along with her pearl necklace highlighted her trim figure, her brown hair tastefully arranged. She smiled at her son and Mrs. Grey as her husband also made his appearance.

"Hello, Dr. Longworth," Mrs. Grey said, putting her glass of ginger ale down on an end table. She felt as though she should rise to greet him. "Thank you so much for inviting me to your luncheon for Mrs. Brennan."

"You're welcome, Mrs. Grey," Simon told her, smiling. He too was dressed exquisitely in a three-piece suit, an immaculate navy-blue tie, and leather shoes, very business-like, although his expression did not match his appearance. Rodney thought his father looked drawn, perhaps too much stress from the recent events. But then he didn't recall his father showing any real emotion over the murders or even his attack. Never one to openly show his feelings, Rodney wondered if his father was hiding something that nobody, not even his mother, knew about. He listened as his parents and Mrs. Grey made idle chatter, not wishing to intervene.

The grandfathers' clock chimed the hour and soon the doorbell rang quite frequently; the Banks arrived, followed by the Brennans. Soon Mr. and Mrs. Lennox appeared. Greetings were exchanged, coats and hats were left on hallway chairs, and ginger ale and coffee were served by Alice and Rodney while their guests chatted and enjoyed the music. The doorbell rang again, and upon opening the door, Rodney saw Olive Mae and behind her, Dr. McIntyre and his wife, and Dr. Bennett and his wife. He welcomed them in and after taking their coats, directed them to the living room, where the gathering was in full swing.

Entering the living room, Rodney stood near the far wall, sipping ginger ale and taking in the scene before him. He was surprised none of the animosity he knew existed was present, although he assumed it was kept dormant. He noticed his Aunt Agnes talking quite animatedly with Mrs. Hayes, laughing and smiling, both quite pretty in floral dresses, with pearls and bracelets, lipstick, and rogue. His gaze traveled to Mr. Banks, chatting with his father and Uncle Jerome. His large figure was clad in a dark gray suit, a white silk shirt and collar, and a gray tie with a silver tiepin. Above his collar, his round face rose like a large balloon. His Uncle Jerome was dressed casually, without a suit, as though he wished he hadn't come and was only there for his wife's sake. Rodney noticed Wilma Banks chatting with Olive Mae and his mother. He thought Wilma looked cheaply dressed, with a simple frock that downplayed rather than augmented her figure, little make-up, and strands of her auburn hair escaping from a clip in the back. Olive Mae wore a fashionable black dress with a string of pearls, little make-up, although she looked fresh and pleasant.

He noticed Dr. McIntyre and his wife talking with Mrs. Grey, rather seriously, he thought by their expressions. Dr. McIntyre gave the appearance of having come out of the military, rather soldierly, but very professional in a three-piece suit. He was surprised to see Steven, always dapper, arrogant and a little crude, chatting and occasionally laughing with Dr. Bennett and his wife. Steven looked handsome in a three-piece suit like his father, although he displayed more of his youthful physique and overall vitality. Dr. Bennett was handsome in his own style with a modest, low-keyed suit. He noticed he was listening to Steven, but he seemed bored by whatever he was saying, despite the brief bursts of laughter. Rodney's glance went to Mr. Lennox and his wife talking animatedly with Mrs. Grey and the McIntyres. Alice excused herself from her guests to check on the food in the kitchen.

Rodney still wondered if there were heated emotions smoldering underneath the pleasant veneer. He couldn't imagine Mrs. Hayes, Steven, or Wilma being particularly glad to see Mrs. Grey. He wondered if Mrs. Hayes and his mother would exchange pleasantries before the afternoon was over. He didn't think Mr. Banks would be glad to see Mrs. Grey, either. Funny, he thought, how there was so much discontent and yet no one displayed any signs of it.

Rodney realized Steven had joined him near the far wall. He started talking about General Electric and his recent experiments, but Rodney only made polite comments as appropriate. Frankly, he wasn't interested in Steven's work at the facility but kept a brave face while he talked practically nonstop. Soon Olive Mae came over to them, sipping ginger ale and eyeing Rodney appreciatively, which he found rather uncomfortable. At that moment, his mother returned from the kitchen, announcing that lunch was ready.

They followed her into the kitchen, where the table was arranged in a buffet style, with the beef stroganoff at one end and the plates and utensils at the other. Garlic bread and a large bowl of salad complimented the entrée, along with plenty of coffee and more ginger ale. Flora commented on how lovely the food looked. Eagerly a line formed, to partake of the delicious stroganoff. After filling up on the offerings, they took their plates and returned to the living room, to enjoy the meal and the lively jazz on the radio. More conversations and laughter ensued. Rodney looked around and noticed everyone enjoying the luncheon. It turned out a great success after all!

After almost an hour, Alice told her guests to join her in the kitchen to wish Agnes a happy birthday. Entering the kitchen, Rodney saw his mother had already lit the candles on the large cake. Agnes was speechless by the sight and hugged her sister affectionately. Mr. Banks jokingly commented about too few candles and Agnes kidded him about it, causing laughter to go around the room. The atmosphere was lively as the guests sang happy birthday to Agnes. She blew out the candles, everyone clapped and then Alice helped her sister cut the cake and serve up portions on dessert plates.

Alice suggested they return to the living room, where Agnes would open her gifts. Settling in chairs, the guests watched as she opened several boxes, one containing elegant stationery and a ball-point pen, another was a chiffon blouse, while another, from Mrs. Grey, contained a book on Cicero and Horace. Wilma and Olive Mae commented on the lovely chiffon blouse. Agnes was delighted with her gifts and expressed her heartfelt appreciation.

It was later than Rodney realized, glancing at his watch when the doorbell rang again.

As though enraptured by the frivolity of the luncheon and the opening of the gifts, Rodney, Alice, and Simon looked at each other, wondering who would be calling now. Rodney, coming to his senses, realized it was most likely Mr. Sheppard. Before his parents could go to the door, he excused himself and entered the hallway. From the curtained windows flanking the front door, he saw not one but three men on the doorstep. He opened the door cautiously and saw Mr. Sheppard, Inspector James, and Sergeant Eberhart. Taken aback momentarily, Rodney looked at them as though in a trance, then composed himself and invited them in. He asked why the police were with him, but Sloane told him to wait until he addressed everyone present. Rodney led them down the hallway to the living room. Upon seeing Sloane and the policemen, a dreaded hush fell over everyone, with the only sounds coming from the radio console, still playing jazz and the ticking of the grandfathers' clock from the hallway. No one spoke until Alice got up from the sofa and addressed the men in the doorway.

"What's the meaning of this, Mr. Sheppard? We're having a birthday party for my sister. I knew you'd be coming as Rodney's guest, but why are the police here?"

Simon also demanded to know what was happening. Alice and Jerome, seated on the sofa, along with the others, remained silent and rather dumbfounded, as though they didn't know what to expect. Police at a birthday party? Alice didn't invite them to sit or to partake of the food. She directed her gaze at her son, as though blaming him for this inexcusable intrusion. Sloane sensed the discomfort, cleared his throat, and began to speak.

"Thank you, Mrs. Longworth, for allowing me to come here today. Rodney invited me and although I do know it's your sister's birthday, I'd like to address everyone regarding the murder of Miss Theresa Hayes."

"We're having a celebration, Mr. Sheppard," Jerome told him.

"Perhaps another time," Agnes suggested.

"If Mr. Sheppard has news about my daughter's murder, I'd like to hear it," Flora spoke up, rather forcibly. She was standing in front of the fireplace, alongside Russell and Wilma.

Sloane acknowledged that he did have credible information, appearing official and even threatening, looking at the faces before him.

As though she had no other choice, especially with the police present, Alice reluctantly sat down next to her sister and brother-in-law on the sofa. Sloane noticed the strained faces and an uncomfortableness permeating the room.

"Again, I'm not here to disrupt your celebration, Mrs. Brennan," he addressed Agnes, who nodded and seemed to appreciate his candor. "I brought with me the police investigating the recent murders in Cucumber Alley, as well as a witness."

Everyone looked at each other, not sure what to expect. Against the far wall, Rodney wondered what Mr. Sheppard meant. There was no one else here unless there was a witness he wasn't aware of. He listened as Sloane continued.

"Rodney first came to me to investigate the murder of Miss Hayes. Before her murder, there was the murder of Mrs. Stella Bradshaw. Not long after Rodney was attacked while in Cucumber Alley late at night, followed by the murder of Mr. John Tucker."

"Mr. Sheppard, we know about the murders and the attack on Rodney," Alice interrupted, clearly perturbed. "Must you rehash it during my sister's birthday party?"

"I will get to the point soon, Mrs. Longworth. I began my investigation into the murder of Miss Hayes by inquiring about her character. From nearly everyone I spoke with I was told Miss Hayes was not an agreeable person both here in the community and at the college library."

"Theresa was basically a good girl," Flora said in her daughter's defense. "She endured a lot when she was younger."

"I knew little about Mrs. Bradshaw," Sloane continued. "As she had no family, I could only draw conclusions from something Rodney told me he observed at the hotel." He glanced at Rodney as he stood against the far wall. "While at the hotel and from a distance, he saw Miss Hayes speaking to Mrs. Bradshaw. There was nothing unusual in that, of course, but what was said was of interest to me. We'll never know what exactly transpired between them, but I can make a good guess what Miss Hayes told Mrs. Bradshaw."

"Mr. Sheppard, please," Alice said impatiently. "This is my sister's birthday."

Sloane continued. "Miss Hayes discovered incriminating information that could lead to ruin and possibly even arrest. She found an easy way to use the information. She decided to blackmail the person involved."

From his vantage point near the far wall, Rodney felt a stiffening of his limbs, unsure what would happen. He glanced out the living room windows and noticed two people on the doorstep.

At that moment, and without waiting for Rodney, Sergeant Eberhart went to the front door, and returned with Boris Ivanov and his sister Ludmilla Kalamanov.

"Who are these people?" Alice demanded. "I want them to leave immediately!"

"You have no business bringing strangers to our house, Mr. Sheppard," Simon said.

"This is a murder investigation," Sloane reminded them. "It's imperative that they're here today." Having managed to silence Simon and Alice, he then turned to Boris and Ludmilla. "Thank you, Mr. Ivanov and Mrs. Kalamanov for coming here and for waiting outside." He looked at everyone as they stared at Boris and his sister questioningly. "This is Mr. Boris Ivanov and his sister, Mrs. Ludmilla Kalamanov. They work at General Electric in the facilities department." Sloane paused. "Mr. Ivanov, you were walking around the village on the evening of March eighth, is that correct?"

Boris nodded slowly, not sure what would happen next.

"On that particular evening, you walked down Cucumber Alley, correct?"

Boris nodded again, feeling overwhelmed with so many people looking at him.

"You saw someone in the alley that night. Would you look around this room and tell me if you see that person here today?"

Sheepishly, his face flushed, Boris pointed toward the center of the living room, near the fireplace. "I saw her," he told Sloane.

At first, no one was sure who he was pointing to until Alice and Flora realized it at the same time before anyone else. Flora tried to contain her wrath, but her venom unleashed a torrent of invective.

"You, you miserable bitch!" she spattered at Mrs. Grey, who sat placidly in the armchair near the fireplace, neither fazed nor moved by her outburst nor Boris's revelation. "You killed my daughter, my only child! You're responsible for the murders!"

"Lies, such fabrications," Mrs. Grey said, calmly maintaining her composure. "I never saw that man, until he was standing outside my house, trying to break in."

"Mr. Ivanov was not trying to break into your house," Sloane said. "He saw you killing Mr. John Tucker in Cucumber Alley, where you left him for dead, as you did Miss Hayes and Mrs. Bradshaw. I assume Mr. Tucker witnessed you killing one or both women and decided to blackmail you. You must've agreed to meet him in the alley, where you killed him to keep him silent."

"Nonsense," Mrs. Grey said with tight lips. "I refuse to listen to these insinuations."

"Mr. Ivanov was afraid to go to the police, as he was concerned about his immigration status. The size twelve shoe print in the snow belonged to Mr. Ivanov. He recognized you the night of Dr. Alexanderson's presentation. He saw you around the village and knew where you lived. On the evening of March eleventh, he approached your house, hoping to get another glimpse of you, because he wanted to be sure it was you he saw in the alley that night. He didn't plan to blackmail you, like the others. He wanted to tell the police he witnessed you killing Mr. Tucker."

Everyone stared at Mrs. Grey, aghast, not believing what Sloane was saying and yet believing it at the same time. Flora and Russell were hard put to keep their anger at bay.

"How could I inflict harm on these people?" Mrs. Grey asked. "I'm an elderly woman."

"Part of your cover, Mrs. Grey," Sloane continued. "For an elderly woman, you're quite strong." He paused. "I'd like to review what occurred with Miss Hayes. While working in the president's office, Miss Hayes was responsible for reviewing old files. She discovered incidents in your past that had gone unchecked, including your lack of nursing credentials. Years ago, there was suspicion you were responsible for the sudden death of a patient. I don't know the exact circumstances, but you fooled many people at the hospital. No one reviewed your credentials, records were never verified. Either you never finished or didn't attend nursing school. You were incredibly lucky, to have been employed as a nurse without the proper credentials or license."

Still Mrs. Grey sat, unmoved by the accusations.

"She *is* a quack!" Steven interjected. "She doesn't know a damn thing about nursing!"

Rodney thought back to the little girl on Washington Avenue and Mrs. Grey's insistence she didn't have a fever. But the girl died. Now he understood what he had only suspected.

Sloane continued addressing Mrs. Grey. "Most likely Miss Hayes told Mrs. Bradshaw about her findings. I assume Mrs. Bradshaw confronted you with this knowledge. You met her in Cucumber Alley as she must have demanded hush money. You worried the truth would lead to public disgrace and possibly dismissal from Union College, and even lawsuits of malpractice. This information could also have been leaked to the local newspapers. You feared your good standing in the community would be tarnished if the truth came out.

"You attacked Rodney, I assume, when you went to Cucumber Alley to meet Mr. Tucker. You didn't want to kill Rodney, but just enough to render him unconscious. You eventually killed Mr. Tucker, as I assume he also demanded hush money. When you and Mrs. Norris walked around Cucumber Alley that evening, you had already killed Mr. Tucker. Mrs. Norris told police you suggested a walk down Cucumber Alley. You needed her as a witness, so she'd verify you found the body. You didn't realize Mr. Ivanov witnessed you killing Mr. Tucker."

Sloane finished speaking, shocking everyone into horrified silence. Only Inspector James spoke, authoritatively as he addressed Mrs. Grey.

"Mrs. Edna Grey, I arrest you for the murders of Miss Theresa Hayes, Mrs. Stella Bradshaw, Mr. John Tucker as well as the assault on Mr. Rodney Longworth."

Mrs. Grey got up slowly and wearily, as though in considerable pain. She looked at Sloane and at the policemen. "Of course, I'll come, Inspector. Please give me a moment."

She walked carefully out of the living room. The front door suddenly opened and then closed, surprising everyone. Sloane and the policemen reacted quickly and rushed to the hallway, Rodney and Steven joining them.

"There she is!" Rodney exclaimed, standing on the front steps as he looked down Washington Avenue, toward Cucumber Alley. "There's Mrs. Grey!"

Sloane, Inspector James, and Sergeant Eberhart ran in that direction. Sloane called out to her to stop, but she paid him no attention. She quickened her pace, and without realizing a trolley was in the middle of Washington Avenue, stepped onto the road, and was then instantly and horribly crushed by the grinding wheels, a bloodcurdling scream ending her mendacious life.

CHAPTER NINETEEN

I don't understand about the red paisley scarf," Rodney said.

It was several hours later. Most of the guests had departed, but the Banks and the Brennans remained. Inspector James, Sergeant Eberhart, Boris, and Ludmilla also left.

The Schenectady police and an ambulance were called to the scene of the trolley accident on Washington Avenue and Mrs. Grey was soon pronounced dead, her body removed to the hospital morgue. A crowd of bystanders approached, including Mrs. Norris, and exclaimed disbelief, shock and horror over what occurred.

In the Longworth house, the surprise revelations about Mrs. Grey stunned everyone, leading to more questions. Sloane was seated on the sofa, looking at his assembled audience. Alice brought him a cup of coffee and an ashtray. He looked at Rodney as he sat in the armchair Mrs. Grey vacated.

"The red paisley scarf was her first mistake," Sloane said. "Rodney, you told me your mother, your aunt, and Mrs. Grey often had lunch together at the hotel. When Mrs. Grey saw the red stains on her scarf, she knew it was blood from when she killed her first two victims. She saw your aunt had the same scarf and knowing the bloodstains would incriminate her, she switched the scarves without Mrs. Brennan knowing it."

"When did that occur?" Agnes asked.

"Most likely not the last time you had lunch with her, but the time before. When the red stains were noticed on the scarf, she made it seem like it was your scarf all along."

"How foolish I was not to notice earlier," Agnes said regretfully.

Alice remembered the dates. "We met Mrs. Grey for lunch on March the second the last time. I think the time before was February twenty-first or twenty-second."

"Mrs. Grey was a clever woman," Sloane continued. "I first grew suspicious of her when she told me she graduated from the State Normal School in Albany."

"I don't think they offer nursing," Agnes said, always the educator.

Sloane nodded. "You're correct, Mrs. Brennan. I learned its primary function is the training of teachers. In her file at Union College, I read how the president's office was unable to procure a manuscript of her academic work. She managed to continue employment at the hospital and the college without her credentials being verified. I don't think Mrs. Grey knew records were kept detailing the discrepancies questioned by professors."

"She fooled a lot of people," Simon said.

"We'll never know the exact details," Sloane continued. "She could've told the hospital she was in nursing school and would soon graduate. The hospital personnel director told me few files were maintained during those years. At a time when doctors and nurses were in short supply, especially during the Great War and the flu pandemic, she was able to secure and maintain a position on the nursing staff. The years went on and she continued her employment at the hospital, but nothing was ever questioned until years later at the college, when a few professors had concerns which they brought to the president's attention."

"I'm surprised she didn't kill me, too," Rodney said. "I knew I saw red right before I blacked out."

"The red paisley scarf. Most likely she was waiting for Mr. Tucker to pay him hush money. She didn't want you to witness her meeting with him."

"Why would she worry about the past being revealed?" Steven asked. "After all, so many years had gone by. Surely it wouldn't have mattered."

"To Mrs. Grey, her reputation did matter," Sloane said. "She was held in high regard in the village and as a volunteer at her church. Regardless of the passing years, it would have been scandalous and may have ruined her good name in the community."

"Would she have been arrested for fraudulent practice?" Wilma asked.

"Quite possibly," Sloane said. "Malpractice is a serious matter, especially as there was suspicion she may have been responsible for a patient's death. If it was revealed she was an unlicensed nurse, that death could have been investigated and she would have been subjected to an investigation. It may have appeared in the newspapers, too."

"Remember I told you Mrs. Grey said you had secrets, Steven?" Rodney asked him.

Steven nodded. "She never cared for us, Rodney. She was a meddling busybody and a murderer. She told you that to throw suspicion on us."

"Of course, why else would she say it?" Wilma said.

"I have no remorse for her," Flora said bitterly. "She was a cruel, ruthless woman. She knew what she was doing. She thought only of herself."

"And Theresa was killed because of it," Russell murmured.

An uncomfortable silence settled over everyone until Rodney spoke, addressing Agnes.

"I'm sorry for ruining your birthday party, Aunt Agnes," he said, feeling guilty.

Agnes turned to her nephew and smiled. "Rodney dear, you're a brave young man. You consulted Mr. Sheppard who found out who was responsible. You should be commended!"

Rodney smiled, then blushed slightly. "No, I think Mr. Sheppard should be commended."

Simon suggested they finish the luncheon. Alice mentioned she'd reheat the beef stroganoff and there was plenty of birthday cake, too. She asked Sloane to stay and enjoy the delicious food.

"Please join us, Mr. Sheppard," Rodney said, following everyone to the kitchen. "The beef stroganoff is the bee's knees!"

Sloane smiled. "It'll be a pleasure, Rodney."

CHAPTER TWENTY

On Monday, Rodney awoke to a morning of brilliant sunshine. He stretched luxuriously in bed and was prepared to turn over and fall back to sleep when the alarm clock signaled the time to rise. He paddled to the bathroom and after showering and shaving, he ensured his shirt, tie, and his usual vest were pristine, his dress pants and shoes immaculate. Before descending the stairs, he smelled the coffee and oatmeal, so he knew his parents were already up.

Upon entering the kitchen, he noticed his mother had opened the kitchen window, overlooking their city garden. The fresh air was invigorating and there was a definite feel of spring in the air. Alice turned and saw her son in the doorway.

"Good morning, dear. I made your favorite again, oatmeal with nutmeg."

Simon put the morning paper down on the table and addressed his son seriously.

"Rodney, your mother and I owe you an apology. Your insistence in hiring a private investigator to learn the truth about Theresa's murder was a wise decision."

Rodney sat down, lit a cigarette, and poured himself a cup of coffee. "No worries, Dad. But I'm glad I hired Mr. Sheppard. He's the bee's knees, to be sure." Glancing at his parents, he knew they had also endured much during the ordeal. He admired their perseverance.

Alice brought over a steaming bowl of oatmeal, gently sprinkled with nutmeg. Rodney put down his cigarette and as though famished he ate the hot cereal, relishing the taste and asking for more coffee. After reading the morning paper, chatting with his parents, and finishing the oatmeal and the coffee, he wiped his mouth on a napkin and told them he needed to leave for work. He crushed his cigarette in the ashtray, said goodbye to his parents, grabbed his plaid jacket and cap from the hallway closet, double-checked that his cigarettes were in his pocket, and left the house.

It was a fine early spring morning and Rodney felt rejuvenated. He took his time walking up Washington Avenue, feeling unburdened. So much had happened within the last month, but the nightmare was over. He doubted he'd ever look at Cucumber Alley quite the same again. But he reminded himself, that the nightmare was over.

He walked to State Street, crossed at the light, and stood before the imposing Hotel Van Curler. Upon entering, he saw it was quite busy; General Electric executive meetings, tour groups, guests checking in, and others relaxing in the lobby. He greeted Olive Mae at the registration desk, then went to his office in the back, where he left his jacket and cap. Straightening his tie and vest in a wall mirror, he then joined her at the front desk.

"There've been mix-ups with some reservations," Olive Mae told him.

Rodney was eager to assist, excelling in his usual role as a problem solver. The morning wore on, as more guests checked in, and issues needed to be addressed. Mr. Lennox arrived at the front desk, noticed Rodney was alone and saw it was past noontime.

"Rodney, why don't you join Olive Mae for lunch in the restaurant?"

Rodney was surprised Mr. Lennox would mention lunch, which he never did before. He was so busy he didn't notice Olive Mae had left the front desk. He thanked him and then decided to walk over to the elegant restaurant, already filling up with the lunchtime crowd. He spotted Olive Mae, at a center table, waiting for him, smiling. Rodney joined her and returned the smile.

THE END

CPSIA information can be obtained
at www.ICGtesting.com
Printed in the USA
LVHW010351190922
728665LV00007B/458